Rachel Vincent is the *New York Times* bestselling author of many books for adults and for teens, including the Shifters, Unbound, and Soul Screamers series. A resident of Oklahoma, she has two teenagers, two cats, and a BA in English, each of which contributes in some way to every book she writes. When she's not working, Rachel can be found curled up with a book or watching movies and playing video games with her husband.

Visit Rachel online at
rachelvincent.com

Follow Rachel Vincent on

THE FLAME
NEVER
DIES

RACHEL VINCENT

MIRA Ink is a registered trademark of Harlequin Enterprises Limited, used under licence.

First Published in Great Britain 2016
By Harlequin Mira Ink, an imprint of HarperCollinsPublishers
1 London Bridge Street, London, SE1 9GF

© 2016 Rachel Vincent

ISBN: 978-1-848-45451-4
eBook ISBN: 978-1-474-04521-6

0816

Our policy is to use papers that are natural, renewable and recyclable products and made from wood grown in sustainable forests. The logging and manufacturing processes conform to the legal environmental regulations of the country of origin.

Printed and bound by
CPI Group (UK) Ltd, Croydon, CR0 4YY

*To every intrepid real-world heroine out there
who knows that one girl can make a difference.
You, fearless ladies, make the world go round.*

ONE

I crouched, tense, in the derelict remains of a high school gymnasium, one of the last buildings still standing in the town of Ashland, which had been mostly burned to the ground during the demonic uprising more than a century before. Though *standing* might be giving the gymnasium too much credit. The walls were upright. The floor was buckled, but intact, and dotted with rotting insulation that had fallen through the ceiling long before I was born. A few weak beams of daylight shone through small holes in the roof, highlighting dust motes in the air, and as I turned slowly, I marveled at how still and quiet the huge room felt.

A footstep whispered behind me and the sound of my pulse swelled in my ears. I spun and drove my heel into my attacker's solar plexus. He flew backward with a breathless "Oof!" and landed hard on the warped wooden floor, scraping the last flakes of paint from what had once been standard basketball court markings. Or maybe a cartoonish depiction of the school mascot, like the one still clinging to the gray brick wall.

The assailant tried to get up, but I dropped onto him, straddling his hips, and shoved my left palm down on his chest. My right fist was pulled back, ready to punch him in the face, just in case.

Maddock held both hands palms-out between us, his hazel eyes wide as they stared up at me. "Nina, I give!"

I laughed as I climbed off him, wiping sweat from my forehead in spite of the cool spring morning.

"You're getting good at this." He pushed himself to his feet for the sixth time in ten minutes, rubbing his flat stomach where my boot had connected with it. "You're almost ready to take on Devi."

I turned my back so he couldn't see me roll my eyes. "I'll try to contain my joy."

We'd been sparring for nearly an hour, burning energy we had no way to replenish in order to hone skills we couldn't survive without on our own in the badlands.

Growing up under the tyrannical thumb of the Unified Church had been no picnic, even before we'd discovered that we were actually being governed by demons, raising human citizens like cattle for the slaughter. But at least food had been easy to swipe from the corner store less than a mile from my house.

Outside the Church's walled-in cities, survival required much stricter planning. And vigorous self-defense. After five months in the badlands, we were all lean and ragged from the meager diet and frequent exposure to the elements, yet I was faster and stronger than I'd ever been in my life.

Maddock used the short sleeve of a sun-bleached blue T-shirt to wipe sweat from his forehead. "Maybe we should take a break," he said, in the quiet way he had of making a suggestion sound like an imperative. I'd been impressed by that ability from the moment I'd met him. Devi could shout and make demands, and, truth be told, she probably could have taken him in a fair fight if she weren't until-death-rends-me-from-your-side in love with him. But she could not lead Anathema because we would not follow her.

Devi did, however, get credit for naming our motley band of outlaws. When the Church had declared us anathema—cast us out, claiming we'd been possessed—Devi had insisted we make the label ours. We'd been wearing it like a medal ever since.

Finn stepped out of the shadows behind a crumbling set of bleachers, the sun shining on his short-cropped dark curls. My pulse spiked when he pulled me into an embrace in spite of the layer of sweat and grime coating my training clothes. "If he's too tired to take you to the ground, I'd be happy to step in," he whispered into my ear, and warmth glowed beneath my skin at the scandalous subtext. My connection with Finn had grown bolder with every mile that stretched between Anathema and the authority of the Church, until daily, unchaperoned conversation with boys no longer made me glance fearfully over my shoulder.

Yet the novelty of that easy contact lingered, intensifying the excitement of my first serious relationship. As it turned out, indecency was terribly exhilarating. Devi had been right about that all along.

"Sounds like fun," I whispered in return, and Finn's embrace tightened. "If I weren't afraid of hurting you, I would have been sparring with you in the first place." But when his arms tensed around me, I recognized my mistake.

"I hate this fragile body," he growled against the upper curve of my ear, and I felt his frustration like a gulf opening between us, widening with every reminder that unlike my own, the flesh he wore was borrowed, and limited by ordinary human abilities. He'd been in the body of a gate guard named Carter since the day we'd escaped New Temperance five months before, and though the guard was strong and fast, and tall enough that I could comfortably rest my chin on his shoulder, his body was no match for an exorcist's speed or strength.

"I like this body," I whispered, sliding my arms around his neck as I stared up into green eyes that looked even greener against the smooth, dark skin of his appropriated face. "And I like you in it. Strength and speed aren't everything." And even a weak "civilian" body was better than no body at all, which was Finn's natural state. At least this way I could see him and talk to him and kiss him . . . when we weren't surrounded by our fellow outlaws.

"We should save our energy for the raid anyway," Maddy added with a sympathetic glance at his best friend. "Assuming there's anything to raid."

But there had to be. "If Reese and Devi don't find a supply truck today, we're screwed," Finn said, and neither of us argued. "The disadvantage of having a body full-time is that it's hungry all the time."

We'd taken everything both vehicles could hold during our most recent heist, but a month later we were running on empty again. As were both cars. Most of us could go a couple of days without food, but Melanie . . .

My little sister and her unborn child had to eat every day. Several times a day. They needed good food—protein and vitamins we just didn't know how to find in the badlands on our own, especially during the winter months, when there'd been little edible vegetation growing in the largely abandoned national landscape.

Now that spring had come we had hopes for foraging, but we were new to the art, and the learning curve was steep.

Yet Mellie and her baby faced an even greater challenge

than hunger, and it was that need that kept me awake most nights. . . .

"Here. Hydrate." Finn pressed a bottle of water into my hand and I gulped half of it. Fortunately, Ashland had several creeks, and they all ran clear and cold. The world's water supply was probably cleaner than it had been before the war, now that humanity had stopped poisoning the planet.

The demon apocalypse had been good for the environment, if nothing else.

I pulled Finn closer and inhaled deeply, letting the feel of his arms around me and the scent of his hair—pilfered shampoo and fresh river water—push entrenched fears to the back of my mind. He'd been my anchor during our chaotic life on the run, and I'd grown comfortable with the arms that held me, even if they weren't really his.

But the guilt from having stolen an innocent man's body wore on Finn constantly. Unfortunately, we couldn't let the guard go in the middle of the badlands. Within hours he'd be torn to pieces by degenerates—deranged demons trapped in mutated human bodies, roaming what was left of the United States in search of a fresh soul to devour.

I'd just finished my water when the growl of an approaching engine put all three of us on alert. Maddy raced for the exit and squeezed through a set of doors immobilized in the ajar position by the warped floor. Finn and I were right behind him, dust motes swirling around us.

We got to the sidewalk just as the black SUV slid to a

halt on fractured pavement, inches from the bumper of the car we'd fled New Temperance in, which still bore the bullet hole and spiderwebbed glass from our escape. Dust puffed beneath the tires and settled onto our worn boots as Reese emerged from the passenger side. Maddy, Finn, and I practically strained our necks looking up at him.

Reese Cardwell was six and a half feet and two hundred thirty pounds of solid muscle, even after months of our paltry badlands diet.

"Maddy. Heads up," Devi called as she climbed out of the driver's seat and pushed her long, dark braid over her shoulder. She tossed a crowbar to him over the hood of the SUV. "Church caravan, ten minutes out. Two supply trucks and an escort vehicle. They've stepped up the security in response to our raids."

That was inevitable. We'd hit three supply trucks in the past five months. The Church was evil, not stupid.

"We can't handle a security escort," Maddock insisted, testing the heft of the crowbar. "There aren't enough of us."

I propped my hands on my hips. "But we're outnumbered by degenerates all the time."

"Exorcising degenerates is easy," Maddock said, though I had a knot on my head and a bandaged gash on my left arm that would argue otherwise. "Disabling innocent people without killing them—that's the hard part. If the security detail's all human, this'll get complicated."

"We don't have any choice." Reese grabbed a set of

binoculars from the passenger-side dashboard. "They've posted guards at the gasoline depot"—a prewar relic kept functional by the Church to fuel their deliveries—"and they probably won't be shipping provisions one truck at a time anymore. We need a haul big enough to let us lie low for a while, and we'll have to siphon all three tanks to get us five hundred miles south."

"South?" When had that been decided?

"We've worn out our welcome here." Finn shrugged borrowed shoulders, but the green eyes that watched me were all his own, no matter whose body he wore. "The cities down south won't be expecting us, so raids will be easier until they catch on."

"Okay. So how many people are in this caravan?" I asked as Maddock counted the empty gas canisters lined up in the back of the battered black vehicle.

"About eight. Maybe more." Devi tossed Reese the keys to the SUV. "All armed. Not sure how many are possessed. We'll need Finn."

And the assault rifle that had come with the gate guard's body.

Devi slid behind the wheel of the smaller car and adjusted the mirrors. Maddock got in next to her and stuck the key into the ignition while Finn and I climbed into the backseat. Reese got into the SUV behind us, and as we took off across the badlands, Finn pulled the semiautomatic rifle from the floorboard and checked to make sure it was loaded.

"What's the setup?" I asked, staring into the rearview mirror at the front of the decrepit school library, where my sister waited with the other two civilian members of our group, in the safest location we could find for them. Mellie was easily persuaded to stay out of the action if she had something to read.

"Roadblock on the main drag of Palmersville." Devi took a turn too fast on the splintered pavement and the tires squealed beneath us as I slid across the backseat into Finn. "They'll have to go right through on their way to the gas depot, and the road's narrow enough that Reese can block it with just the SUV. When the trucks stop, Finn will shoot out the tires of the rear vehicle to block their retreat. Then we melee."

"That's the best way to fight." Maddock twisted in his seat to shoot a gleeful grin at us. "Trap them, then force them to brawl hand-to-hand. Because chaos—"

"—favors the militia," I finished for him. "I know." Obviously, we were the militia.

I'd never been in a fight in my life until the week of my seventeenth birthday, five months earlier, when I'd discovered I was an exorcist by frying a demon from my mother's body. Naturally, she'd died in the process, and the Church had accused me of matricide, to cover up the fact that their army of "exorcists" was full of fakes. I'd gone from high school senior to the country's most wanted fugitive in a single instant.

Since then, Melanie and I had been on the run with the

rest of Anathema, armed with the dangerous knowledge that the all-powerful Unified Church, which claimed to have "saved" humanity from the invading demon horde a century before, actually *was* the demon horde, disguised with human faces and authorial robes.

Minutes after piling into the car, we raced down the main drag of what was once a tiny town called Palmersville, which boasted a grand total of four mostly paved streets. Devi turned right onto one of them, and behind us Reese parked the SUV sideways across the entire two-lane road.

Finn got out of the car with his rifle and took a quick look around the derelict town. He pointed at a crumbling storefront across the street. "I'll be in there. Center window, bottom floor."

"Be careful." I pulled him close for an adrenaline-fueled kiss, and when we let the moment linger, Devi grabbed the tail of my shirt and hauled me backward.

"Priorities," she snapped as Finn grinned at me, then turned to jog across the street.

"We'll take out the escort vehicle first." Reese towered over the rest of us, in a group too varied in height to form a true huddle. "Then Nina and I will take the first supply truck and you two take the second one."

Maddock and Devi nodded, then headed into an alley across the way while Reese and I hid behind an industrial trash bin half-eaten with rust on our side of the street.

Seconds later we heard engines.

Our haphazardly parked SUV was dusty and dented enough to pass for abandoned, and I knew for certain that the ploy had worked when the caravan's escort vehicle, a police car, stopped ten feet away. The police car bore the stylized emblem of the Unified Church—four intertwined columns of flames—and the men who got out of it wore the long navy cassocks of police officers.

Even from a distance I could see the white embroidery on their full, bell-shaped sleeves. They were both consecrated Church leaders.

Which meant they were possessed.

A jolt of excitement shot up my spine, anticipation laced with an edge of fear, and I felt Reese tense beside me. He was as eager to fight as I was.

The cops were already headed toward our SUV, obviously intending to push it off the road, when a passenger got out of the second cargo truck and shouted, "What's the holdup?" He wore civilian clothes—a green jacket bearing the logo of the shipping company that owned the truck.

"Abandoned car," the first cop shouted over his shoulder. "We'll have it out of the way in a minute."

"We came through here last week and there was nothing in the road," the civilian called, and both cops turned to eye our vehicle warily.

A gunshot thundered from Finn's hiding place as the civilian was climbing back into his truck. One of its tires exploded, and shouts erupted from both trucks.

The cops dove for cover behind their open car doors,

pulling pistols from their holsters while they scanned the storefront for the source of the gunfire. Finn took two more shots in rapid succession, and one of them hit a second tire, effectively disabling the second cargo truck and trapping the two vehicles in front of it.

My pulse raced, my left fist clenching and unclenching in anticipation.

Maddock and Devi burst from their hiding place and crossed the distance quickly and quietly.

Reese and I came at the lead vehicle from the opposite direction, running crouched over, and the driver got out of the car when he saw us coming. Even if his robes hadn't been embroidered, I'd have known he was possessed from the way he moved, inhumanly quick and impossibly nimble. Daylight hid the demonic shine in his eyes—visible only to exorcists and fellow demons—but I saw recognition in his expression when he skidded to a stop in front of me, already reaching for the gun at his waist. He knew me.

But then, everyone knew Nina Kane. I was public enemy number one.

I lunged forward and pressed my left hand to his chest before he could pull his weapon. Light burst between us, and the demon screamed as he was burned from his human host while the body dangled from the fire kindled in my palm, weightless beneath the power of exorcism.

On my right, Maddock grunted. A form flew past me and crashed to the ground, unmoving. The light from my hand faded and the body suspended from it crumpled to the cracked pavement. I turned and found Maddy fighting a second possessed police officer, but before I could get to them, I was suddenly yanked from the ground and thrown backward through the air.

I screamed and flailed in flight, then crashed onto a patch of grass ten feet from the road. Before I could stand, another navy-robed demon sprang at me with an odd, squarish gun in his hand. I rolled out of the way, and the demon shoved the weapon into the ground where I'd been an instant earlier.

The weapon buzzed, and I realized it was a stun gun. They'd come armed not to kill, but to capture.

The Church still wanted us alive.

"Watch out! Stun guns!" I shouted as I rolled over and leapt to my feet.

The demon was on me in an instant. I tried to kick the weapon from his grip but missed his hand entirely. He was too fast. Too strong. After fighting only mutated and relatively weak degenerates in the badlands, I was out of practice battling demons in their prime, and the number of pained grunts bursting from my fellow exorcists said I was not alone.

Time to step up my game.

The demon cop lunged again and I blocked his gun arm, then kicked him in the chest as hard as I could. Breath exploded from his mouth and the demon flew backward several feet. I was on him before he could stand, my palm already alight with the force that would scorch him from his stolen body and eject him from the human world. For just a second, as I pressed that living flame to his chest and listened to his flesh sizzle, I felt . . . peaceful.

Useful.

I was born for this.

Behind me, the grunts and thumps were winding down, and when the body beneath my hand fell limp, I turned to see that we had won the fight.

It wasn't even close, really. I counted six men in white-embroidered navy police cassocks, each now sporting a scorched and smoldering hole in his chest. The two survivors were the human deliverymen who'd been driving the cargo. Both now stood with their backs against the first of the two green supply trucks with their hands in the air, while Finn aimed his rifle at them.

"What's the plan for these two?" he asked, his aim unwavering.

Maddock considered the question for a moment. "Cuff 'em and leave 'em in the escort vehicle."

"I'm on it." Devi squatted next to one of the dead cops, then stood with his handcuffs. While she and Finn restrained the civilians, Maddock searched the bodies until he found the keys to the cargo compartments. He unlocked the rear of the first truck and rolled the door up to reveal the shipment.

Relief eased the most immediate of my fears. Our famine was over, at least for a while.

Reese rounded the back of the vehicle. "Holy hellfire."

The truck was stacked full of boxes, floor to ceiling, front to back. Even if the second vehicle was empty—and it wouldn't be—we'd found way more than we could carry.

Each box was clearly labeled, and at a glance I noticed crates of canned and dry goods, boxes of clothing bound for department stores, cleaning supplies, textbooks, and more toiletries than I'd ever seen in my life.

"They put all their eggs in one basket," Maddock said, his voice hollow with surprise. "They must have thought we wouldn't attack an armed caravan."

"Or they were hoping we would," I guessed. "They came armed with stun guns, prepared to capture, not kill."

"Well, too bad for them." Devi stepped in front of me and pulled a clipboard from a hook on the wall of the cargo area. The inventory was several pages long.

"It'll be easier to drive this back than to try to unload it," Reese said, and no one argued. We took turns siphoning the gasoline from the truck we wouldn't be taking, and then Maddock and Devi drove off in the other cargo truck. Reese followed them in our SUV, which left Finn and me to drive the shot-out car we'd "stolen" from a sympathetic cop back in New Temperance. As we passed the police vehicle on the way to our car, one of the cargo truck drivers stuck his head out of the backseat window.

"Carter?" he called, leaning at an odd angle because his hands were bound behind his back. The other civilian sat in the front seat, his left wrist handcuffed to the steering wheel. Neither man could get out of the car, but they would be able to drive it to the nearest city. "You used to be Heath Carter, right?" the man in the backseat repeated, staring at Finn. "I knew I recognized you."

We'd ditched Carter's ID along with his unembroidered church cassock months ago, because even when Finn eventually released his body, returning to New Temperance would be a death sentence for the real Carter—he would know things the Church wouldn't want him to share.

"He's not possessed," I said. "He just switched sides once he learned the truth." Telling my little lie was much easier than trying to explain that Carter actually was possessed, but not by a demon. Beyond that, we didn't want the Church to know about Finn and his ability to inhabit any human body not already occupied by a demon. He was as close to a secret weapon as we had.

"What truth? What the hell happened out there?" the man cuffed to the steering wheel demanded, and I followed his gaze to where we'd lined up the scorched corpses on the grass. "What did you bastards do to them?"

The drivers didn't recognize us as exorcists because their only exposure to the practice had come from the Church's army of fake exorcists, who marched around in dramatic black robes, wearing crosses and chanting nonsense in Latin for show.

"Those cops were possessed," I said. "We exorcised them."

"Nina," Finn whispered, warning me to shush, because just like with Carter, the more these civilians knew, the more danger they'd be in from the Church. But they'd already seen enough to get themselves killed, so my explanation might actually save their lives.

"You expect us to believe you're exorcists and the cops were demons?" the man in the backseat spat. "Bullshit." He leaned forward, appealing to his coworker in the front. "Demons are pathological liars. You can't believe a word she says."

"If we're possessed, why would we let you live?"

Backseat Man lifted his eyebrows at me in challenge. "If they were possessed"—he nodded at the bodies lined up on the ground—"why were they going to let you live?"

"So they could deliver us to the Church." I shrugged. That should have been obvious.

"Deliver you . . . ?" Front Seat Man stared up at me, surprised. "Where exactly were they going to put you?"

I frowned, considering the question. The backs of both cargo trucks were full of goods, and most of the available seats had been filled by the cops and drivers. They wouldn't have had room to bring more than two of us back.

So why had they come armed with nonlethal weapons?

Before I could come up with any reasonable theories, Backseat Man made a show of glancing around what he could see of the ghost town. "Where's your sister? She lose that baby yet?"

Finn held me back when I took an instinctive, aggressive step toward him. Melanie and her unlicensed, underage pregnancy, which constituted multiple prosecutable sins, had risen to infamy when the Church publicly questioned her humanity and broadcast her boyfriend's immolation—death by fire—to the entire country.

For once, Finn's hand on my shoulder failed to calm me. "She's not going to lose the baby," I growled through clenched teeth. Making sure of that had become my mission in life since escaping New Temperance. Mellie's unborn child was the only family she and I had left in the world—thanks to routine sterilization by the Church, I could never have one of my own.

"Oh, we both know that's not true," Backseat Man taunted. "Even if it's born breathing, how long will it live? The well is empty, and you have no donor. Without a soul, that baby will die out here in the dirt, and there'll be nothing you or your sister or your gang of flame-wielding assassins can do about it."

Assassins? My heart thumped harder. Only demons called exorcists assassins.

I squinted against the sunlight for a better look at Backseat Man, and that time when I stepped toward him, Finn didn't try to stop me. He'd heard it too. The Church had sent one of its demons in disguise as a deliveryman—no official cassock, no telltale embroidery.

"Melanie's baby will live." I held my left hand out so he could see the flame cradled in my palm. His eyes widened, and he tried to retreat across the bench seat but was trapped by the seat belt. "I will find a soul for it." I shoved my fiery hand through the open window, and the demon screeched, an inhuman sound of agony, as the flame met his flesh. "And if I can't find a soul for my sister's baby," I whispered so softly that no one else could hear me above the crackle of crisping skin, "I will damn well give that kid my own."

TWO

We caught up with the other two vehicles on the way back to Ashland, and Finn must have known something was wrong, because he didn't tease me about my lead foot. "Try not to let them get to you," he said, plucking my right hand from the wheel so he could intertwine his fingers with mine. "They're demons. They live to cause us pain."

But I wasn't upset about what the backseat demon had said—I was upset because he was almost certainly right. The well of souls *was* empty. It had been quietly drained over the past millennia by demons secretly living among us. The soaring infant mortality rate at the end of the previous century had finally clued humanity in, leading to the war against the unclean, which had decimated two-thirds of the world's population.

Now pregnancies were licensed and regulated by the Church. People who were declared unfit to reproduce were sterilized at age fifteen, as I'd been because I was slightly nearsighted and prone to seasonal allergies. To make sure that every baby conceived would actually live, elderly citizens were expected to give up their souls in simultaneous birth/death events carefully orchestrated by city officials. What the rest of the world didn't know was that the Church only wanted those babies to live so they could be possessed and fed from as adults.

Escaping New Temperance had spared Melanie's baby—and the rest of us—from that fate. Theoretically, at least. Unfortunately, our escape had also drastically lowered the chances of finding a soul for the baby. Without one, the youngest and most vulnerable of my two remaining family members would die within hours of his or her birth. We'd all known that from the beginning.

What I hadn't told the rest of Anathema was that I was fully prepared to make the necessary sacrifice myself if I couldn't find a willing donor before the birth.

"It'll work out, Nina." Finn squeezed my hand as I pressed on the brake to keep from rear-ending the cargo truck in front of us. "One way or another, it'll all work out."

But I knew better. Nothing in my life had ever just worked out. Good things never happened unless I *made* them happen, and five months spent wandering through the badlands hadn't changed that.

Before we'd even pulled to a stop in front of the library, Grayson James burst through the cracked glass doors and raced down the crumbling steps without so much as a precautionary glance in either direction. I groaned as I shifted into park. One of these days her enthusiasm was going to get her killed. Or worse—possessed.

Reese got out of the SUV and pulled her into his massive embrace, then lifted her for a long, deep kiss. For a moment I was caught off guard by their demonstrative affection—a transgression worthy of arrest had we still been in New Temperance, or any other city. If Finn and I had become comfortable with our relationship, free from the enforced modesty of the Church, Reese and Grayson had grown *bold*.

Maddock and Devi's connection had already been scandalous when I'd met them.

"Grace, you can't just keep throwing yourself into unknown situations." Reese set her on her feet on the crumbling concrete, and her head barely reached his shoulder. "Until you transition, you're vulnerable."

We'd seen an increase in degenerate activity over the past month as her seventeenth birthday approached, bringing with it the emergence of her exorcist abilities—a genetic inevitability because her brother and both of their parents had also been exorcists.

"I knew it was you," Grayson insisted. "I didn't hear any monsters."

Degenerates could sense an exorcist in transition, like

a cat scenting a mouse. Albeit, a mouse that would soon be able to burn the cat alive with a single touch. Grayson could "hear" degenerates in her mind, in the same way she could hear Finn talking even when he had no physical form. We didn't understand her ability, but we couldn't deny its existence.

Devi scowled, her dark brows drawing low over expressive black eyes that only seemed to venture beyond skepticism and disapproval when she was looking at Maddock. "Degenerates aren't the only threat out here."

"I was right, wasn't I?" Grayson demanded.

Reese closed the SUV's driver's-side door. "That's not the point."

"That *is* the point. I'm not a civilian," she whispered fiercely, trailing him around the vehicle as Melanie and Anabelle finally followed her out of the library now that they knew we weren't under attack. "In a couple of weeks, I'll be as strong and fast as the rest of you."

"And we welcome the day," he said. "But it's not here yet." Reese would willingly throw his own overgrown frame in front of her as both shield and weapon, but he worried that Grayson was vulnerable when he wasn't around. I had the same concerns for my sister. And for Anabelle. Fortunately, neither of them was eager to start battling demons.

"It's never too early to start training." Devi shrugged. "Maybe if she knew what she was doing, she wouldn't throw herself into unknown situations."

That was one of the few things Devi and I agreed on, but Reese was afraid that training would encourage Grayson to put herself in danger.

Maddock unlocked the back of the cargo truck and rolled the door up as the last two members of our outlaw band made their way down the crumbling library steps. Anabelle had one arm around Mellie to help steady her. Every day Melanie's stomach grew larger while the rest of her appeared to shrink, and the unborn child seemed determined to upset my fifteen-year-old sister's balance. And to keep her up all night. And to make her feet swell, her ribs ache, and the circles beneath her eyes grow darker with every day spent on the run with inconsistent nutrition and nonexistent prenatal care.

Anabelle let go of Mellie on the bottom step. "That's quite a haul!"

"This is only half," I said, scanning the labels on the top row of boxes. "Cross your fingers that there's a crate of vitamins in here, or we'll have to go back for the other truck."

Devi groaned—returning to the scene of the crime would be a huge risk for the group—but she didn't argue. I'd made it clear since our escape from New Temperance that the health of my sister and her unborn child came first.

"We can't carry all that." Melanie stared with huge brown eyes up at the stack of crates.

Finn shrugged, and I could practically hear gears

turning as he considered the problem. "We can if we ditch the shot-up car for this truck."

"You want to drive across the badlands in a marked Church cargo truck?" My brows rose. "I guess that *would* be faster than actually painting targets on our backs."

Maddock chuckled as he scanned the inventory, and I glanced from face to face. "By the way, am I the only one who didn't know we're heading south?"

"It's news to me," Anabelle said, but that was no surprise. I'd known her since I was a kid, but the others didn't trust her like they trusted me, because I was a fellow exorcist, and they didn't like her like they liked Melanie, because everyone liked Melanie. My sister's gift—and her curse—was charisma. Which was how she'd wound up in love with and pregnant by a sweet but ultimately doomed boy two years her senior.

The oldest of our group by several years, Anabelle was a former ordained Church teacher who'd had to follow us into the badlands because knowing the truth about her superiors was as good as having a noose around her neck. She'd lost everything and everyone she'd ever had, just like the rest of us. But like Mellie, she was largely defenseless against the dangers of the badlands, and she was eager to earn her place in the group any way she could.

"First things first." Finn pulled the collapsible stairs from a hidden shelf beneath the cargo hold, then stepped up into the truck. "Food. We'll decide everything else once our brains are fueled."

While Maddock, Devi, and I stood watch, Reese and Finn began pulling boxes from the truck and stacking them on the ground. Mellie and Anabelle made notes on the inventory sheet until they came to a crate of canned goods, and the chore was suspended in favor of lunch in the library's vestibule, from which we could watch over our haul through tempered glass walls that appeared to have shattered, yet remained in place.

Finn and I sat down with a jar of peaches and a can of unidentifiable processed meat apiece. Next to us on the granite floor, Anabelle and Melanie shared cans of twisty pasta shapes in red sauce and a box of cheese-flavored crackers.

The remaining four members of Anathema paired off on the other side of the vestibule so that they could see the road leading into Ashland from the larger American wasteland.

Melanie tugged her bag closer and pulled out one of the books she'd scavenged from the library, then flipped through the yellowed pages while she chewed.

"How are your feet?" I asked around a bite of peach.

"Still kind of swollen, but they don't hurt," she answered, without looking up from the book. "My hips ache, though."

"What about that mark on your back?" At first we'd thought it was a bruise—a small spot at the base of her backbone, slightly darker than the rest of her pale skin. But then it had started to stretch along her spine like the inverse of a skunk's stripe.

Melanie shrugged, and sun-bleached blond hair fell over her shoulder. "I can't feel it, and all the pregnancy books say some skin discoloration is normal. It'll fade after the baby's born." When she found her place in the book, her pale brows furrowed and she settled in for the read.

"What's she learning now?" Finn asked, eyeing Mellie with a brotherly affection that made me smile.

I tilted my sister's book up so I could read the title. "Um . . . *Hunting and Gathering for the Modern Paleo*." Another in her small collection of survivalist literature, rescued from multiple crumbling libraries across the small stretch of badlands we'd explored.

Mellie shrugged and held the book up so we could get a better look. "Plants are starting to grow, and we need to know which ones are edible." She and Anabelle had already taught us to fish, to set basic traps for small game, to start a fire without matches, and to cook our meat evenly on a homemade spit. "Soon we'll be able to spot wild-growing roots, tubers, and nuts to supplement all this aluminum-flavored cuisine." She tapped the side of her pasta can and smiled. Then her gaze dropped to the page.

And with that, I lost Mellie to her book. Again.

* * *

In the end, we decided to leave the rusted, shot-up car in favor of the cargo truck.

It took nearly two hours to unload the boxes and set aside the ones we couldn't use—mostly household cleaners and clothing that fit no one—then divide the food and usable supplies between the truck and the back of the SUV in case we got separated.

None of our previous raids had yielded as much as this latest haul, but the new goods wouldn't last forever. We'd need the hunting and foraging techniques Ana and Mellie were learning in order to make it through the summer.

But what we needed even worse was fuel. The SUV and truck both guzzled gas at a rate we could not sustain, and the Church had crippled us by cutting off access to their fuel depots. Reese siphoned all the gas from the car we were abandoning while Mellie and Anabelle stocked backpacks full of "up front" supplies. Then Finn and I squeezed into the cab of the cargo truck with Ana and my sister, and we took off into the badlands again on yet another fractured strip of highway, this time headed south, with the descending sun on our right.

I sat as close to Finn as I could get, both to give Melanie more room and because touching him, even casually, still made my head spin and my stomach flip, like when I'd played on the swings as a kid. At first I'd thought that was because touching a boy I wasn't related to, for any reason other than medical necessity, was strictly forbidden by the Church. But even as the thrill of rebellion had faded, the rush I felt every time Finn looked at me had only grown.

We'd been on the road for about an hour, his arm stretched across the back of the seat so he could play with my hair, when Ana looked up from her book and sucked in a startled breath.

"Holy Reformation . . . !" she swore, and as Finn pressed on the brake I followed her gaze to a car parked on the side of the road a few hundred feet ahead. The windshield was generously splattered with mud, but I couldn't see any obvious damage to the vehicle. It had probably run out of gas, like dozens of other abandoned cars we'd come across in the badlands.

"Is that—?"

Static crackled from the handheld radio on my lap before I could finish the question, and I picked it up as Reese spoke into a matching radio from the SUV behind us. "You guys see it?" he asked, and Mellie nodded, though he couldn't see her.

"Yeah," I said into the handset.

"It's a long shot, but let's pull over and check the tank for gas," he said, and that was when I realized that those in the SUV couldn't see the detail that had drawn the exclamation from Anabelle. The detail that had captured my attention and Mellie's heart, and led Finn to put his right blinker on, even though there was no other traffic to warn of his intent to pull over.

"There's a kid," I said into the radio, holding down the button with my thumb. The boy standing in the dirt beside the car was small, with dark skin and long, tightly curled hair. His navy pants might have been part of a uniform, but his arms were crossed over a faded, striped short-sleeved shirt instead of the white button-down required for school. "He's six or seven years old. Appears to be alone."

Stunned silence dominated the radio channel.

"He can't have been there long," Anabelle whispered, as if the child might overhear her through glass and steel from a good hundred feet away. "Where on earth are his parents?"

"In the car." Finn pulled onto the side of the road several yards from the blue sedan. "Look closer."

I squinted, and chills popped up all over my skin when I saw two forms slumped over in the front seat. What I'd mistaken for mud sprayed across the outside of the windshield turned out to be blood splattered across the inside.

It was too dark to be anything else.

"Oh *no* . . ." If the kid's parents were in that car, they were either dead or dying.

"Stay here." Finn shifted the truck into park and opened his door, then pulled his rifle from behind the bench seat on his way out of the vehicle. He tried to close the door, but I stopped its swing with my foot.

"Stay here." I passed his instruction on to Mellie and Anabelle as I climbed down from the truck after Finn.

Seconds later Anabelle's door squealed open at my back; she'd ignored my instruction as readily as I'd ignored Finn's.

"Don't aim that thing," I whispered when I caught up

with him. "He's probably terrified already, and if there were still anything dangerous nearby, he would be dead."

We stared at the car for one long moment, but the splatters were too thick to reveal anything except vague shapes behind the blood.

"This isn't right, Nina," Finn murmured, and I knew he wasn't just talking about the gory windshield. Excursions beyond city walls were rare and discouraged, but they weren't actually prohibited by the Church as long as the proper permits were secured in advance. But . . . "If his parents are dead in that car, how'd they die? Demons in their prime don't pull people apart. That'd be wasting potential hosts. And degenerates wouldn't have left the boy alive."

I shrugged. "Maybe he hid."

Finn lowered the rifle but didn't engage the safety. "And maybe whatever killed his parents is still around."

His words still hung in the air when Anabelle jogged past us, her blond curls flying, her jeans hanging low on her newly narrow hips. "Are you okay?" she called to the child, and I grabbed for her arm but missed.

Finn followed her to the car, the rifle aimed at the ground, and he peeked through the windows while Ana knelt in front of the boy without checking under or behind the vehicle.

I groaned on the inside. Why were the members of our group who were the least able to defend themselves always the most likely to put themselves in danger?

The boy nodded slowly.

"What's your name, sweetheart?" she asked, and I realized there would be no teaching her caution where children were concerned. Ana had spent five years as a grade-school teacher, and she'd found it harder than any of the rest of us to let go of what she'd learned during her Church ordination—not the bullshit creeds and oppressive rules, but the ways of life as we'd known it. Modesty. Service. Sacrifice.

"Tobias." The boy's voice was soft and hoarse, as if he'd been crying. His gaze slid from Anabelle to me, and I decided the glazed look in his eyes was from shock.

He reminded me of the kindergartners I'd spent my service hour with every day of my senior year, until the Church had declared me a cancerous wart on mankind's collective hind end. Tobias could have been any kid in my class, terrified and traumatically orphaned.

We couldn't leave him alone in the badlands. Yet ours was no life for a kid.

The irony in that thought hit home when my sister waddled past me, one hand on her huge belly. "Melanie," I called, but she waved off my warning. When I glanced at Finn, he nodded to give me the all clear, the rifle still aimed at the ground. He'd inspected the car from the outside and squatted to peer beneath it, and had found no immediate danger.

Still, Mellie was too pregnant to fight or to flee from sudden danger, so I followed her, ready to pull her out of the path of evil should a demon burst from the bloody car.

"Are you okay, Tobias?" my sister asked, kneeling in front of the child with Anabelle's help.

For a moment he only stared at her, studying her pale skin and even paler hair. Finally he nodded, his gaze fixated on her stomach, while I tried to calculate the mileage his family must have traveled in that doomed blue car. "You got a baby in there?"

Melanie laughed, and I marveled at the fact that she could find joy where the rest of us saw only tragedy and hardship. "Yes. And I like your name, Tobias." She laid one hand on her stomach. "Maybe I'll borrow it if this little one's a boy."

Assuming it lived.

Melanie was a tireless optimist, not blind to the dangers of the world, exactly, but not quite concerned enough about them. She refused to think about the overwhelming odds against her child's survival, and neither she nor Ana had even glanced at the carnage inside that blue car.

And I hadn't heard her mention Adam, the ill-fated father of her child, in weeks.

Reese pulled the SUV to a stop beside our truck, right in the middle of the road, and the other half of our group poured out of the vehicle. "What the hell?" Footsteps crunched in the dirt behind me, and then Reese and Grayson stopped at my side. She carried a plastic jug and he had a hose wrapped around his massive left arm.

"Looks like the parents are dead in the front seat," I whispered. "Not sure what happened yet, but Finn hasn't found any immediate threat."

"Poor thing!" Grayson cried.

Devi rolled her eyes and scuffed her boot in the dirt on the side of the road. "What the hell are we supposed to do with him?"

"We can't leave him here." Maddock threaded his arm through hers, frowning as he watched the little boy. "It's a miracle he's still alive. He must not have been here long."

"We're not even going to *think* about taking him with us until we know what killed his parents." Devi circled the car toward the driver's side and used one hand to shield the sun from her face while she bent to peer through the window. When she stood a second later, she looked sick. "Nothin' but blood."

While the rest of us took a closer look at the car, Grayson, Ana, and Mellie lured Tobias toward the cargo truck with promises of water and chocolate from a box of sweets that had been intended for the general store in New Temperance.

As Devi and Finn had said, the front windows were too caked with blood to show anything at all, and through the rear windshield we could see little more than the outlines of two bodies sitting in the front seats. The trunk door stood open a couple of inches, and when I lifted it, I saw that the narrow center seat had been folded down, creating a small path into the trunk from the backseat of the car. A path just wide enough for a six-year-old.

My stomach twisted at the thought of what Tobias must have witnessed. How could any kid see that much carnage without being psychologically destroyed?

When the child was out of sight behind the cargo truck, Maddock opened the driver's door while Finn aimed his rifle at the interior just in case. Nothing jumped out at us, but after one glance inside I gasped and stepped back. Finn's jaw tightened, and even Devi covered her mouth in horror.

The man and woman, still buckled into the front seats of the car, were drenched in blood fresh enough to glisten in the afternoon sunlight. The dashboard, windows, windshield, and floorboard had all been heavily splattered with what could only have been an arterial spray.

Yet even through all the gore, two things were clear.

First, the man and woman in the blue car were not Tobias's biological parents—their skin was as pale as mine, even accounting for the pallor of recent death. And second, based on the blood and bits of flesh caking their right hands, the couple's wounds appeared to be self-inflicted.

The man and woman had simply pulled onto the side of the road, then ripped out their own throats.

THREE

"Who are they?" Grayson whispered, glancing at the gore-splattered car.

"They didn't have any IDs." Maddock ran one hand through his thick brown hair in a rare display of nerves. But then, the contents of that car had bothered us all. "They're not his biological parents, but aside from that, who knows?"

Grayson sipped from a half-full bottle of water, then passed it left in our huddle, to Reese. "There's not a drop of blood on Tobias." She shrugged. "If he was far enough away to avoid the spray, I'm betting he didn't see much of what happened."

"I think he was in the trunk, but who knows when he crawled in there?" I'd fought demons, degenerates, and humans on a regular basis since finding out I was an exorcist, but I'd never seen *anything* like the carnage in that car.

"Why is no one asking the most obvious question?" Devi demanded, and Grayson shushed her with a sharp look. "Why the hell would a normal couple just pull onto the side of the road and rip their own throats out? I don't even see how it's physically possible!"

Finn accepted the water bottle from Reese but hardly sipped from it before passing it to me. "They hadn't been normal for a long time. And they probably weren't a couple."

"But they *were* possessed." Maddock's voice was so soft that at first I didn't even register the words. "They'd already started to degenerate."

Devi frowned. "I didn't notice anything weird about them. Other than their mutilated throats."

"Their fingers were too long." Finn exhaled slowly and propped his rifle over his left shoulder. "And their chins were too pointy." He glanced at Maddock, who nodded to confirm some unspoken concern; Maddy and Finn had known each other for so long that sometimes they each seemed to know what the other was thinking. Which left the rest of us in the dark. "The mutations were subtle. They'd be hard to detect, especially under all that blood."

"How did you two notice?" I asked, passing the water bottle to Devi.

"They've had a lot of practice." Grayson turned to

Maddy and Finn, and her eyes held a profound sadness that seemed to stretch even beyond the scope of the carnage we'd just discovered. I started to ask what she meant and how she knew that, but—

"Okay, but how do you know they weren't a couple?" Devi demanded, frustration sharpening the ends of her words.

Maddy shrugged. "Demons don't make commitments unless they need to blend in." Like Grayson's parents, whose simulation of a human marriage had allowed them to breed her and her older brother as future hosts to be possessed at maturity. "And there's no one to blend in with in the badlands."

Devi rolled her eyes. "That doesn't mean any—"

"We should get going, unless you all want to sleep in the open tonight." Finn swung his rifle down and aimed it at the ground, then headed for the cargo truck, where Mellie and Tobias sat snacking on the bench seat while Anabelle leaned on the open passenger's-side door.

"What's got his gun sling in a twist?" Devi grumbled while we watched Finn walk off.

Maddy accepted the bottle from her and drained the last inch of water. "He's being cautious. The blood's still wet, which means that whatever bodies the demons are wearing now, they're probably still close." Maddock gestured toward our vehicles, urging us all forward, and I jogged ahead of the group to catch up with Finn.

"Hey. You okay?"

"Yeah," Finn said, too quickly to have given the answer any thought. "I just haven't seen anything that gruesome in a really long time."

"Wait." I reached for his arm and pulled him to a stop facing me. "How long is a really long time?" When had he *ever* seen something that gruesome? "What are you and Maddock not telling us?"

Finn shot an anxious glance at the others over my shoulder, then lowered his voice. "If it were my secret, I'd tell you, but there are things Maddy's not ready to talk about." His conflicted gaze begged me to understand. "But it has nothing to do with whatever happened in that car. That dead couple just . . . they remind him of something."

"Something you saw too," I guessed. Because Maddy and Finn were never apart.

"Yeah, but . . ." His shrug made him look vulnerable, in spite of his soldier's powerful build and the rifle slung over one shoulder, and I wanted to pull him into a hug.

"Just because you didn't have a body at the time doesn't mean you went through any less than he did." Finn had spent countless nights curled up in the sleeping roll next to mine, listening to stories about my mother's escalating abuse and neglect while a demon Mellie and I knew nothing about had ravaged her body and devoured her soul. I wanted Finn to trust me enough to let me return the favor. "Whatever it is, it's your childhood trauma too," I insisted.

"But not like it is his."

"You know you can tell me anything, right?" I whispered as the footsteps at my back grew louder.

"Yes." Finn pulled me into a hug to speak directly into my ear, and in spite of the grim circumstances, the feel of his body pressed against mine made my pulse rush. "And as soon as Maddock is ready to talk, I'll tell you everything."

Before I could argue, we were overtaken by the group again.

When we pulled back onto the abandoned highway, Mellie rode in the SUV so she could stretch out for a nap on the third-row bench seat, and Tobias sat in the truck between Anabelle and me, while Finn drove.

I wasn't sure how to approach the questions we needed him to answer, but Anabelle—bless her heart—was finally in her element for the first time since we'd escaped from New Temperance.

"How old are you, Tobias?" she asked, and I could hear teacher-Ana in her voice again.

"Almost seven," he said around a mouthful of chocolate, which Devi had vehemently objected to "wasting" on a kid.

"What grade are you in?"

"Second."

"I used to teach second grade!" Anabelle said, and when Tobias's eyes widened, she laughed. "I don't look much like a teacher without my cassock, do I?"

Tobias shook his head and sucked the bit of chocolate on his tongue.

It had taken Anabelle nearly a month in the badlands to finally give up her Church robes in favor of a pair of jeans and a few T-shirts we'd liberated from our first supply raid, and she still didn't quite look comfortable in the causal clothes.

"Look, I can prove it." Ana held out her right hand to show him the brand on the back—four stylized, intertwined columns of flame, each representing one of the sacred obligations of the people to the Church. Together, those individual flames formed the symbolic blaze with which the Church claimed to have rid the world of the demon plague.

Though, as it turned out, that was a lie, the brand was a lie, and pretty much everything the Church had ever told us was a lie.

But Tobias didn't know that. His eyes widened when he saw the brand, and trust opened his expression in a way that even chocolate hadn't been able to.

Anabelle set him a little more at ease with a few funny stories from her days as a teacher, and then she gently switched gears. "Where did you go to school, Tobias?"

"At the Day School."

"Which day school? Where are you from, sweetie? Solace? Diligencia?" Those were the two closest cities, other than New Temperance, and we knew for a fact that he hadn't come from my hometown, because Anabelle would have recognized a second grader, even if he hadn't been in her class.

"Verity," he said at last, and Anabelle's gaze snapped up to meet mine over his head, while Finn stiffened on the seat next to me. Verity was more than a thousand miles west of New Temperance, in the mountains of what was once called Colorado.

I'd never heard of anyone traveling so far, except as part of an armed Church caravan. How the hell had a little boy wound up so far from his hometown, with two possessed adults who were not his biological parents?

"Tobias, there were two people inside the car we found you next to," Anabelle said, her voice almost fragile with tension. "Were those your parents?"

He nodded again. "They picked me over all the other boys at the children's home." His small chest puffed out with pride. "They said I could live with them in their house. Out east."

Chills raced the length of my spine, then settled into my stomach. Tobias's new "parents" couldn't have adopted him without a parenting license. Were they unable to have children of their own? Had they adopted him for the same reason my mom had given birth to Melanie and me? If so, why would they rip out their own throats so soon after the adoption—much too soon for either of them to inherit their newly adopted host?

The answer suddenly seemed obvious: they'd found other, older potential hosts, already ripe for harvesting.

We'd seen evidence of a few nomads roaming the badlands. They were few and far between, but it was entirely possible that Tobias's parents had run across a small band and killed their mutating human hosts so they could claim fresher bodies. Maybe they'd planned to come back for Tobias and raise him as a future host. Or maybe they'd abandoned him entirely in the face of a new opportunity.

Finn clutched the steering wheel, and I realized he hadn't said a word since we'd resumed our trek south. Something was wrong, but he wouldn't talk to me about it until we had privacy.

"What were their names, sweetie?" Anabelle asked.

"Mommy and Daddy," Tobias said, and I had to swallow a groan. They hadn't told him their real names? "They died, didn't they?" he asked softly, and my heart ached for him. I nodded, and when he only blinked at me, somber but accepting, I wondered if maybe losing another set of parents just didn't come as much of a surprise to a child who'd already been orphaned once.

Though the *manner* of their deaths was obviously traumatic.

What if that were Mellie's baby?

The sudden thought sent a new kind of terror slithering through my veins: helplessness.

What if Mellie's baby were one day orphaned in the

badlands—not a far-fetched scenario, since he or she would be raised among fugitives who sought out demons on a daily basis. How would my niece or nephew survive without Anathema's protection and provision?

The inevitable, horrifying answer chilled me from the inside out: Melanie's orphaned child would be little more than a snack for the first degenerate to find the poor thing. Giving the baby a soul wouldn't be enough. Someone would have to teach him or her how to *survive*.

"Did you see what happened to your parents?" Finn asked Tobias, drawing me out of my own terrifying thoughts, but when Anabelle scowled at him, I realized she'd planned a more gentle buildup to that particular query.

Tobias shook his head. "Mommy told me to climb into the trunk and be as quiet as I could. She said if I won the quiet game, she'd open the trunk and give me a surprise. But she never came, so I had to open the trunk with the safety latch." He bowed his head, reminding me of my kindergarten students when they were in trouble. "I guess I wasn't quiet enough."

"I'm sure you weren't the problem, honey," Anabelle said, and outrage burned deep in my soul as I thought of the boy hiding in the trunk while his new "parents" ripped out their own throats and abandoned him in the badlands in favor of other hosts.

But then I realized that the poor kid was actually pretty lucky—his worthless "parents" had left Tobias alive, which was a mercy, considering how his life would have ended if he'd grown up in their custody.

* * *

"You want to *what*?" Devi demanded, and I laid one finger over my lips to shush her. Across the dusty second-floor den of a long-abandoned house, Tobias was curled up on my bedroll in the glow of twice the number of candles we would normally have burned at night, in case he woke up and was afraid of the dark.

He'd fallen asleep in the truck around the time the sun set, so I'd carried him up the stairs myself.

Melanie slept just feet from him, on her own mat on the hard floor—we avoided carpet whenever possible, because after a century of neglect, most soft materials had become havens for mold, mildew, and entire colonies of parasitic insects.

We'd been lucky to find a ghost town so soon after the sun went down, and luckier still that that particular town had been abandoned during the war, rather than razed or torched. It wasn't safe to drive across the badlands at night, because headlights could lure degenerates from miles away.

"I want to take him home," I repeated. Then I held my breath, watching the others for their reactions as candle-light cast dancing shadows on the six other faces in our huddle.

"Okay, first of all, he doesn't *have* a home," Devi insisted, and though her voice was softer, it had lost none of its bite. "He's an orphan twice over. He must be the unluckiest damn orphan in the *world*. I mean, who gets adopted by demons?"

"They spared his life, but you want to abandon him," I pointed out. No need to note that demons only spare children so they can be possessed once they've suffered through puberty and can reach the high shelves. "Sounds like meeting *you* was his unluckiest blow yet."

Grayson covered a grin with one hand, but Devi only scowled at me and continued. "Second of all, I'm not sure that returning him to a Church children's home would be much of an improvement. Those are run by demons too. All we'd be doing is delaying his inevitable possession."

"So your solution is to keep him?" Reese whispered, intentionally misunderstanding her to support my point, and I could have hugged him.

She abandoned the rest of her argument in surprise. "Of course not. A kid's the last thing we need."

My brows rose, and I aimed a pointed glance at my sister.

Devi pulled a long rope of dark hair over her shoulder and leaned back against a couch too musty to risk sitting on. "We don't have any choice about that one. But that doesn't mean we should start collecting more of them!"

But I could practically hear the part she hadn't said out loud. Devi wasn't worried about life in the badlands with an infant—in fact, she rarely even thought about that impending challenge—because she didn't think Mellie's baby would survive.

Despite my determination to see that baby live at all costs, the heartbreaking truth was that Devi was probably right. But Tobias *was* alive, and we couldn't just leave him for the degenerates. So I took a deep breath and forged ahead. "Look, I know you all wanted to head south, but we don't have a destination in mind, so what difference docs it make if we head west instead?"

Finn squeezed my hand. "It's nearly a thousand miles, Nina." Because in our wanderings, we'd never strayed more than a hundred miles or so from New Temperance.

"So what?" I stared into the deep green of his eyes, trying to understand his reluctance. "Are we on some schedule I don't know about?"

Maddock exhaled slowly as he painstakingly peeled the label from an empty bean can as if it deserved more of his attention than my suggestion did. "No, but it's not safe. There's too much empty space between the cities out west. Caravans will be few and far between."

"We've never been better prepared for that," Reese argued, and I gave him a grateful smile. "We just scored the biggest haul we're ever going to have. That'll give us some breathing room while we learn to spot those plants Mellie and Ana have been reading about. And it's spring." He shrugged. "Hunting will be easier."

"Nina, what does it matter where we leave him?" Finn asked softly, stroking my knuckles with his thumb. "I hate to say it, but Devi's right. He'll be raised by demons no matter where we take him, so why not drop him in one of the cities on our way south?"

"Because he's lost everything! Twice! The least we can do is return him to the only home he's ever known, where at least he'll have some friends."

Maddock set his can down with a firm clank against the wood floor. "We're not going west, Nina."

I glanced at him in surprise. He'd always been a good leader precisely because he never made illogical, unilateral rulings, but something had changed. Something was *wrong,* and Maddock might not be willing to talk about it, but that didn't mean the rest of us had to stop talking. "I say we vote on it."

"No vote." Maddy leaned back against the couch next to Devi and crossed his arms over the new T-shirt he'd found in the cargo shipment. "We're not going."

My gaze narrowed on him and I let go of Finn's hand. "We're a team. We decide together." I glanced around our candlelit circle, hyperaware of the sudden tension in our ranks. "All in favor of taking Tobias back west, to Verity, raise your hand." I held my left hand high above my head, and a second later Reese did the same.

Devi crossed her arms over her chest and raised one eyebrow at me in challenge. That was no surprise, and neither was Maddock's nay stance, but what I couldn't understand was why he looked genuinely sorry to be voting against me.

Anabelle raised her hand, and I smiled at her.

"You don't get a vote!" Devi snapped.

"The hell she doesn't! There's a price on her head too, and she lost just as much as the rest of us when we fled New Temperance," I said hotly.

"She gets a vote," Maddock said. But he didn't seem very pleased with his own ruling.

Fair enough.

But when Finn's arm remained at his side, my chest suddenly felt tight. "Sorry, Nina. I vote we go south." His deep gaze pleaded with me to understand, and I tried not to be hurt that he'd sided with Maddock rather than with me.

"That's three to three," Devi said, irritation flashing in her candlelit dark eyes, and we all turned to Grayson, who would have the deciding vote.

After a couple of seconds of contemplation, she raised her hand.

"Damn it!" Devi snapped.

Grayson only shrugged. "If we don't go with Nina, she'll go on her own, and we're safer together than apart, no matter where we wind up."

She was right on all counts.

Maddock glanced over my shoulder to where my sister lay snoring lightly on the wood floor. I could see what he was thinking, but I shook my head. "If you wake her up, she'll vote to take him home," I said, and no one disagreed.

Maddy sighed. "I'll take first watch. The rest of you get

some sleep." His eyebrows dipped low. "In the morning we're westward bound."

* * *

When everyone but Maddock and Finn had curled up on their sleeping mats, I checked on Tobias and found him fast asleep on my bedroll, which meant I'd have to double up with someone. I grabbed Finn's mat and tossed my head toward the door, silently asking him to join me in another room.

He nodded with a steamy smile, his pupils dilating as he picked up one of the candles, and heat flooded my cheeks when I realized he'd misread my request for privacy. Finn followed me into the dark hallway, then through another door and into a bedroom where most of the linens had long ago rotted away from the mattress.

"Are you mad at me?" he whispered, pushing the door closed at his back. I turned to find that the candle cast only a small dome of light around us, leaving the rest of the room in deep shadows. The lit space between us felt as intimate as his softly spoken question, and suddenly I realized I could count on both hands the number of times we'd been alone together.

"If I were mad at you, I'd be cuddling with my sister right now." I watched the candlelight flicker in his eyes, thankful that they stayed the same no matter whose body he wore. If the eyes truly were the windows to the soul, at least I could be sure I was seeing some real part of him even when the rest belonged to someone else.

I'd first met him in Maddock's body, and the revelation that his form wasn't really his own had come as a shock to me. But I'd grown used to the guard he'd worn for months now, in part because I had no previous association of those arms or hands or face with another person. And in part because he wore the body easily and used it *well*. As his comfort level had risen, so had mine.

"I would like to know why, though," I confessed as he set the candle on a dust-coated dresser. "Why does it matter whether we go south or west?"

Finn sighed and tucked a fallen strand of brown hair behind my ear. "Maddy was born out west." His hands trailed slowly over my shoulders and down my arms, and I fought the urge to lean into his touch in that rare private moment. "He had it rough as a kid, and he doesn't want to go back."

"I get it. I don't want to go back to New Temperance either." Yet the doubt in Finn's eyes told me that I couldn't possibly understand. Not really. "But we're not taking *him* home. We're taking Tobias home."

"I know. But Verity's too close for comfort."

My brows rose and I studied his gaze. That was the closest he'd ever come to mentioning a hometown. "Is Maddy from Verity? Are *you*?"

"No. And I don't know." He took his sleeping mat from

me and unrolled it on the floor a few feet from the door. "I don't remember anything from before I met Maddock." Which he'd insisted over and over.

His early memories were as strange and inexplicable as his incorporeal state. Though playing with Maddy was the oldest thing Finn could remember, no one else had been able to see or hear him. Maddock's family had assumed he was talking to and playing with an imaginary "friend," which was how Finn got his name—that was as close as toddler Maddock could come to properly pronouncing the word.

Finn sank onto the bedroll and patted the spot next to him. "What I do know is that when Maddy's upset, I'm upset."

"That makes eight of us," I said, settling in next to him, and Finn's green eyes took on a grateful shine as he leaned in to kiss me. He was as glad that I liked Maddock as I was that he liked Melanie. "Mind if I share your sleep roll tonight?" I whispered against Finn's mouth as his hand slid into my hair, gently tilting my head for a more accessible angle. "Tobias is using mine."

"You can share everything I own." Finn's mouth met mine, and he sucked my lower lip between his for one heart-pounding second. "Which is pretty much just this sleep roll," he admitted, his lips brushing mine with every syllable. He kissed me again, and I decided that if the Church was right and carnal contact really was a sin, it was a sin well worth paying for. . . .

* * *

It was still dark outside when I woke up with Finn's hoodie folded beneath my head for a pillow. I turned back one of the blankets from our recent Church raid, and when my hand brushed his warm, bare chest, my touch lingered. I didn't want to leave our private cocoon, but nature called.

Finn stirred when I stood, but he didn't wake up, so I draped the blanket over him.

While we'd slept, our candle had burned out, which meant I had to feel my way down the hall in the dark.

Two candles were burning in the den, and by their light I saw that Maddock still stood watch, though my biological clock told me hours had passed since the rest of us had gone to bed. Since we had no *actual* clocks and I didn't own a watch, my body and the sun were all I had with which to measure the passage of time.

Those and the rate at which a candle burned.

Maddock sat on the arm of an ancient, mildewy couch, peering behind a dusty set of blinds at the street out front. He didn't notice me until I sank onto a wooden desk chair two feet from him. "Need a break?" I whispered, and when I shifted on the chair, peeling flakes of varnish caught on the seat of my worn jeans.

"I don't think I could sleep if I tried," he admitted, and I squinted for a better look at his face. Maddock looked tense and sad, but what worried me was the new edge of fear lining his brow and crinkling in the corners of his eyes.

"Finn told me why you don't want to go west."

He turned sharply to look at me. "What did he tell you?"

I shrugged. "That you were born out west and that Verity is too close for comfort."

Maddock relaxed visibly, and I frowned.

"There's more to it, isn't there?" I said, and he nodded but offered nothing more. "We'll head back east as soon as we've dropped Tobias off," I assured him. "None of us is eager for a family reunion. Except maybe Reese." His father had been burned as a heretic—otherwise known as a skeptic—in Diligencia, and his mother had sent him with Anathema to save him from the same fate.

"Or maybe Grayson," Maddy added, and a sudden memory burned bright from the back of my mind.

Grayson's parents had been exposed as breeders when her older brother, Carey, came into his exorcist abilities earlier than expected. The Church executed her parents and took her brother. Grayson was the only member of the James family to escape intact, and if not for Anathema, she'd probably be in Church custody, just like her brother.

Except that Carey James was no longer in Church custody.

During our escape from New Temperance, I'd discovered that the Church had lost him in a raid by a group of demons led by someone named Kastor.

For a while, I'd debated telling Grayson what I'd learned about her brother, but in the end, I'd decided not to say anything because I'd uncovered more questions than answers about Carey, and I was afraid that would only make his absence harder to bear. Then we had become overwhelmed by constant cold and hunger, and roaming degenerates, and I'd forgotten I even had that unfortunate bit of information.

Until Maddock's mention of her family sparked the memory.

A flash of light caught my eye from between two of the slats in the mini blinds, yanking me from my thoughts. "What's that?" I stood and peeked through the glass, my heart thumping rapidly. Usually Grayson woke up when she sensed that degenerates were closing in on us.

But Maddock didn't seem worried. "I think they're nomads."

Supposedly, after the war several groups chose a dangerous, migratory life in the badlands over the totalitarian protection of the Church-run cities. In school we were taught that the nomads had succumbed to starvation and degenerate attacks decades ago, yet the half-dozen abandoned campsites we'd found seemed to suggest otherwise.

Maddock shifted uncomfortably on the arm of the couch. "They've been on the edge of town for hours and they don't seem to know we're here." Which was why he hadn't alerted the rest of us. Any movement we made now would only bring us to their attention.

The only people we'd actually seen in the badlands were uniformed Church cargo drivers and scavengers sent to "reclaim" resources from our past. They tended to work quickly and scurry back to the safety of tall steel walls, and they never veered off course.

By contrast, the nomads weren't scared of the landscape they lived in, but they did seem to be shy. "That's the closest they've ever come."

Maddy shrugged. "It was bound to happen sooner or later."

"Maybe we should make contact." After all, for more than a century nomads had been living off a landscape the Church told us could not be conquered. They'd been fishing, hunting, and harvesting—surviving among roving hordes of degenerates, presumably without exorcist abilities. "They could probably teach us a lot faster than Mellie's books have."

Maddock shook his head, still staring out the window at the bright flicker of what looked like a single candle. "Helping us would put them on the Church's radar. If the 'exorcists' find us with those nomads, they'll kill every one of them to get to us."

FOUR

"Incoming!" Reese shouted, and I ducked as a degenerate flew over my head, its tattered cassock trailing through the air behind it. The torn and filthy Church robe was once navy blue, which meant that the host had been a policeman before he'd been possessed by the Unclean.

The mutated monster landed barefoot on the crumbling sidewalk four feet from me. His elongated toes were broken and oozing fresh blood, but he didn't seem to notice. He howled, his sharply pointed chin dropping to reveal a mouth full of broken, rotting teeth. Then he lunged.

The beast slammed into my chest, driving me onto the chipped steps of an abandoned small-town courthouse. A chunk of concrete dug into my back, just left of my spine. The monster's jaws snapped at me, drool dripping onto my shirt, and I shoved my right forearm against his emaciated throat, narrowly preventing him from tearing mine out with his teeth.

I pressed my left hand against the beast's chest, and bright light surged between us. The monster screeched, his bald head thrown back, dark hollows stretching beneath his cheekbones, and the fire from my palm blazed deep into his flesh, burning the demon from its soulless, mutated human host.

When the light faded and the monster sagged against me, I shoved him onto the fractured courthouse steps, then rose to assess the fight still going on all around me. Finn stood guard with his rifle in front of the courthouse's massive double doors, which no longer quite closed because the building had both settled and begun to rot in the century since it last saw use. Ana, Grayson, Mellie, and Tobias watched from a first-floor window, despite instructions to stay on the top floor, at a safer distance.

Reese, Devi, and Maddock were each locked in combat with other degenerates in the street—Reese was fending off three at once—and as I took stock, one of them abandoned the fight and darted across the overgrown lawn on all fours, her thin, matted hair flying out behind her.

As she hit the courthouse steps, I grabbed her by the tail of her torn, filthy shirt, then shoved her facedown onto the concrete and pressed my glowing hand against the back of her ribs. She screamed and flailed beneath me, and I could only ride out her violent death throes even as another monster lunged at Finn.

He swung the rifle like a bat—reluctant to kill a human host, because that would free the demon within—and the thunk of the steel barrel against skull made me flinch.

I backed away from the dead host beneath my hand and grabbed the degenerate he'd just bashed, then pressed my still-burning left palm against its bare, filthy flesh. The demon thrashed, caught by the flames blazing between us, and on the edges of my vision the other members of Anathema gathered to watch me burn out the last of the small horde.

Grayson pushed the courthouse door open as the monster crumpled to the ground. She ran past Finn and down the steps to throw herself into Reese's arms. "I'm a walking monster magnet," she groaned into his shoulder while he stroked her brown curls. "They won't stop coming until I exorcise one and trigger my transition."

I knew how she felt. During my transition a few months before, two small hordes of degenerates had managed to breach the walls of New Temperance, drawn to the emergence of my exorcist abilities like fish to a wriggling worm. But in the badlands, there was no wall standing between Grayson and the monsters. There was nothing but us.

Unfortunately, she was right; that wouldn't stop until her hand began to burn in response to their presence, allowing her to actually exorcise a demon, which would usher in the full speed and strength that came with her new ability.

"Maybe if I help fight them, the close proximity will trigger my flame?" She held out her left hand with a hopeful look up at him, but he only shook his head.

"I'm not going to put you in danger to test a theory. When you're ready, it'll happen."

Until then, all we could do was wait.

"Lemme see the bodies!" Tobias tried to run down the steps but tripped over a loose chunk of concrete and crashed to the ground instead. When he stood, blood welled from a gash on his right knee.

"Careful!" Anabelle knelt to examine the cut. "Hold still and let me get a bandage." We'd found a crate of them in the cargo truck, and Tobias had gone through half a box in the two days since we'd found him.

"It doesn't hurt," he said while she rummaged through her satchel. "I can't even feel it."

"You've got to hand it to him," Melanie whispered from my right, rubbing her belly with one hand. "That kid's tough. Last night he burned his arm when he got too close to the campfire. It blistered, but he insists it doesn't hurt at all."

"This one's still smoking!" Tobias squealed as Anabelle pulled him away from a corpse lying in the street. It was indeed still leaking smoke from the hole in the center of its back.

"Don't touch," Mellie scolded, leaving my side to tug

him even farther from the body. "They're probably crawling with germs." Not that we were exactly clean since leaving the abundance of clear creeks and small lakes behind.

"Does the hole go all the way through? Let's roll it over!"

Melanie distracted Tobias with a bottle of water and the bag of cookies she now kept at the ready. I wasn't sure what we'd do with the precocious little boy when we ran out of sweets with which to bribe him.

"You okay?" I asked Finn when I noticed blood dripping from his arm. He blinked, then frowned at me until I showed him the long scratch across his forearm. "That last one had claws."

"Oh. Yeah. I'm fine." He swiped at the blood with the sleeve of his other arm, and then his focus strayed back toward the road. I followed his gaze to find Maddock staring westward into the setting sun, both fists clenched at his sides.

* * *

"I said *no*." Anabelle plucked the chocolate bar from Tobias's grip and tucked it into the front pocket of her backpack. "That's the last one, and you can't have it until you've eaten some real food."

"I'm tired of beans for breakfast." Tobias poked at the contents of his can with a stainless steel spoon. "I want bacon."

Devi rolled two half-burned candles in an extra T-shirt,

then stuffed them into her bag. "Do you see any pigs running around?"

Tobias's bright brown eyes widened. "*Bacon* comes from *pigs*?"

"And from little boys who don't do what they're told," she said, supporting my theory that she probably hadn't liked children even when she'd been one of them. The child stuck his tongue out at her. Devi laughed and knelt to roll up her sleeping mat.

"I gave you beans because you said you were tired of stewed tomatoes," Anabelle pointed out as she wiped her own spoon clean with a damp rag.

"They don't taste good anymore." Tobias pouted. "They don't taste like *anything*. I think they went bad."

I picked up his nearly full can of beans and read from the back. "They're two years from their expiration date, like all the rest. You just don't want to eat anything that's actually good for you."

"Yet he never grows tired of candy." Reese winked at the boy and slid him a secreted chocolate bar from his own bag. Tobias grinned at him and took another small bite of beans.

I stood to gather the cans we'd emptied at breakfast and at dinner the night before, and my gaze fell on Melanie, still lightly snoring on top of her sleep roll. The further her pregnancy progressed, the more easily she tired, yet the harder it was for her to rest. We let her sleep late whenever we could afford to.

As I cleaned up I noticed that Maddock and Finn were both staring out the window. "What's up?" I said, plucking the empty peach can from Maddy's grip.

"They're back." Finn scooted to make room for me at the window, and I saw the problem immediately. We'd slept on the third floor of what was once a small-town courthouse, and the vantage point gave us a view of half the town, and of the crumbling two-lane road leading into the badlands.

About a mile outside of town the nomads had set up camp with four vehicles, two dozen tents, and about twenty horses. They hadn't been there when we'd settled in the night before.

"Two days in a row." Maddock frowned. "We can't keep calling it a coincidence. They're following us."

I picked up the empty can at his feet. "Maybe they want to help us. Or warn us about something."

"Or rob us blind and kill us in our sleep," Devi offered from across the room, where she was stuffing her bedroll into her bag.

"If that's the case, why make their presence so obvious?"

She shrugged. "It can't be easy to hide an entire herd of horses."

I stood by my theories, but Finn and Maddock hardly seemed to know I was there. The farther west we'd come—two-thirds of the way in two days, thanks to pre-war roads kept passable by the Church—the more tense they'd grown.

Tobias, on the other hand, seemed happier with each mile that passed beneath our tires.

"How are we fixed for gas?" Reese added Devi's duffel to the three others hanging from his shoulders.

"Too low to pass by the next station without filling up," Finn said. "If I remember correctly, there's a fuel depot a couple of miles south of town. With any luck, it'll be locked but unguarded."

Assuming the Church hadn't anticipated our westward shift.

Maddock stood and hefted his pack onto his back. "Devi and I will take the SUV. Reese, you take the truck."

"I'll go with him." Grayson rushed ahead before anyone could object. "I'll stay in the truck, but I'm going. You can't keep leaving me behind."

"Oh, let her go," I said. "Finn and I will hold down the fort here."

Reese only relented when he realized he was outvoted.

"Watch the nomads," Maddock said on his way out the door. "If they come any closer, call on this." He tossed me one of our handheld radios.

I gave him a mock salute and clipped the radio to my waistband. As soon as they were gone, Finn took up watch at the window while I knelt to help Tobias with his—formerly *my*—sleep roll.

"Hey, Tobias, how long had you been with your new parents before we found you? Do you remember?"

He shrugged, and I held my finger in place over a length

of black cord holding the bedroll closed so he could form a clumsy bow. "I dunno."

"And you don't remember your new parents' names?"

Anabelle shook her head at me from across the room, where she was taking inventory of our hygiene supplies. But I couldn't leave it alone. If demons adopting kids was going to be a new trend, I wanted to know as much as I could about how they were pulling it off.

"They just said to call them Mommy and Daddy." Tobias stood from his messy but functional nylon bow and pressed his knees together in a stance any first grader would recognize. "I gotta *go*."

The courthouse had half a dozen restrooms, but none of them had been functional in decades. "Hang on, and I'll take you out—"

But he was out of the room and halfway down the first of two dusty marble staircases before I could even stand.

"Tobias, wait!" I called, and Mellie rolled over on her bedroll but didn't quite shake off sleep.

The rapid patter of the child's footsteps echoed below me as I stomped down the spiral stairs after him. A second later Finn's boots clomped from above as he followed both of us. "Tobias!" he shouted, but the boy's footsteps didn't slow.

When I hit the first-floor landing, I stopped to listen for the echo of small shoes to figure out which way he'd gone.

Down the back hall, toward the rear door.

I followed Tobias into the back of the building,

marveling at how well the courthouse had held up under a century of neglect. Stone floors and walls didn't crumble or mold like carpet and drywall, and though many of the windows were broken, most of the doors were still intact, which had kept out the larger animals. And because the building had been stripped of furnishings shortly after the war, there was nothing left inside to rot or mildew.

"Tobias?" I called, my boots nearly silent on the grimy marble tiles.

Muffled footsteps whispered against the floor at my back, and a grunt exploded behind me, followed by a blunt crack. My heart hammering, I spun to find an unfamiliar man splayed across the floor at my feet, the short end of a crowbar lodged in the side of his skull.

I jumped back, startled, and my pulse raced so fast my vision swam.

Standing over the dead man was a boy about my age, wearing torn jeans and a dusty black cowboy hat, his feet spread for balance, his jaw set in a firm line. He wore prewar vintage Western boots, absent the spurs I'd seen in history textbooks, and despite my shock—or perhaps because of it—I wondered how he'd managed to walk so softly in footwear that looked stiff and unyielding.

His skin was dark, his eyes a piercing golden brown, and he wore a simple silver cross on a thin chain around his neck.

With a startling bolt of intuition, I realized the boy

was one of the nomads—and he'd just killed the stranger who'd snuck up on me.

"Don't move." Without looking away from me, he braced one boot on the dead man's jaw and wrenched the crowbar free with a wet sucking sound. Then he wielded it like a bat on one shoulder, ready to swing again, blood dripping from the short, bent end of the metal.

"I am Eli Woods, sentinel in the Lord's Army." His gaze narrowed on me. His grip tightened on the crowbar. "You have ten seconds to convince me you're not one of the Unclean, or I *will* bury this in your skull."

Uh-oh.

I took a step back and my spine hit the cool stone wall.

Eli wasn't a demon, so I couldn't exorcise him, and I wasn't going to hurt a fellow human in anything less than self-defense. Which was starting to look like a distinct possibility.

"Five seconds." He studied me, and I found no recognition in his eyes. "Who are you?"

Obviously nomads didn't watch the news. They didn't have television. But if they had a radio and had picked up any of the Church's broadcasts proclaiming the infamous Nina Kane to be possessed, giving him my name wouldn't help him trust me.

"Um . . ."

"Three seconds."

I sucked in a deep breath and held his gaze. Then I spat

out the truth. "I'm Nina Kane. But I'm not a demon, and I can prove it."

Eli's dark brows rose beneath the wide brim of his hat. "You can prove you're not a demon?" He was either surprised or skeptical, but I couldn't tell which because his face only seemed capable of scowling. His grip on the crowbar tightened. "That's a new one. Start talking."

But as I tried to figure out what to say, I realized that without a demon there to exorcise, proving my claim would be nearly impossible. I held my hands up, palms out, to remind him that I wasn't armed. "Okay, I could prove it if there was another demon here for me to kill, but since there isn't, you'll just have to take my word for it." In my whole life, I'd never wished for a demon, but in that moment, I got close. "I'm an exorcist."

"There *are* no exorcists." He pulled the crowbar back to swing, and my heart fell into my stomach. "They're all demons the so-called Unified Church uses to hunt down its enemies." He shifted his weight and leaned into his swing. Pulse racing, I dropped to the ground on my knees. Pain radiated up my legs. The metal bar swung over my head with a fierce whoosh. I scrambled around the dead guy's feet and stood, backing away from Eli with my arms out. Trying to look harmless.

"No, wait! I'm not one of *those* exorcists." I would have been relieved that he knew about the Church's black-robed fakes if he didn't think I was one of them. "I'm the real thing! So we're actually on the same side—"

"Drop it!" Finn shouted, and I turned to see him in the doorway, aiming his rifle at Eli.

"Who are you?" the sentinel demanded, crowbar still held at the ready.

"That's a complicated question." Finn's focus on Eli never wavered. "Come any closer to her, and you won't live long enough to hear the answer."

"Eli, *please* put the crowbar down." I forced my voice to remain low-pitched and calm. "This is Finn. He's with me. He's not going to hurt you." I turned to Finn. "This is Eli Woods. He killed the demon who snuck up on me, and I think we should all be friends."

Finn glanced at the corpse on the floor but looked unconvinced.

"Finn, put the gun down," I said.

"Him first." His aim at the center of Eli's worn-thin button-up shirt was a steady threat.

"Okay, boys, someone has to go first." I turned back to the self-professed sentinel. "Since you obviously don't recognize my face or my name, I'm guessing you haven't seen or heard the news recently?"

He shook his head. "We don't have television or radio."

"We who? The Lord's Army?" I said, and Finn gave me a confused look. "What is this army?"

"We are the last of the true believers." Eli's words had the formal cadence of an official pledge or creed. It sounded a little too much like the Church for comfort, but Eli—and presumably his nomadic army—were no more fans of the Unified Church than I was. "We are a beacon of light and truth, shining in a world of darkness and corruption."

"Humble too," Finn muttered.

I ignored him and focused on Eli. "It's nice to meet you. And your army." I cleared my throat and tossed a warning glance at Finn. "Are you familiar with the saying 'The enemy of my enemy is my friend'? Because that's kind of what we're looking at here. The Church has been hunting you guys for decades, and now they're hunting us too because of what we know and what we can do. Since we're on the same side, maybe you could reconsider lowering your weapon?"

Eli took one hand from his crowbar long enough to reseat his black cowboy hat, briefly revealing short, tight curls. Then he reclaimed his expert grip. "You're exorcists." It wasn't a question. He was repeating the part he obviously found hard to believe.

"We're *true* exorcists. We hunt demons, just like you." I gestured to the body at my feet. "But instead of puncturing skulls, we incinerate the bond between parasite and host and fry the demonic bastards back to hell."

His eyes widened. "You're serious."

I nodded. "It's kinda badass."

"Though most of us don't object to blunt force trauma when the occasion calls for it." Finn shrugged and gestured with the rifle he was still aiming. "Or bullets."

I glared at Finn, then turned back to Eli. "I need both

of you to put down your weapons so we can focus on our mutual enemy." I shrugged, aiming for casual confidence. "You know. Evil."

Both of them glanced at me. Then they glared at each other. Neither boy lowered his weapon.

My temper spiked. "We're in the middle of the badlands with a corpse on the floor and the Church on our tails. We are *not* each other's biggest problem. So, Finn, put the damn gun down!"

Finn's bright green eyes narrowed and his jaw tensed. "Not until you back out of his reach."

"Striking a human would be a blight on my honor, and she's obviously not possessed," Eli said as I moved closer to Finn. "The jury's still out on you."

Finn's glare grew colder, but he flicked the safety switch on his rifle, then lowered it. But he didn't sling it over his back.

I turned back to Eli. "Your turn."

When the sentinel took a deep breath, I realized that trusting Finn and me was as much of a risk for him as the reverse was for us. Maybe more. He lowered his bloody crowbar but didn't put it down, and I decided that was the best we were going to get.

"Now I have to go find—" Something moved in the shadowy doorway behind Finn, and I exhaled in relief as Tobias stepped into the marble foyer from the back hall.

But he wasn't looking at me. He wasn't gloating over having escaped my custody, nor did he look chagrined. He didn't even seem surprised to see the body on the floor, or Eli, with his gore-covered crowbar.

Eli's gaze tracked down from Finn to the boy now at Finn's side. His eyes narrowed and his arms tensed as he raised the crowbar like a bat again. "Step away from the Unclean."

I tried to move in front of Eli, to shield Finn, but he pushed me aside.

Finn lifted his gun again. "Do *not* touch her!"

"I'm fine," I insisted, my pulse racing as the tension between the two of them resurged. "Finn's not possessed. He would never hurt—"

"Not him," Eli growled through clenched teeth. "The little one."

Chills rose the length of my spine as I turned to follow his intently focused gaze. He was staring right at Tobias.

FIVE

"No." Panic tightened my throat as the sentinel focused his destructive zeal on the child I'd committed all of Anathema to helping. The child I'd begun to think of as an older version of my unborn niece or nephew—an innocent, dependent upon us for survival. "*No*. He's just a kid."

"Tobias was my nephew," Eli said, and shock surged like fire through my veins. I hadn't told him the boy's name. "Then an Unclean raiding party ambushed our division four days ago and took him. You've been traveling in the company of a demon, Nina Kane."

I glanced at Tobias, expecting the child to deny the accusation. But then, he probably didn't even understand what he was being accused of. "We found him on the side of the road. He'd been abandoned. Left to *die*."

"He wasn't left. He was *bait*," Eli insisted.

"No." I stepped toward Tobias, intending to shield him with my body, but Eli pulled me back again, and this time Finn didn't object. I jerked free of the sentinel's grip and reached for Tobias.

"Nina." Finn suddenly turned and aimed his rifle at the child, backing slowly toward me and away from Tobias. "Eli's right. The kid's possessed."

I froze. If anyone would know for sure, it'd be Finn. All he had to do was give a little psychic push in Tobias's direction—as if to take over the child's body—and he would only meet resistance if something else was already occupying that space.

A demon.

"But . . ." My pulse raced even as I tried to deny what I was hearing. A demon traveling in the company of exorcists, and not *one* of us had realized? How was that even possible? We hadn't suspected him because . . . "Demons don't take over children's bodies," I mumbled, still trying to come to terms with what I was hearing. "Everyone knows that." The limitations were too great. The hosts failed to mature properly. Degeneration came much faster.

Tobias smiled slowly, eerily, and chills crawled across my skin. There was nothing left of the little boy we'd spent the past two days with. "Which is exactly why you'd never suspect a child." His gaze—his very awareness—appeared to age right in front of me, and suddenly his chubby cheeks seemed an absurd and disturbing disguise.

"He's your nephew?" I asked Eli, without taking my gaze from the pint-sized demon. No wonder the nomads were following us. We were traveling with the human husk of one of their children.

"He was," Eli corrected, and I could practically feel the tension in his bearing. I could hear it in every word he spoke. "Until four days ago."

Four days. That meant his division of the Lord's Army—whatever *that* was—had been raided the very day Anathema had turned south to leave the New Temperance area. That *couldn't* be a coincidence.

"You weren't leading us to Verity, were you?" My words echoed in the empty foyer, my voice deep and still with the weight of the question. I knew Verity was out west, but without a map I'd never realized the child had led us off course. "Where were you taking us?"

Tobias's smile decayed with a cloying sweetness, like fruit gone bad. "Ask your boyfriend."

Finn cursed so passionately the words actually compromised his aim. Not that he would shoot a demon unless he had no other choice.

"Finn?" I said, but his jaw remained clenched.

"I didn't recognize you at first," Tobias said, still watching Finn, and even his speech sounded different. Ageless. His voice was infinity, granted sound. "Where did you find such a pretty host?"

75

Finn bristled at the comparison of his incorporeal state to that of a demon, but I was too startled by the implication to be offended for him. Tobias *knew* about Finn.

How the hell could he know? We'd been so careful not to reveal Finn's uniquely incorporeal state in front of the monster we'd mistaken for a child.

"Identify yourself," Finn whispered, and there was something strange in the demand. Some ageless formality, as if the words carried more power—more imperative—than I could possibly understand.

"Don't you recognize me, child?" Tobias's small brows arched over eyes that had once shone with human joy and innocence, and the irony was staggering.

"Aldric," Finn said, and it didn't sound like a guess. "And who was that?" He tossed his head at the man Eli had killed with the crowbar.

"Meshara. And you *know* how she abhors wearing the male form."

"Finn?" My hands opened and closed, my left palm burning with the flames my body wanted to unleash, and I was suddenly hyperaware of every opportunity I'd had to burn this Aldric from Tobias's young form. I'd given him my bedroll. I'd sung to him in the cab of the truck and shared my chocolate ration with him. He'd slept *inches* from *my sister*.

"What's happening, Finn? Where was he leading us?" I hadn't felt so distressingly uninformed since I'd discovered that my own mother was possessed.

Eli stepped closer on my right, crowbar still ready to swing. "He was taking you to Pandemonia."

The name was unfamiliar, but I knew the meaning of the word.

Pandemonia.

All demons.

My chills became a full-body quaking I had to fight to restrict to my insides. "A city full of the Unclean?" In truth, all the surviving US cities were being governed by demons in the guise of Church officials, but a city *populated* by demons, advertising its presence with its very name? "When the Church finds out, they will wipe your demon city from the map."

Aldric laughed, and the sound seemed to freeze as it slid down my spine. "She's adorable, Finn. One doesn't usually find such naïveté in an exorcist."

Naïveté? "The Church *knows*?" The very existence of Pandemonia was a threat to the Unified Church's biggest secret. Why would they let the city stand?

The answer came as soon as I'd thought the question. *Because they can't take it down.* If the Church *could* raze Pandemonia, it would.

"Why are you here?" Finn demanded.

"Why do you think? He wants to see Maddock." Aldric's eerie smile slid my way. "He wants to meet *all* of Maddy's little friends. Especially the exorcists."

"Who's *he*?" Eli asked, and if he hadn't, I would have. But we got no answer. Whoever "he" was, he was obviously a demon, and his interest in the exorcist members of Anathema was painfully clear. Exorcists made much stronger, hardier, longer-lasting hosts than did normal people. Which was why my mother had chosen an exorcist to be my father—so that the child she raised to be her next host would be as durable as possible.

"He'll never see Maddock again," Finn growled. "And neither will you." He turned to me. "Nina?"

I lifted my left hand, already cradling its flame.

"Grayson's transitioning," Aldric said, and I froze in the middle of my first step toward him, confused by the non sequitur. "No matter where you go, degenerates will flock to her, and he will follow them to you. How do you think *we* found you?" The child-demon nodded at the corpse of his former peer—obviously the other half of "we."

"We'll fry everyone he sends after us," Finn promised.

"And your sister?" Aldric turned to me. "Is Melanie an exorcist? Will her baby be one?"

"Stay away from my sister and her—"

Finn lifted his rifle, revising his aim.

Aldric spread his chubby arms, inviting Finn to shoot. "Go ahead." His focus found me and lingered. He looked . . . hungry. "I'm due for an upgrade anyway."

Surely he was bluffing. It wasn't easy for a disembodied demon to claim a healthy, conscious human host. But I wasn't confident enough to bet on that, and neither was Finn.

"Nina!" Finn glanced at my hand, and then his gaze skipped to the demon.

I flipped a mental switch, and a handful of flickering flames kindled in my palm.

Aldric's grin widened—a farce of childhood joy. "Kastor is going to *love* her."

"Kastor?" I said, and Finn gave me the smallest, subtlest shake of his head. The "he" from Pandemonia who wanted to see Maddock was *Kastor*?

Finn looked sick. I'd told him in confidence that Kastor—whose name the former Deacon of New Temperance had invoked to scare us—had stolen Grayson's brother from a Church caravan. But Finn had never mentioned that he *knew* this demon that other demons feared!

"You told her about Kastor?" Aldric said, then he read the answer in my expression. "You *haven't* told her. Yet she knows something. . . ."

"Kastor is the wolf," I said. And we were the sheep.

At least, that's how Deacon Bennett had put it. She'd seen the Unified Church as a shepherd, slaughtering only the sheep they needed to survive, while the wolf, she'd claimed, would butcher us indiscriminately.

"Yes, the wolf." Aldric's eyes narrowed as they studied me. "I don't suppose you own a red hooded riding cloak?"

"What?" I frowned.

The demon child shrugged. "No matter. He will devour you just the same, and Finn will be forced to watch. Eli knows all about the torment of spectators, don't you?" Aldric said, and I felt Eli tense at my back. "He saw poor little Tobias wake up from an afternoon nap with a wicked smile and a voracious appetite for pain."

Eli grunted, and something whistled through the air, end over end, so fast my gaze couldn't quite track it.

"No!" Finn's hand shot out, and Eli's crowbar slammed into his palm hard enough to throw him off his feet. He landed in front of Aldric, his eyes shut tight, clutching the steel bar in his left fist and the barrel of the rifle in his right. Pain was drawn in every line of his face.

Aldric pounced, straddling Finn, his tiny hands around Finn's throat. The muscles in his small arms bulged with more strength than a child should have had. He hardly looked human in that moment, and I didn't understand why Finn didn't fight back, until his eyes opened and they were no longer Finn-green.

They were Carter-brown, and terrified. Sudden, excruciating pain had driven Finn from the body of the New Temperance gate guard.

Eli lunged for them, and his movement broke through my shock. I lurched in front of him and shoved my left hand down on the demon child's back. Light exploded between us. Aldric threw his head back. The screech that erupted from his small throat filled me with a savage satisfaction, and I was certain all over again that even on the run in the badlands, I was doing what I was meant to do.

Aldric's hands loosened around Carter's throat, then fell

away as his scream died. When he finally collapsed on top of the poor, shocked guard, I fell with him.

For a moment no one moved. Then Carter gasped for air, blinking rapidly, and I scrambled off him on my hands and knees. "Are you okay?" I asked, disoriented by the lack of *Finn* in the guard's features and mannerisms.

"Where am I? What's going on?" Carter shoved Aldric onto the floor with his swollen left hand, and flinched from the pain. Then he pushed himself to his feet with his good hand and backed away from the child's still-smoking corpse, which—fortunately—put the rifle out of his reach.

"What the *hell* just happened?" Eli demanded, and I stood to find him staring at us in total bewilderment.

"Um . . . exorcist." I laid one hand over my chest, while both of them stared at me. "Incineration of stolen souls. Sending demons back to hell." I turned to Eli as he knelt to pick up his crowbar. "We've been over this."

Carter cradled his left hand, where an inflamed red streak spanned his palm. "Son of a bitch!" He tried to flex his fingers, then flinched again. "What happened to my hand? Where am I? Who *are* you people?"

Eli stared, his jaw slack. "What's wrong with Finn?"

"Well . . ." I rubbed one hand over my face in frustration. "That's not Finn anymore. That's Heath Carter."

The guard glanced around, and when he noticed his rifle, I slid it out of his reach with my foot, just in case. "What happened to that kid? What the *hell* is going on?" His brown eyes were wide and glazed with shock.

81

"Finn!" I called, hoping he could hear me. "You can come back anytime!"

"Who's Finn?" Carter demanded.

"Nina . . ." Eli retrieved his crowbar, then backed away from the guard, and I could see that his confusion was making him dangerously nervous—he would start swinging again any second.

"Calm down," I said. "Carter's human. So is Finn. He just doesn't have a body of his own, so he's been borrowing Carter's. For several months."

"What?" Carter glanced at the rifle behind my heels, and Eli looked back and forth between us, one frayed nerve away from throwing his crowbar again—and I wasn't sure I could catch it, even if I were willing to risk a broken hand.

"Finn!" I shouted, and Carter closed his eyes. When they opened, they were green. Finn was back.

"Sorry." He blinked again, then stretched his arms as if testing the fit of a new shirt. "The pain woke him up and I got ejected." He started to flex the guard's injured left hand, then flinched and hissed in pain.

Eli gripped the crowbar until his knuckles paled with the strain. "What in the *holy hellfire* is going on with you people? What kind of demon are you consorting with?"

Finn snorted. "If I were a demon, Carter wouldn't have been able to toss me out. He's human. *I'm* human—but without a corporeal form of my own. Just like Nina said."

Eli eyed Finn warily as Finn picked up the rifle with his right hand. "Only demons lack bodies."

Finn bristled again, and I had to remind myself that I'd had a similar thought when I first found out about his . . . state. Then he braced the butt of the rifle against his chest with his left forearm and racked the slide to chamber a round.

Eli's eyes widened.

"Look, there's a lot of it that we don't understand," I said, before Finn's temper could explode all over the sentinel. Not that he would have fired, even without a broken hand, but he wasn't above scaring the immortal soul right out of anyone who implied he was one of the Unclean. "But what we *do* know is that Finn's not a demon. He doesn't eat souls. He has no access to his host's memories. He doesn't originate from hell. He's just—"

"Missing one of the defining characteristics of humanity?" Devi said, and I looked up as she and Maddock marched through an archway on the other side of the foyer, dust clinging to their combat boots, bold loyalty shining in their eyes. "Yeah. It's endearing. Who the hell are you?"

Maddock's pistol was aimed at Eli's head.

Reese and Grayson weren't with them.

"I am a sentinel in the Lord's Army," Eli began. "We are the last of the true—"

"This is Eli Woods. He saved my life"—I gestured at

the dead man on the floor—"with the crowbar that just tenderized Finn's hand. Eli's one of the nomads," I added, in case they couldn't tell from the cowboy boots and hat.

"Wha—?" Maddock started to ask a question, but then his gaze found Tobias and his aggressive stance crumpled beneath a devastating comprehension. "The kid was possessed?" His expression seemed caught in the battle between what experience had taught him—that demons don't possess children—and the irrefutable singed hole in the boy's chest.

Maddock lowered the pistol. "Why would a demon abandon an adult body to take a *child*?"

Eli lowered his crowbar, but his grip on it did not loosen. "The boy was bait."

When Finn swung his rifle over his shoulder with his good hand, I exhaled slowly, relieved now that no weapons were being aimed. "It was Aldric," he said. "He knew we wouldn't suspect a kid. Kastor sent him."

Maddock froze. "He was leading us to Pandemonia."

Finn nodded.

"Who's Kastor?" Devi asked, and I was oddly reassured to realize that Maddock had been keeping the same secrets from her that Finn had been keeping from me. That made the wound feel much less personal—it wasn't that Finn didn't trust me specifically; it was that neither of them truly trusted anyone but the other.

"How did he know where to look?" Maddock asked, as if he hadn't even heard Devi's question.

"You were on the news in New Temperance." Finn shrugged. "That probably told them where to start. They followed the degenerates flocking toward Grayson to narrow it down."

"Okay." Maddock closed his eyes, the pistol hanging at his side. "Kastor will send more. I need to think."

"Maddy, what's going on?" Devi demanded.

When he seemed too lost in his own fears to answer, I turned to Finn. "Who's Kastor, and why does he want Maddock? And does that have anything to do with him taking Carey James from a Church caravan?"

"Carey, Grayson's brother?" Devi scowled at me, clearly irritated that I knew more than she did.

Finn gave us an apologetic glance. "Just give him a second to process." He turned back to Maddock. "We have to tell them. They're all involved now."

Maddy nodded slowly but made no reply.

Eli slid the long end of the crowbar through a belt loop on the left side of his jeans, evidently satisfied that we weren't a threat. "I don't know any Kastor, but I can tell you exactly where this demon child was taking you." He pulled a rag from his pocket and began scrubbing at the blood on his hands. "The Lion's Den. And no matter what it says in the Bible, nobody walks out of there alive."

"The Lion's Den. The Meat Market. Pandemonia." Maddock thumbed the safety on the pistol and tucked it into his waistband. "Whatever you call it, we're headed as far away as we can get, as fast as we can get there." He turned to Finn and me. "Get everyone packed. Devi and I will help Reese and Grayson with the gas run—we turned back when we saw Eli headed this way."

"I don't think I'll be much help with the packing." Finn stepped closer to the nearest window and held his hand in the pool of light. The red mark across his palm had widened, and the surrounding tissue was already turning a dark blue. "Damn it!"

"Why did you catch the crowbar?" Eli asked. "It would have put a sizable dent in that little demon's skull."

I suppressed a shudder at the thought, even though we'd never actually met the child. "Killing demons just releases them to look for another body," I explained. "Finn was trying to stop you from releasing Aldric, so I could send him back to hell."

Finn groaned, trying to flex his fingers. "I think it's broken."

"How did you catch it?" Eli began wiping blood from the crowbar with his rag. "I've never seen anyone move that fast."

"I spar with exorcists."

"So you're really an exorcist? A *true* exorcist?" Eli qualified. "We didn't think there was any such thing."

"But you've been following us for days," I pointed out. "How did you *think* we were burning holes straight through degenerates?" They hadn't come close enough to actually see us fight, but surely they'd seen the results.

Eli shrugged. "We assumed your guns were some new technology."

And our disposal of the mutated monsters wouldn't have convinced them that we weren't possessed. Church demons kill degenerates too, to keep them from killing humans, which they saw as a waste of precious resources.

"Are *all* of you exorcists?" Eli asked, and I realized that the nomads hadn't just been following us. They'd been *watching* us, probably trying to decide how many of us were possessed, like his poor little nephew.

"No. Just me, Maddock and Devi . . ." I gestured to each of them as I said their names. "And Reese. The big guy."

"Soon Grayson will be too," Maddock added. "She's the little one, with curly hair."

"And your other two women?"

"Anabelle and Melanie are human," I said, grateful that neither of them had come to investigate whatever noise our confrontation had made. And if Grayson were there, she would have come running and might have gotten hurt.

"Which one is pregnant?"

"Mellie. She's my sister." And the thought of losing her or her baby terrified me almost beyond words. "I'm so sorry about your nephew." And even sorrier that Eli had been prepared—by necessity—to cave in the poor child's skull himself. "I assume he's the reason you and your army were following us?"

"Not just for Tobias." Eli stood straighter and shoved

his blood-smeared rag into his back pocket. "When we were kids, my brother, Micah, and I swore that if either of us was ever taken by the Unclean, the other would personally find him and free his soul." Eli's fingers traced the short end of the crowbar hanging from his belt, as if touching it brought him comfort. "They took my brother and my little nephew four days ago."

His gaze fell heavily on the demon who'd snuck up on me. "Today, I've fulfilled my childhood oath."

SIX

"Well, I don't think it's broken, but it's badly bruised and swollen." Devi sat on the marble floor across from Finn, examining his hand more gently than I'd have thought her capable of. "What we really need is some ice to ease the swelling. A couple of months ago we could have just given him a handful of snow." She glared at me across the candle lit in the middle of our circle, as if Finn's injury were somehow my fault. "But for today, we're out of luck."

"Wait. Maybe I can help." Eli stepped over the candle and headed into the hall while we all stared at him in surprise, and a second later his boots clomped down the stairs.

"I can't believe it." Anabelle sniffled, her eyes still red from crying. "I can't believe Tobias is dead."

"I can't believe we never actually met him." Melanie's voice sounded strained, and she'd been staring at the floor, tears in her eyes, ever since we'd told her the news.

"Don't be sad for him," Devi snapped. "Be disappointed in us. We've spent the past two days feeding chocolate to a pint-sized monster when no one on the *planet* was more qualified to see through his disguise than we were."

Melanie sobbed, and I slid my arm around her, glaring at Devi. "Well, maybe if we hadn't developed a tolerance to everyday malice from overexposure to *you,* we would have recognized the real danger."

Devi stood, her fists clenched, and Finn grabbed the back of her shirt with his good hand to halt her angry advance, unfazed when she turned her glower on him instead.

"So, what's the story with this Lord's Army?" Grayson's subject change was less than subtle, but it broke the tension.

"They think killing the Unclean is their life's calling," Maddock said, without looking away from the window, where he'd been watching both the nomad camp and the western horizon for nearly an hour. And largely ignoring the rest of us. "Yet they had no idea that by killing the hosts, they were actually just contributing to the problem."

Finn flexed his hand carefully. "They were moving in on Aldric when we found him and fell for his ruse. Only, Eli wasn't sure whether we'd fallen for it or were part of it."

"And his brother?" Mellie was no longer even pretending to read the botany textbook lying open in what remained of her lap.

"Meshara and Aldric didn't actually possess Micah and Tobias until they got close enough to us to stage that scene at the car by killing the hosts they'd worn during the raid," I explained. "Aldric was the bait, and Meshara hung back in Micah's body to watch from afar. Eli followed her into the courthouse, evidently on her way to talk to Aldric, and killed her as she snuck up on me."

"Who is this Aldric?" Devi stared at Maddock as if she could *will* him to rejoin the group, and I almost felt sorry for her. He'd withdrawn from all of us, except for Finn, but she was taking it the hardest.

Finally, Maddock turned from the window and laid Finn's rifle on the floor at his feet. "Aldric was Kastor's right-hand man. Now he's just one of millions of demons crawling over one another in their native world, desperate for a way back into ours. But he's not going to find one, because what Kastor doesn't want anyone to know is that whatever interworld rift they crossed to get here in the first place doesn't exist anymore. No new demons have come into our world in more than a decade."

What? No more demonic immigrants?

That would have been news worth celebrating if there weren't already millions of them roaming the world in stolen bodies, devouring one human soul after another.

The rest of us were still staring at the ground in stunned

silence when Devi spoke again. "And Kastor would be . . . ?"

Maddock glanced at Finn, who gave him a subtle shrug, and I wondered what they'd just agreed on.

"Kastor runs Pandemonia," Maddock said. "He's not a deacon, or a president, or a king, or any kind of leader you guys would ever recognize. He's more like a precariously perched celebrity-slash-despot. He's in charge because the other demons are afraid of him and entertained by him, but if either of those ever stops being true, he will lose control of Pandemonia, and its Unclean citizens will be unleashed upon the rest of the world."

Finn cleared his throat while the rest of us tried to absorb what we were hearing, and then he continued their statement as Maddock turned back to the window. "The only thing worse than Kastor being in control of hundreds of demons who don't play by the Church's rules would be Kastor *not* being in control of hundreds of demons who don't play by the Church's rules."

For several long seconds no one spoke.

"The Lion's Den," I whispered, and both Finn and Maddock nodded.

Or the wolf's den, if Deacon Bennett's description of Kastor was more accurate.

And Kastor had Grayson's brother. If I thought there was a chance in hell that he was still alive, I would have told her right then, but the last thing she needed was to think about her brother dying in a city Maddock had described as a demonic meat market.

"So, what does he want with Maddy?" Devi asked before I could vocalize the same question.

Maddock's mouth opened but no sound came out, so Finn answered for him. "Kastor wants the same thing from Maddy that he wants from every exorcist. The same thing the breeders want. The same thing the Church wants. A stronger, longer-lasting host. Specifically, one capable of producing a couple more just like him."

Which was exactly what my mother had wanted with me—until the Church had me sterilized and ruined my demonic sire's evil scheme. Ironically, my pregnant sister was *not* an exorcist, and her child wouldn't be one either.

A scuffling sound echoed from outside the courthouse, and Maddock turned to look out the window. "Eli's back."

A moment later boots clomped up both flights of stairs, and then Eli appeared in the doorway carrying a worn-soft cardboard box. Melanie looked up from her can of breakfast pears and watched him in silence, one hand rubbing her bulging stomach. She couldn't seem to trust the new stranger after having been betrayed by the child she'd doted on for two days.

"The demons who raided our division had to abandon some of their supplies to get away. We've found these particularly useful." Eli set his box on the floor and pulled out a small, stiff-looking plastic bag. He shook it for a few seconds, then tossed it to Finn, who caught it out of instinct. With his bad hand.

"That's the kind of impulse that got you hurt in the first place." Eli chuckled while Finn ground his teeth together against the pain, still clutching the bag.

"A cold pack?" I peeked into the box and found several more, along with a roll of gauze and some loose adhesive bandages.

Eli shrugged. "Hardly a fair trade for my brother and my nephew, but we take what we can get."

Devi nodded. "We too observe the 'finders, keepers' principle—the universally acknowledged law of the badlands, and of kindergartners everywhere."

"Thanks." Finn tried to curl his hand around the bag cradled in his palm. When he flinched, I scooted closer and threaded my fingers through his so he could feel the warmth of my skin around the cold pack pressed between our hands. He smiled and laid his free hand over mine, stroking my knuckles with his thumb, and the heat building behind his eyes echoed deep and low in my stomach.

I hated seeing him in pain, but I relished the excuse to touch him.

Eli turned to Melanie. "When is your baby due?"

"Just over a month," she said as Anabelle put one protective arm around her shoulders.

"Is it moving often?"

She only nodded, and I frowned, watching her. Normally, Mellie was a chatterbox, eager to tell us what she'd learned from her most recent book or to run baby names by us for opinions, but now . . .

The boy's death had hit her especially hard. Or maybe Aldric's infiltration had scared her in a way the endless dangers of the badlands hadn't been able to. It saddened me to see her spirit dampened, but maybe that was for the best. A mother can't protect her child from threats she doesn't see.

"That's good." Eli gave her a pleasant nod, then turned to Maddock. "How—"

"Why is that good?" Melanie demanded.

The nomad turned back to her in surprise. "Because healthy babies move a lot, and the healthier the infant, the longer it can survive outside the womb while it waits for a soul." He shrugged again. "I've seen a couple of them last nearly an hour."

Melanie rubbed her stomach in a slow circular motion that was surely more comfort to her than to the baby. "That's nothing, compared to the average human life span."

The average human life span? Was she quoting one of her childbirth books?

"Every second counts." Eli sank onto the floor next to his box, and Grayson watched him solemnly. "Who will be delivering the baby?" His gaze fell to me, but I shook my head. We'd already decided that when the time came, all of the exorcists should be ready to stand guard and fight in case Melanie's screaming attracted trouble.

The best way I could help my sister was to protect her. That had been true her entire life.

"Grayson and I will give it our best shot," Anabelle said. "We've read every book we could find on the subject."

Eli looked puzzled. "Have you never delivered a child before?"

They both shook their heads. "Have *you*?" Grayson asked, her brown eyes wide.

"Of course," he said, and suddenly the nomad had our full attention. Even Maddock looked away from the window in surprise. "I've delivered two on my own, and I've assisted with three more. We *all* learn to deliver babies and care for children, just like we learn to hunt, scavenge, gather, and fight."

We could only stare. In the cities everyone had a specific job, and most people had been trained to do little outside of duties within the home.

"Wait, *everyone* in your group fights?" Grayson's brown eyes brightened, and she turned to Reese to make sure he'd heard.

Eli shrugged. "Everyone old enough and healthy enough to hold a weapon."

"As it should be," Devi said, with a nod of approval. "If people in the cities weren't dependent upon the Church for protection, this would be a different world."

Grayson frowned. "I *never* get to fight."

"Why not?"

"She's still transitioning," Reese said. "She won't have

any enhanced abilities until she becomes a full-fledged exorcist, and I can't let her get hurt."

Eli watched Grayson, who stared at him, fascinated. "She may get hurt, but then her scars will be a badge of honor. Or she will succumb to her injuries and we'll remember her as a noble warrior. None of us could ask for anything more."

"Um, yeah, we could," Reese said through clenched teeth, but Eli didn't seem to notice his anger. "I don't want to *remember* her, I want to *be* with her." He wrapped one arm around Grayson's waist, and she snuggled against him like always, but Eli held her gaze.

"This life comes with no guarantees," the nomad said. "We fight, we believe, and we hope for an honorable death. I would hate to see you deprived of any of that."

Though I wasn't sure he understood what he was doing, my stomach pitched as I watched Eli drive a wedge between two of my friends by offering Grayson exactly what Reese kept trying to protect her from. And I couldn't blame her for wanting it. I never felt more alive than when I was burning demons from their human hosts.

She turned to Reese. "I want to fight."

"And I'm sure Reese would love to teach you," Devi said. She and Maddock had been watching the oddly intense exchange with as much unease as I felt, and when she gave Reese a pointed look, he nodded reluctantly.

Grayson's eyes lit up, and she threw her arms around him.

"There's no time like the present!" Eli declared, clearly caught up in her excitement. "I'd be happy to—"

Reese growled from deep in his throat.

Before he could say something we'd all regret, I stepped in with a change of subject. "So, back to the delivering of babies. What's your infant mortality rate?"

Eli sat straighter, puffed up with pride. "We're down to sixty-six percent!"

"Wait, you lose *two-thirds* of your entire population as infants?" I glanced at my sister, and the terror squeezing my chest like a giant fist was reflected in her wide, stunned eyes. I'd known Mellie's baby's chances were slim in the badlands, but I'd assumed that a community with elders would have much better luck.

"Only because they lack souls. Most of them are born physically healthy." Eli took in our matching horrified expressions and frowned. "Do more survive in the cities?"

"Nearly one hundred percent," I said. "But that's because the Church limits the number of pregnancies and requires that senior citizens become soul donors." Which was considered both a privilege and a duty of the elderly in Church-run society.

"Soul donors." Eli's words echoed with horror. "You kill adults so infants can live?"

"We don't kill them!" Reese insisted, and though I'd heard him openly criticize the system several times, he seemed determined to disagree with Eli on everything. "They're volunteers."

"That's a total crock of shit," Devi snapped. "They don't have any more choice about dying than Nina had about having her tubes snipped. It's part of the price you pay for the Church's 'protection.'"

And as painful as her casual mention of my most traumatic memory was, she was right. I hadn't chosen sterilization. But I would *damn well* decide what happened to my soul after I was done with it, and if giving it to Mellie's baby meant I had to die before I reached "elderly," then so be it.

I had nothing more valuable to give the child, and no one could take *that* choice from me.

"You let infants die so the elderly can live?" Anabelle's horrified question pulled me from my unspoken determination. "But they've already *lived* their lives."

"It's not . . . It doesn't work like that out here." Eli frowned. "The elderly—even those with arthritis and cataracts—are better able to fend for themselves and to contribute to society than an infant. If we killed an adult every time a baby was born, the average age of our members would never rise above ten. We wouldn't stand a *chance* in the badlands."

I stared at Eli as his point sank in. He was right—survival in the badlands would require not just different skills, but different *sacrifices* than the Church had taught us. I understood that.

But my unborn niece or nephew would *not* be one of those sacrifices.

I tried to catch my sister's attention, to give her a reassuring smile, but her unfocused gaze was aimed at the candle flicking in the center of our circle. Worried, I took her hand and squeezed it. When she looked up, her smile seemed forced, but all I could do was return it.

Melanie could *not* find out what I was planning until looking into the face of her child made her more willing to accept my decision.

Grayson let go of Reese's hand and scooted across the floor toward Eli, studying him the way she studied Finn every time he took on a different body. As if he were suddenly a whole new person to get to know. "Tell us about your army. How many soldiers do you have?" She peeked into his box like a curious kitten.

"Well, we're not that kind of army. We don't have guns or anything. We fight with what we have. There are almost sixty in our division, with a new one due any day."

"How do you feed that many people?" Anabelle asked.

"We travel south in the winter because plants bloom longer, but food is always sparse in the cold months, and we're all a little thin right now. But things will get easier soon, when more vegetation is ready to harvest."

"You *do* look thin." Grayson frowned, evidently unaware of the irony. We were thin too. "We have food, and we'd be happy to share!"

Devi scowled, but before she could object, Eli's face erupted into a broad smile. "That would be much appreciated!"

"Grayson is obviously misinformed about the concept of 'finders, keepers,' so let me explain," Devi said to Eli. "In this scenario we're the 'finders,' so we will 'keep.' Try to carry out your weeping at a reasonable volume."

"You'll have to excuse Devi. She's just . . . horrible," I finished, when no more accurate description came to mind. "Of course we'll share our food." I glared at Devi. "If not for Eli and his army, we'd be headed toward Pandemonia in the company of a bite-sized demon right now."

Devi tried to incinerate me with her gaze. "And who will we be sharing with, exactly? What's the deal with you and this 'army'?"

Eli squared his shoulders. "I am a sentinel. It's a position of great honor and responsibility. And we're—"

"They're nomadic religious relics who believe that when a human host is killed, its soul returns to the well." Reese glanced at each of the rest of us, and I recognized the soapbox he was about to step up onto, though usually his hot button was Church conspiracy theories. "During the war, when the Church offered us protection in exchange for walls, rules, and service, Eli's people struck out on their own, believing that obedience to their holy imperative would save them."

"Holy imperative?" Anabelle turned to Eli for an explanation.

"We believe it's our duty to return as many souls to the well as possible by slaying every demon we meet."

Reese huffed. "The Church says it put you guys out of business fifty years ago."

Actually, the Church said it had hunted the nomads into extinction to rid the world of a false faith almost as threatening to the human spiritual condition as were demons themselves.

"The Church lies," Eli said through clenched teeth. No one argued. "Our numbers have dwindled along with the rest of humanity. But our mission is clear, and those who commit to it will find peace in the next life."

"Well, in *this* life, you've lived in the badlands a lot longer than we have, so if we're going to share our food"— Devi aimed a pointed glance at Grayson—"why don't you share the details about how you've survived out here on your own for a century."

"They haven't," I said softly, and everyone turned to look at me as the vague mental connection I'd made came into sharper focus in my head. "You're not surviving out here, are you? Your way of life is dying, and that's why the Church doesn't kill you anymore. They know the badlands will do that for them. But the problem isn't the degenerates, is it?"

Eli shook his head slowly, and I knew I'd guessed right. "We can handle the monsters, even a dozen at a time," he said. "Watching for degenerates has become second nature. Killing them is routine." He waved one hand at the floor, indicating the corpse still lying two stories below. "*They* are the problem."

Grayson frowned. "Kastor and his people?"

Eli nodded, and Maddock watched him closely. "They're pillagers. Raiders. Savages. They're smarter and quieter than degenerates, but less predictable than the Church. They stalk us. They strike when food is scarce and we're weak. They take those in their prime. Older bodies don't last as long, and kids are too much work—the pillagers would rather let us raise them."

"They steal your *people*?" Grayson's voice trembled, and Reese put one arm around her.

"We fight, and we usually kill a couple of them, but we lose a few of our strongest young people in every raid," Eli said. "Our division can't survive any more loss."

"Where do they take them?" Annabelle asked.

Melanie watched the entire exchange wide-eyed.

"To the Lion's Den. We followed them once, but the city is too big. Too . . . dangerous."

"It can't be breached?" Reese sounded doubtful, and both Maddock and Finn were noticeably quiet.

"They would probably throw the gates open for us if we actually knocked. It's getting back out that would be the problem. No one leaves the Lion's Den alive." Eli shrugged. "After every raid we pack up and move on, hoping they won't find us again for a while. But they always do eventually. We don't really have anywhere to go."

"You stay in the south and the east to avoid most of the Church cities," I guessed, and Eli nodded. "But it's too cold in the north for most of the year, and if you go west . . ."

"The lion pounces," he finished.

"So let us travel with you," I said as soon as the idea hit me, and Finn turned to me in surprise. "Just until the baby is born. We can protect you from Kastor's people. You can teach us. None of us has ever delivered an infant, and we've only survived in the badlands by robbing Church supply shipments. We can't do that forever."

"Nina . . . ," Maddock began.

"We need them," I insisted. "We need to know what they can teach us." I turned to Eli. "And you need *us*. We don't just release demons back into the world, we vanquish them, which denies them the opportunity to possess any more of your people. And any one exorcist"—I gestured to Reese, Devi, and Maddock in turn—"is faster and stronger than your best five soldiers combined. If you don't believe me, give us a test."

"It's not me you'd have to convince," Eli said. "I've seen you in action. Let me return Tobias and Micah to my family, and then I'll present your offer to Brother Isaiah. If he says yes, you've got a deal."

I smiled at Melanie, truly hopeful on her baby's behalf for the first time in weeks.

SEVEN

As soon as Eli left, Maddock tried to undermine my plan. He wanted to put distance between us and Pandemonia as soon as possible, and he knew we could move faster on our own.

I understood his fear, but *nothing* was more important to me than Mellie and the baby. Fortunately, everyone but Reese agreed with me that we stood to gain as much from the Lord's Army as they stood to gain from us.

After he was outvoted, Maddock stared out the window, watching both the nomads' temporary camp and the western horizon closely until Devi shoved an open can of white-meat chicken into his hand. "Hey," she said. "Remember me?"

When Maddock blinked and struggled to bring her

into focus, I realized he was fried. "Why don't you two go take a nap, or . . . something," I said. "I'll take watch for a while."

"I'm fine," Maddy insisted.

Devi rolled her eyes and took the rifle from him. "You're not fine." She handed me the gun, then pulled him up by one arm. "You're gonna rest, and I'm gonna help."

I didn't want to know how she planned to help, and for once I didn't care that she hadn't thanked me for my offer. My motive wasn't entirely altruistic.

I took the rifle and Maddock's metal folding chair— we'd been carrying two of them because so many of the buildings were empty—out onto the courthouse balcony, then went back in for a can of soup and some reading material. Between bites of my cold lunch, I checked to make sure there was no round in the chamber, then propped the rifle up on the balcony railing and stared through the sight at Eli's camp.

The rifle didn't have a scope, but the sight was magnified enough to give me a much better look at the Lord's Army. I couldn't bring individual faces into focus, but in a span of ten minutes, I counted twelve white-haired individuals, about half of whom walked either hunched over or with a walking stick.

Eli's group had at least a dozen senior citizens, and each one of them represented a potential lifeline for Melanie's baby. I'd meant what I'd said about what our two groups could offer each other, but those twelve gray-haired souls were the real reason I'd insisted we stay with the Lord's Army.

Since I knew how Eli—and presumably his entire society—felt about the concept of donating souls, I had no intention of asking anyone else to make such a huge sacrifice, and though I was still more than willing to do what had to be done myself, if my new plan panned out I wouldn't have to.

Ironically, I'd gotten the idea from the Unified Church.

For decades, the Church had been peacefully, painlessly inducing death in elderly volunteers, timed to coincide with the birth of each baby because when a child is born the nearest unclaimed soul will be drawn to it. If there is no soul nearby, one will be drawn from the well instead.

But except for the occasional drop or two, the well of souls ran dry long ago.

I wouldn't schedule someone else's demise even if I could get away with it, but maybe I *could* schedule Melanie's labor to coincide with the imminent natural death of one of the Lord's Army's elderly members. The baby wasn't due for more than a month. In that time, surely *some*one would succumb to old age and the physical demands of such a rough, migratory lifestyle.

What exactly was the average human life span without Church intervention, anyway? Melanie would know, but if I asked, she'd figure out what I was up to. So instead,

I added that question to two others rolling around in my mind as I set the rifle down and picked up the pregnancy book.

To my relief, according to the book, Mellie's baby had already passed the most critical milestone—namely, lung development—and with each week spent in utero, the infant's chances of survival increased dramatically. So in another couple of weeks I could cross premature birth off my list of concerns, barring unforeseen disaster.

Unfortunately, the book didn't list any surefire way to induce labor without a hospital, a doctor, and an intravenous oxytocin drip—an IV full of hormones. The authors did suggest several "home remedies" for an overdue birth, including walking, variations of an herbal tea, and intercourse, of all things, but none of that sounded very reliable to me. Maybe the experienced midwives in the Army knew of some herb or plant that could—

"Hey, whatcha doing out here alone?" Finn asked as he pushed the balcony door open.

"Learning what to expect." I closed the book and held it up for him to see.

Finn leaned against the balcony rail. "I thought you were going to be standing guard with the rest of us when she gives birth."

I shrugged and set the book on the ground, then stood. "I might not have to, with sixty other trained soldiers there to help out." I smiled and stepped into his embrace when he held his arms out. "That's got to be worth at least, what? Eleven exorcists?"

"We'll be lucky if half of them can fight like Eli." Finn stretched his sore hand for emphasis, and I ran my fingers lightly down his palm. The swelling looked a little better and much of the redness had faded. Still . . .

"You may have to stick to touching soft things for a while." My cheeks flamed over my innuendo, but the heat in his eyes rewarded my bold words. After seventeen years under the Church's puritanical social rules, I still found it much easier to snuggle in the dark than to flirt in broad daylight.

"Now, that is one piece of advice I'd be happy to follow. . . ." Finn leaned down, and my heart began to pound when his lips met mine. I'd seen and touched him every day for the past five months, yet every time we kissed, I felt like we were starting something new and wonderful. Something daring and bold, and completely ours.

Something that made my entire body feel alive and—

The balcony door flew open and slammed into my back, shoving me against Finn so hard that his teeth cut into my lower lip.

"Ow!" I cried.

Finn shoved the door off us and pulled me out of its path.

"You're both relieved of duty," Devi snapped as I turned to find her peering over the railing. "I get how you might not see the flames, with your vision so clouded by lust . . ." She turned and pointed toward Eli's campground. "But can you honestly not *smell* the *smoke*?"

Maddock joined her at the railing, and I followed their gaze to see a dark plume rising into the sky from the center of the Lord's Army's camp. "Fire!" Maddy shouted, already on his way back into the building.

"Stay here," I said to my sister as I ran after him, with Devi on my heels. Finn grabbed the rifle with his good hand on his way into the building.

"You stay with her." Reese handed Grayson the pistol, then raced into the hall and down the stairs after us. We piled into the SUV and took off toward Eli's camp on the eastern edge of the small, abandoned town.

Three miles later Reese slammed on the brakes and the car slid to a dusty stop ten feet from a grimy four-person tent. Two horses neighed and rose onto their hind legs, startled by our sudden appearance, but they were prevented from bolting by the ropes securing their bits to the bumper of a dented white camper.

We piled out of the car and ran toward two distinct plumes of smoke rising from the center of the makeshift camp. I kept my eyes open for degenerates, or anyone moving too fast to be human, but could see no visible threat.

"Eli!" Maddock shouted as we ran. We rounded the end of a short line of campers, and he came to a halt so suddenly that Devi nearly slammed into his back.

"What—" I demanded, but the rest of the question was

ripped from my tongue by surprise when I found several dozen people staring at us in shock, most holding dusty cowboy hats in their hands out of respect for the dead.

Eli's entire community was gathered around the source of the smoke: two flaming pyres built of scraps of wood scavenged from the abandoned town. Many of the faces studying us were flushed and still wet with tears, and near the center, his wrinkled face flickering in the light from the flames, stood an elderly man with a head full of tight white curls, still speaking softly with his eyes closed, as if he hadn't noticed our arrival.

He was praying.

We'd just interrupted a funeral.

*　*　*

"Again, we're *so* sorry," I whispered as Eli led us around one of the campers. "We thought you guys were under attack. We were trying to help."

Eli's jaw remained clenched until we were out of sight of the mourners, where he pulled up sharply and turned on us, anger flashing in his golden-brown eyes. "Have you never seen a funeral before?" he demanded.

Reese's brows rose. "More than I care to count, actually."

"But in civilization, we *bury* our dead," Devi added.

Eli's expression hardened. "Your 'civilization' is led by demons in church robes."

"Fair enough." Devi shrugged. "But burials don't

111

usually attract hordes of degenerates. Huge columns of flames *will*. If you're not careful, you're going to wind up with several more bodies to bury."

"This isn't our first rodeo," Eli snapped. "There are never more than a handful of degenerates in any one area, and by the time they get close, we'll be ready for them."

"Wrong." Reese spun and glanced toward the south, scanning the horizon for whatever he could hear. He had the best ears in our group by far. "Grayson's in transition. Every degenerate within range was *already* headed this way, and that smoke is like shooting up a flare, so they know exactly where you are."

"We didn't . . . This has never . . ." Eli gripped his crowbar and glared at all of us at once. "This is *your* fault. You brought them here!"

Reese nodded. "Which we tried to tell you."

"How many?" Maddock squinted at the southern horizon.

"Ten or twelve, by my best guess. It's hard to get a good count with no buildings to funnel the sound of their approach."

Finn turned to Eli. "Go finish your funeral. We'll keep them off you."

"Five of you against a dozen? You sure you can handle it?" Eli asked, already backing toward his gathered community.

"Even if we were half-asleep and hungover." Devi held

up her hand, already glowing with the flames ready to burst from her palm in response to the approaching horde.

"Let's confront them before they get into town," I said. "That way we can retreat if we need to without drawing them toward either the funeral or the courthouse." If there was one thing I'd learned from several months of training with Anathema, it was that she who chooses the venue has the advantage.

We piled back into the SUV, then drove directly south, ignoring the cracked and crumbling streets for the more direct, off-road route. But we were too late to stop the horde from entering town. We found them barreling down a residential street in a neighborhood near the edge of the long-abandoned suburb.

Adrenaline fired through my veins as Maddy slammed on the brakes and the SUV skidded to a crooked stop in an overgrown field just outside the neighborhood. We poured from the vehicle and took off toward the degenerates. I'd never run faster in my life. I didn't gasp for air and my lungs didn't burn. I *became* speed and strength, and every bit of both was aimed at the monsters galloping toward us, most on all fours.

There weren't twelve. There were fifteen.

Their arms were too long, their legs too thin and knobby. Torn clothing flapped in the wind as they ran. Dirt streaked their grayish faces. Grime matted their hair.

I could smell them almost as soon as I could hear them,

panting like dogs on the scent of prey, misshapen feet and hands pounding against the ground, heedless of abuse from grass burrs and rocks. Several of the degenerates drooled, spittle flying from loose lips and rotten teeth.

Maddock got to them first, his left hand blazing and ready. Devi and I were still several feet away when the first of the demons lunged at Maddy and Reese. Reese caught one by the throat, and while it tore at his sleeves, hissing and screeching, he shoved his glowing left hand at the chest of a second. The frying demon seemed suspended there, arms seizing, jaw opening and closing, knees bent as if they'd no longer hold him up.

When that one hung limp, Reese pulled his hand back. "One!" As the body crumpled to the ground he shoved his still-glowing palm at the chest of the deformed and snarling woman he had by the throat.

On my left, Finn stopped running and lifted his rifle with his uninjured—yet nondominant—right hand. He rested the barrel on his left forearm to steady it, then peered down the sight and fired.

The shot echoed all around me and I turned just in time to see a degenerate crumple to the ground.

"No—" I shouted, skidding to a halt.

"I'm taking gut shots," he said. "Just slowing them down for you. Go!"

I raced toward the nearest degenerate, my hand already beginning to warm with the flames that would burn it from its deformed and decaying human host.

Maddock leapt up from a body on the ground. "One!" he called as another pounced on him. Devi pulled the monster off him and shoved her glowing hand at its back, and in the second before a woman with long, straight blond hair reached for me, I realized that all the degenerates were dressed alike.

Their clothes hung on them strangely, thanks to their mutated, angular physiques, and some were more threadbare, torn, and stained than others, but every last one of them wore gray jogging pants and a white T-shirt.

The blond host's knobby hand tangled in my hair, and I screamed as she jerked my head toward her mouth. I shoved my left hand at her chest and flames flared between us. She screeched, and her hand fell from my hair as her body dangled—seemingly weightless—from my burning palm.

When the demon crumpled to the overgrown grass, I turned and quickly assessed the fight. Reese, Maddy, and Devi were each frying demons of their own as more galloped bizarrely toward us from the neighborhood adjacent to the field. A crack like thunder rang out from behind me, and the degenerate racing toward me fell backward into the knee-high grass.

"Thanks!" I shouted to Finn, and was rewarded with another crack. A third demon dropped farther away, and I squatted next to the closest one, which was hauling itself toward me hand over hand because its left leg had been blown open by Finn's bullet.

I'd dispatched the two closest of the incapacitated de-generates and was headed for a third when something hit me from my left side, driving me to the ground.

Grass scratched my face, and hands tore at my cloth-ing. Teeth snapped an inch from my forehead as a balding man with sagging grayish skin tried to rip me apart in his frenzied search for my soul. I shoved him with both hands, and my left burst into flames, immobilizing him as he thrashed above me.

By the time I threw the empty shell of his host off me, the action was over. Footsteps pounded closer as Finn came to check on me, and when he pulled me upright, I found Devi smirking at me. "I got four," she said.

"So did Nina," Finn pointed out.

"The ones you incapacitated don't count," she insisted, and I didn't bother to argue.

"What's wrong?" Reese asked as I knelt in the grass next to the monster I'd just vanquished. I turned the body over, looking for some kind of label or insignia on its cloth-ing, but I found none. Devi came closer, curious, but Mad-dock backed away from the corpse, his forehead furrowed.

"They're all wearing—" The sudden thunder of hooves stole my voice. I looked up to see nearly a dozen horses galloping toward us across the overgrown field, each car-rying a man, woman, or child wearing a cowboy hat. The riders were mostly thin and dark-skinned, wearing sun-bleached, dusty clothing, their faces shielded from the sun by their wide hat brims. Most wore pouches over one shoulder—openmouthed satchels made of stitched-together strips of leather.

Cowboys. The thought seemed absurd—according to my former history teacher, Wild West cowboys hailed from even deeper in our past than shopping malls and hand-held telephones. Yet there they were, in saddles and stir-rups, staring down at us without a hint of horror over the corpses littering the ground around us.

"Did we miss all the excitement?" Eli was the first to dismount, but the moment his boots hit the ground, he turned to help an elderly man from his horse. The man wore a gray hat with a diamond-shaped fold at the top, but visible beneath the brim was a head full of tight white curls. I recognized him as the man who'd been leading the prayer at the funeral.

"Yes, there weren't that many—"

A young girl in a faded pink cowboy hat suddenly reached into her pouch and pulled out an unedged butter knife. She hurtled it toward me, end over end. My pulse spiked and I dropped to the ground. My friends gasped all around me.

A thud echoed at my back, and I turned to see the knife embedded up to its scrolled silver hilt in the eye of a de-generate still bleeding from a gunshot wound.

I stood, stunned, staring at the dead demon.

"You missed one." The girl grinned. Her horse snorted and tossed its head.

"Holy shit!" Devi knelt next to the degenerate. The man

with the white curls scowled at her language, and I might have subtly tried to censor her . . . if I hadn't been too busy staring in utter awe at the demon that had just been dropped with unerring accuracy by a child twelve years old at the most.

The girl dismounted with ease and led her horse behind her while she knelt to look at one of the demons we'd exorcised. "What happened to his chest?" She looked every bit as awed by the still-smoking hole as we were by the knife-through-the-eye trick.

"We exorcised them. Awesome, right?" Devi stood and glanced around at the bodies.

"Indeed." The man with the white curls stepped forward and pushed his hat back on his head, revealing a dark, age-lined face and deep-set brown eyes. He studied the nearest exorcised corpse. "The Lord has delivered a glorious victory today, and that is worthy of celebration. As is the return of our lost sons Tobias and Micah, long may their souls rest in peace." He gave Eli a gregarious pat on the back, and the sentinel's smile swelled as the others dismounted.

"The Lord didn't deliver this," Devi mumbled beneath her breath. "*We* did."

Reese wasn't quite so subtle. "Those souls were——"

I elbowed him before he could derail their celebration with the facts.

"So, the Lord's Army is really more like the Lord's

Cavalry, right?" I said, and the man with the white curls laughed out loud.

"I suppose it does look like that. Our mounts will graze on their own, and fuel's hard to come by out here, so the horses make sense for us." He turned back to Eli. "Will you introduce your new friends?"

"Isaiah." Eli led the man—obviously the tribe's elder— toward us. "Brothers and sisters." He aimed a grand gesture at the others, to include them. "This is Maddock, Devi, Nina, Reese, and Finn. Grayson, Anabelle, and Melanie are . . . somewhere." Eli glanced around for them, visibly disappointed by their absence.

"They're still at the courthouse." I plucked Maddock's radio from his waistband and turned away from the rest of the introductions. "Anabelle?" I said into the radio, hoping that the smoke plumes had been enough of a distraction to keep the degenerates away from Grayson.

A second later she responded. "Yeah. You guys okay?"

"We're fine. The smoke was from a funeral, but it drew a small horde. You three get in the truck and head toward Eli's camp. We'll meet you there." We shouldn't have left them alone. Not while Grayson was in transition.

I turned back in time to hear Eli explaining to his group that the term 'Anathema' meant something different to us. "Something less . . . dishonorable," he finished, and I stifled a laugh. "They're exorcists. *True* exorcists. They wield the Lord's fury in the palms of their hands."

A murmur began among those still holding their horses' reins. Several craned their necks to see the burned-out bodies on the ground.

"Anathema, this is Brother Isaiah, our elder, and these are the most able among our soldiers." Eli gestured to the rest of his group.

Maddock was the first to stick out his hand. "Nice to meet you, Isaiah."

"The honor is certainly mine," Isaiah returned.

"And this is my niece Joanna," Eli said, as the girl in the pink hat knelt next to the demon she'd dropped. The moment she looked up, I realized she was Tobias's sister. The resemblance was uncanny.

"How old are you, kid? That was one hell of a throw," Devi said.

"Eleven." Joanna pulled her dull knife from the corpse's eye, then wiped the gore on its gray pants. "I'm the best in my age group." She didn't seem to be bragging; she was simply stating a fact.

Eli took his hat off and wiped sweat from his forehead with a faded red handkerchief. "She *is* the best," he confirmed. "But there are several ready to give her a run for her money. Some even younger."

"I've asked the rest of our group to meet us at your camp," I said, extending my hand for Isaiah to shake. "Is that okay?"

"It would be our pleasure. We'd love to hear how you

wield the Lord's holy flames"—Isaiah held up his empty left hand—"in the palms of your hands."

Maddock was noticeably quiet, but Devi shrugged. "I'm not sure that's actually what we're doing, but we'd be happy to demonstrate if an opportunity comes up."

"Oh, one always seems to." Isaiah gestured for Joanna to mount her horse, while he pulled himself up into his own saddle with shaking hands. And suddenly, though I was in desperate need of a soul, I hoped Isaiah wouldn't be ready to let go of his anytime soon. Any man who held the respect of his people—not just their fear—for so long must have been worthy of the position. "We don't have much to offer in the way of refreshments, but what we do have, we will gladly share."

"I suspect we could help out on that front," Reese said, and I shouldn't have been surprised. He may not have liked Eli or shared his faith, but he wasn't selfish.

"We'll join you in a few minutes," I said to Isaiah, and Finn glanced at me in surprise. Maddock was already holding the keys to the SUV.

"What was that about?" Devi demanded as the horses galloped toward the columns of smoke still rising into the afternoon sky.

"These degenerates are all wearing the same clothes." I knelt next to the one Joanna had dropped with her knife. "And the clothes are too new." The hosts should have worn a wide variety of clothing. Jeans. School slacks and blouses. Church cassocks. Their clothes should have labeled them as former students, police, teachers, or doctors. Or even nomads.

And their clothing should have been in much worse shape. Yes, the degenerates we'd just exorcised were deformed in the typical ways and covered in dust and grime, but their clothes were only ripped, rather than shredded. They were dusty, rather than matted with mud, blood, and gore.

Something was . . . strange.

Reese knelt next to me. "They almost look like uniforms of some sort."

"That's it!" I stood so suddenly my head spun. "Jail uniforms." The jogging pants and T-shirts looked just like what prisoners at the New Temperance jail wore. Except that these didn't have the words *New Temperance Jail* printed on the back. "They're generic jail uniforms."

"They were prisoners?" Devi's tone bled skepticism. "From where?" There was no more federal prison system of the sort the United States had had before the war, but each city had its own jail. "Verity's the closest city, right? And we're still . . . what? Half a day away?"

"At least," Finn mumbled, and I noticed that he'd backed away from the monster to stand near Maddock, his rifle aimed at the ground.

They knew something.

"It doesn't make sense for their bodies to be this

deformed but their clothes to be this new. Or for them to have traveled this far in a pack," Reese said.

However they'd escaped from wherever they had been kept, they shouldn't have remained in a single group long enough to have been drawn to the same place. Degenerates were solitary creatures no longer sane enough to choose their company.

"They're not prisoners," Maddock said at last, and I looked up to find Finn frowning at him—a wordless warning to shut up. "They're bloodhounds. *Kastor's* bloodhounds."

Finn closed his eyes and inhaled deeply.

"They're *what*?" Devi turned to Maddy and Finn with tension in every line of her frame. "Okay, it's past time to come clean. How do you know so much about Kastor? Why is he looking for you?"

"Why have you been lying?" I added softly, but my question was for Finn, not for Maddock.

"We haven't been lying." Finn's intense eye contact begged me to believe him. "We've just been leaving things out. Private things."

Things Maddock didn't want to talk about.

Finn wasn't withholding information on his own behalf, but on Maddy's. He'd do anything to protect Maddock, just like he'd do anything to protect me. We were the only family he had.

"That is such *bull*sh—" Devi swallowed the rest of the word in surprise when I put one hand on her arm.

"You were his prisoners, weren't you?" I said, and everyone except Maddock turned to look at me. "But I'm guessing Finn only stayed because Maddock was there."

How else would Maddy know so much about Pandemonia? Why else would Kastor be after him?

"We escaped two weeks before my seventeenth birthday." Maddock spoke so softly I could hardly hear him. "Kastor knew I was starting to transition."

"You were supposed to be his host, weren't you?" Devi said, and there was no hint of anger left in her voice. She sounded *horrified*.

Maddy nodded. "Finn got me out. Just in time."

Devi stepped toward him and slid her arms around his neck. She laid her head on his shoulder and held him, comforting him the same way I'd seen him calm her down countless times. When he wrapped his arms around her in return, my vision blurred beneath tears.

I couldn't even imagine what Maddock had been through at the hands of someone the *Church* had labeled a monster. Surely Finn's lack of a body had been a blessing for once.

"How did he get you in the first place?" Reese asked.

"I'm guessing the Church got to him first, but then Kastor stole him." And I was pretty sure I was right, considering what I already knew about Carey James. "Kastor probably raided a Church caravan."

"The specifics don't matter," Finn said before anyone else could question my theory. "What matters is that we got out, but now Kastor knows we're in the badlands, thanks to the Church's news broadcasts, and he knows how to find us, thanks to Grayson's transition." Finn waved his bad hand at the corpses littering the ground. "That's why he let out the bloodhounds."

"That part I don't understand," I admitted. "I'm assuming he calls them bloodhounds because he uses them like bloodhounds—to hunt. But how is that possible?"

"Because he doesn't just use them like dogs. He *trains* them like dogs." Finn slung his rifle over one shoulder by the strap, and when Maddy showed no desire to take over the explanation, he continued. "It's a punishment and a scare tactic—one of the ways Kastor maintains control. People who piss him off get locked up until they start to degenerate. Once they're too far gone to take another host, he throws them into the 'pound' with the other hounds and he starts training them."

"You can't train a degenerate," Devi insisted. "They hunt humans by nature."

"You can if you start when they're only a little crazy," Maddock whispered. "But the training deteriorates along with their minds."

"It's mostly teaching them not to attack the possessed," Finn elaborated. "He's had marginal success training a few of the fresher ones to corner potential hosts without attacking them, but that bit's inconsistent."

"So, he sent them after us expecting them to kill us?" Reese said. "I thought he wanted us alive."

"He does," Maddy said. "He sent them after us expecting *us* to kill *them*. The whole point of the exercise was to point him in the right direction. Like bloodhounds flushing out prey from the bush."

"But if these are the hounds, that means . . ." Devi didn't seem interested in finishing the thought, so I did.

"That means the hunters will be coming." And they wouldn't be degenerates, they'd be demons in their prime. "We need to be long gone when they get here."

EIGHT

"I want a horse." Grayson slid her knife through the belly of the last trout on her pile. One of Eli's cousins had told us what *kind* of trout it was, but I couldn't remember the fish's proper name, because we'd heard twenty of them in the two hours Finn, Grayson, and I had spent practicing new fishing techniques that morning. "Brother Isaiah's right," she continued. "Horses don't require gas."

She looked up from the fish hemorrhaging its innards on her plastic mat to where Eli was brushing his large tan-and-white mottled mount across the campgrounds. Several feet away Melanie sat with a group of women roughly our mother's age, listening to them discuss their own child-birth experiences while they cleaned wild greens and a few thin, edible roots.

"In the winter horses need hay," Reese pointed out with weary patience from beneath the hood of the SUV. In the five days we'd been traveling with Eli's division of the Lord's Army—only one of several, according to Brother Isaiah—Grayson had become fascinated by them and by the skill with which they subsisted off the neglected American landscape. "And horses can't carry as much as a car trunk."

"Yes, but if and when they die, you can eat them and wear them." Grayson ripped the innards from her fish and dropped them with a splat into the bucket we were sharing. "You can't eat or wear a car."

I refrained from pointing out that Eli's group utilized both horses *and* vehicles, because that wasn't the point. At least, not for Reese.

"And you can't drive a horse eighty-five miles an hour to escape a contingent of Church exorcists." He held the SUV's dipstick up to the sunlight to check the oil level.

"True." Grayson sliced the head from her fish with two confident cuts. "But you can't feed apples and carrots to a car. A car cannot love you back or lick your face. A car is just a hunk of metal that can never need or be needed!" She stood and dropped her fish onto the pile of trout ready to be grilled, and her brown eyes lit up when Eli waved to her from across the park, carrying a leather pouch loaded with dull butter knives.

"Which is it you want?" Reese called after Grayson as she took off for her knife-throwing lesson, leaving me to fumble my way through the last fish alone. "You want to cat a horse or be friends with it? You can't have it both ways!"

When Grayson didn't respond, Reese ducked beneath the hood of the SUV and let loose a soft string of heartily felt expletives.

"There was probably a better way to handle that." I pulled the head off my trout and shuddered when its guts tumbled onto the ground perilously close to my boots. I was fine with burning the souls from deformed demons, but pulling the innards from fish never failed to make me cringe. "She loves you, Reese."

"I know." He unhooked the metal prop and let the hood fall closed. "But *Eli* can drop a degenerate with a crowbar. From horseback. He can live off the land and teach her hymns I've never heard of and stop her from poisoning herself with the wrong mushrooms. I can't do any of that."

"You could learn," I pointed out. The rest of us were learning, but the more interest Grayson took in the Army's lifestyle, the harder Reese resisted the new knowledge. "But Eli can't teach her to pluck a demon from the air or scorch it from its human host. You have to play to your strengths."

He picked up the bucket and held it while I dropped the discarded bits of fish inside. "You think I should help her trigger the transition?"

I shrugged and wiped my hands on a clean scrap of cloth. "Is she ready?"

"Maybe." There was an odd bit of resistance in his voice.

"You've been putting it off. Intentionally," I guessed, and he glanced at me in surprise. "Why?"

"Because once she transitions, she'll be able to take care of herself. She won't need me anymore."

I stood and angled us so that Reese couldn't see Eli teaching Grayson to throw butter knives at a tree trunk. "Even if protection *was* all she wanted from you, keeping her from her true potential will only make her resent you. If she's really ready"—and based on the number of degenerates we'd been fending off, she was—"the best thing you can do for her is help her *reach* her potential."

Reese blinked at me. "Okay, when you say it like that, it sounds kind of reasonable."

"Good." I reached up to give him a pat on one enormous shoulder. "Might I suggest sooner rather than later?"

"I'll tell her tonight. After dinner."

"Perfect." I took the bucket of innards from him and waved one hand at the pile of cleaned fish. "I caught and cleaned. *You* cook and serve."

* * *

"Voilà!" Reese handed Finn and me each a stainless steel camping plate with a raised lip around the edge. Each plate held a grilled trout fillet, a hunk of the flatbread Joanna and her mother had shown us how to make, and a scoop of wilted dandelion greens from the pot Melanie and Anabelle had made under Brother Isaiah's supervision.

It was the best meal we'd made for ourselves since we'd lost access to New Temperance's electricity and kitchen appliances.

I grabbed a steel spork from a can of camping utensils and dug in.

"That *is* impressive," Devi said from the other side of the circle as Reese loaded two more plates from the foldable steel grill straddling our campfire.

"I made the bread!" Grayson used a knife to slice the last batch into pieces on a tray balanced on her lap. We'd been happy to share several bags of flour with Eli's people in exchange for a demonstration of what could be done with it even without yeast.

Firelight flickered over Grayson's wide smile as she handed the next slice to Melanie.

"It smells amazing." Maddock sat on the ground next to Devi and accepted a plate from Reese.

Melanie frowned and held her bread up to her face, where she gave it a delicate sniff. She looked puzzled. "I don't smell it."

"My kingdom for a stick of butter," Devi said around a bite of fish. "I miss hot buttered bread more than *anything.*"

Mellie took a tentative bite, then set her bread on her plate and poked at her fish with her spork.

"She's lost her appetite again?" Finn said from my left. "I thought she was feeling better."

Melanie leaned forward to give him a rare smile. "I'm

fine. The bread's just kind of . . . tasteless." She whispered the last word with an apologetic glance at Grayson, who was oblivious. "Don't you think?"

"Mine was good." He'd finished his hunk in three bites. "You don't like the fish either?"

Melanie shrugged. "Reese is better at killing things than cooking things."

"I heard that," Reese said with a self-deprecating smile. "But I think the baby's messing with your taste buds. Everyone else likes my fish."

In fact, mine was already half gone. Reese's experimental salt, pepper, and thyme dry rub was a culinary triumph, in my opinion.

Melanie's problem probably had nothing to do with the food. She'd been quiet and withdrawn since Tobias had been exposed as a demon, but Eli's mother had assured us that fatigue was to be expected during the third trimester of her pregnancy. Especially for someone so young, who'd been through so much trauma. So I'd tried to leave her alone, watching her from a distance while she studied everything going on around her with eyes that seemed to grow larger every day.

While I watched Mellie, I'd also been getting to know our gracious hosts. Particularly the elders, who had even more to offer than priceless decades of experience. I felt guilty when I asked Brother Isaiah's gray-haired wife to show me how she sewed together scraps of leather to make a knife-carrying pack, but not too guilty to notice that her thin, fragile hands shook and she had to hold the materials mere inches from her face to see them.

The elderly man who taught me how to layer kindling and tinder for a proper campfire couldn't stand straight because of the hunch in his spine, and the sweet old lady who showed me how to prepare rendered animal fat to be used in soap-making had a persistent wet cough.

They were all three in their late sixties, according to Eli, which made them a full decade older than the oldest person I'd ever met in New Temperance, thanks to mandatory soul donations. I didn't want *any* of them to die. In fact, the more time I spent with the army's senior citizens, the harder it became to imagine saying goodbye to them. But if one of them *was* nearing the conclusion of a natural life span, I was determined to make sure that Melanie's baby honored the end of one life with the beginning of another.

The only one who seemed to have noticed my sudden interest in the elderly was Finn, and I was afraid to ask if he knew what I was thinking, because then he might ask me what my backup plan was. I couldn't lie to Finn. I *wouldn't* lie to him.

But even as I watched firelight flicker over our joined hands, I knew I wouldn't let him talk me out of it either.

"Eli!" Grayson called when she spotted the sentinel walking toward his family's campfire, one of several scattered around the clearing. "Come eat with us! I made bread!"

"Are you sure you have enough?" he asked, already headed our way.

Reese shook his head in the dark, but Grayson jumped up and grabbed Eli's arm, then pulled him down next to her. "We're short one plate," Reese grumbled.

She shrugged. "He can share with me."

"No, take mine." Reese shoved the last full plate at Eli. "You're our guest."

Finn and I exchanged glances as we chewed in silence, but neither Grayson nor Eli seemed to notice Reese's irritation. Or the fact that he had no food.

When Eli bowed his head to pray silently over his plate, everyone but Grayson stopped eating to watch.

Grayson bowed her head and closed her eyes.

It wasn't that the rest of us objected to Eli's faith. It was that most of us had little of our own after discovering that generations of our ancestors' souls had been consumed by those claiming to be our spiritual leaders. Everything we'd ever been taught to believe in had been proven not just false, but *foul*.

The only things we *knew* could save us were vigilance and violence. The only people we *knew* we could count on were those gathered around our campfire.

"What did you pray for?" Maddock asked when Eli looked up, and his thoughtful tone caught my attention. Reese would have asked the same question with sarcasm. Devi would have asked it out of skepticism. But Maddock . . .

134

As usual, Maddy was merely curious.

"I was giving thanks and asking the Lord to put more demons in my path so I can strike them down in His name." Eli took the spork Grayson handed him and dug a flake of fish from his fillet.

Anabelle gaped at him. "You were asking for *more* demons?"

Eli laughed at her horrified expression. "I wasn't asking for a second demonic invasion. I just asked the Lord to keep pushing the ones that are already here into my path so I can fulfill my life's purpose by killing them."

"You just mean the degenerates, right?" Reese said. "Because you guys seem to need help with Kastor's people."

"My fellow sentinels and I are perfectly capable of taking on any of the lions from the pit, but the oldest among us have already served their purpose and the youngest— like Tobias—are not yet ready. I ask only that the worst of the horde be put in *my* path rather than theirs."

"Sounds reasonable," I said. I felt the same way about protecting Mellie.

"But do you really think that's your purpose?" Devi asked around a bite of bread.

"It's ours, just like it is yours. There is no more noble pursuit, considering the state of the world. Every demon we strike down is felled through the strength the Lord has bestowed upon us, and—"

"Well, then he bestowed it all wrong." Reese's voice was

135

so sharp I actually choked on a bite of greens and had to cough it up.

Eli's spork clattered onto his plate, his meal suddenly forgotten. "Excuse me?"

"You guys are out there impaling degenerates through the eyeball and calling yourselves warriors, but all you're really doing is setting the demons loose to search for new hosts. *That's* what you did to your brother's killer. You released him. *We* fry the bastards right out of this world."

"I cannot deny that the Lord has blessed you in ways he has not seen fit to bless me, Reese." Eli's glance at Grayson made it clear that he wasn't just talking about exorcist abilities. "Nor can I presume to understand his reasons. I did what I could for Micah, with the gifts the Lord has given me. I freed his soul so he could find peace, and so that somewhere, a new child can live."

"I hate to tell you this," Reese began, though he didn't look like he really hated it all that much. "But your brother's soul is gone. Once a demon starts munching on it, there's no getting it back. On the bright side, that means he's not in pain. He's not . . . anything."

Eli's quiet smile was somehow both peaceful and patronizing. "We believe that the souls of the faithful will be returned to the well upon death—clean, whole, and at rest. I've released his soul. Micah is at peace."

"That's beautiful," Grayson breathed.

"That's horseshit," Reese insisted. "The well is empty.

Babies die within minutes of birth. That wouldn't be happening if you were freeing souls with every kill."

Eli contemplated him somberly. "Only the souls of the *faithful* can be restored. The souls of the faithless will be destroyed. The well is empty because there aren't enough people of faith left to fill it. Which means that disbelievers are just as much of a drain on the well of souls as demons are."

Devi turned to me with both brows raised. "Is he serious?"

Grayson glanced from face to face across the flickering flames of the campfire. "Souls at peace. I think it sounds . . . serene."

"Serenity must be earned," Eli said, setting his half-eaten dinner down in front of the fire. "We fight evil in this life so that we may find peace when it is over. Such is our burden. Such is our faith."

Devi rolled her eyes and tossed her thick, dark braid over her shoulder. Anabelle looked . . . confused.

Reese exhaled heavily. "I'm sorry, Eli, but there is absolutely no evidence of—"

"If there were evidence, it wouldn't be called faith," Eli interrupted, and the sharpness in each word said he was finally starting to lose his temper.

"That's right. It'd be called truth." Reese leaned so close to the fire his knee almost hit the grill. "What you're talking about isn't religion, it's delusion."

"Reese!" Grayson gasped. "There's no need to be rude!"

"Since when is the truth considered rude?" he demanded.

"Okay, everybody calm down." I set my spork on my plate and held both hands palms out, hoping to deescalate the discussion. "Let's not—"

Melanie's piercing scream sliced through my sentence. Everyone stared, and I turned to see my sister clutching her round stomach, firelight flashing over the pain written in every line on her face.

"I think the baby's coming."

NINE

"The baby? *Now?*" I said, and when Melanie nodded, I stood up in a panic and suddenly forgot everything I'd learned about childbirth over the past five months. All I could think about was that the baby was on its way and I hadn't found it a soul.

I would have to say hello and goodbye to my new niece or nephew in the same breath.

"Nina." Finn stood, and when he took my hands, I knew he recognized the fear in my eyes, if not the true source. "Calm down. Mellie's scared enough for both of you."

I couldn't make my heart stop racing. I hadn't had time to teach her everything she needed to know. I hadn't had time to write a letter to the baby. I hadn't had time to say goodbye to Finn. . . .

"It's okay." Eli handed his plate to Grayson, his argument with Reese apparently forgotten. "Melanie happens to be in the company of no fewer than a dozen experienced midwives." He gave us all a firelit grin. "Not including me."

"Nina . . ." Melanie groaned my name as Finn let me go to give us some room. Fear danced in my sister's eyes. "It's too early."

"She still has another month to go," I said, and Eli frowned.

"Okay, let's give her some space," he said, and everyone who wasn't already standing got up and backed carefully away from the campfire, taking their food with them. On his way out of the clearing, Reese picked up the plate Eli had set down and began to eat the meal he'd given away minutes before.

I couldn't really blame him. We all knew we might be in for a very long night.

At least, that was my greatest hope.

"This could just be false labor." Eli spared a moment for a reassuring smile at my sister. "So I'm going to get my mother. She's the most experienced midwife we have. Nina, you and Anabelle sit with Melanie and try to keep her calm. Start timing her contractions. If this is false labor, they'll probably be weak and erratic. But that could be true even if this is real labor. First babies can take well over twelve hours to make their appearance."

Melanie groaned, and I squatted to take her hand.

"What about us?" Finn set his plate on a tree stump, his dinner forgotten. "What can we do?"

Eli glanced at the other members of our surrogate family, who'd gathered to stare awkwardly at my sister, unsure how to help. "The rest of you can gather some pillows and sheets. Blankets. Whatever you have that will make her more comfortable."

While the rest of us were occupied with our assignments—busywork though they may have been—Eli went to get his mother. As I watched him wind his way between the neighboring campfires, I realized that the other members of the Lord's Army knew that Melanie had gone into labor, but as a courtesy, they wouldn't bother us until and unless they were asked for help.

Finn and Maddock cleared away our plates, taking the occasional bite as they worked. Reese wrapped his hands in extra shirts to protect them while he removed the folding grill from the fire and set it where no one would accidentally bump into it in the dark. Devi and Grayson grabbed several of our bedrolls from the back of the SUV and helped me prop Mellie up against them to make her as comfortable as we could.

I kept up a quiet conversation with my sister—assuring her that she and her baby would be fine and asking about the names she'd been considering—while Anabelle counted the passing minutes on her watch, waiting for the next contraction.

When she finished her assignment, Devi excused herself

from the event with a mumble and a graceless gesture I couldn't interpret, then headed for one of the other campfire groups, where several of her new training buddies were waiting for their fish to finish grilling.

Devi had no interest in childbirth, and every interest in a second helping of dinner.

Several minutes after he'd left, Eli returned with a tall, thin woman in her midforties. Her thick, dark curls were cropped close to her head and she carried a worn handstitched leather satchel over one shoulder. "This is my mother, Damaris," Eli said. "Mom, this is Melanie Kane."

Flickering firelight revealed deep wrinkles in the woman's forehead and unwavering confidence in her dark eyes. She squatted on the mat next to my sister. "It's an honor to meet you, Melanie."

"Hi," Mellie returned, then grimaced and clutched at her stomach.

"Eight minutes," Anabelle said, without looking up from the watch she held angled toward the firelight.

Damaris's eyes widened. "Well, that's progressing faster than I expected. What month are you in?"

"We think she's at the end of her eighth," I said when Melanie appeared unable to speak.

"Okay," Damaris said as if she'd come to some conclusion. "That's not great, but it could be worse. We don't have the medication and equipment necessary to stop your labor, so the best we can do is make sure your son or daughter makes it safely into the world. After that, it's up to the Lord. Do you understand?"

Melanie nodded, and I squeezed her hand. If Damaris's Lord didn't step in on the baby's behalf, I would.

And with a sudden jolt of alarm, I realized I had no idea how best to do that.

I'd need to die instantly, to make sure the baby got my soul in time. And I'd need to be near the baby when it happened. But I couldn't do it in front of Melanie—she'd never get over the trauma.

"Is this your first labor?" Damaris asked, and Melanie nodded again. "Where is the father?" Eli's mother glanced at Reese, Finn, and Maddock in turn, and they all shook their heads, then took a couple of steps back, just to be clear.

"His name was Adam," I whispered to Damaris. "The Church had him executed."

"I'm so sorry," she said to Melanie. "But the Lord never gives us more than we can bear, so you must be a strong woman indeed. Even if you don't know it yet." She patted Mellie's denim-covered knee as my sister exhaled slowly through her mouth. "Okay, let's take a look." She reached for Mellie's calves to angle her toward the firelight, but my sister screeched and pressed her knees together.

She turned to me, her eyes wide and shiny with unshed tears. "Nina . . ."

"Okay, hon, I know you're scared, but you have to let

Damaris examine you. If we were still in New Temperance, you'd be used to this already. You'd have been getting checkups once a month."

"I know," Mellie said. But the fear did not fade from her eyes, and she made no move to take off her jeans.

"I'm sorry," I said, turning to Damaris. "She's never had an obstetrics exam."

"I've had one," Melanie said, and we both turned to her in surprise. "At the jail." When they'd held her on charges of fornication and unlicensed pregnancy, as well as suspicion of possession. "They tied me down. Don't let them tie me down again, Nina," she begged, and my heart broke for my sister all over again.

"We don't do things like that here, honey," Damaris said. "I promise. I just need to see how far dilated your cervix is. Do you know what that means?"

"Of course." Melanie looked more than a little offended by the question. "I've read seven books on pregnancy, labor, and delivery. I just . . . the reality feels different than I expected."

"And this is just the beginning," Damaris gave her a comforting smile. "Are you ready to be examined?"

"I want to change into my gown and robe first," Mellie said. We'd found them both—as well as a selection of maternity clothes—in a shipment headed from a factory in Solace to a department store in Constance. Melanie looked up, and her gaze settled on Grayson. "Could you grab my hospital bag? It's in the front of the cargo truck." She'd had it packed for weeks, just like the books advised, even though we didn't have an actual hospital to take her to.

"Of course." Grayson grabbed the large hammer she'd been training with and turned toward the far side of the campsite, but Eli put one hand on her arm.

"I'll go with you."

"I can take care of myself." Grayson let the hammer thunk into her palm.

"Good for you," he said, smiling after her as she took off for the parked truck, which formed part of the perimeter of the campground.

Damaris gave Mellie another gentle smile, then turned to look up at her son. "Eli, go grab my flashlight and see if Brother Isaiah has any batteries left for it. We're gonna have to do better than firelight for this little one."

"We have flashlights," Maddock said as Reese returned from stowing the cooled camp grill. "I'll grab the one from the SUV. Reese, can you catch up to Grayson and have her grab the other one from the truck?"

"She went to the truck? By herself?"

"It's just across the clearing, and she's armed," Eli said.

"She's also a degenerate magnet. A largely *untrained* degenerate magnet." Reese took off toward the truck and Eli jogged after him, while Maddock headed for the SUV.

"Okay, they'll be back with your gown in a few minutes. Let's get you ready to change," Damaris said, and my sister voiced no objection when the older woman began removing her sneakers. "The first thing we're going to do is—"

"Grayson!"

Reese's shout startled me so badly I would have fallen into the fire pit if Finn hadn't grabbed my arm.

"Grayson!" Reese raced into the center of the large clearing from the darkness at the back of the truck, carrying Grayson's hammer. He was lit on all sides by individual cooking fires, so even from across the camp I could see that the hammer glistened with fresh blood.

"Oh no . . ." I felt the warmth drain from my face, leaving cold shock in its place.

Eli appeared from the shadows a second later, dragging something in the dirt behind him.

"Mellie, I'll be right back," I murmured, gesturing for Anabelle and Damaris to stay with her. I jogged across the clearing with Finn on my heels, his rifle in hand, but Maddock and Devi beat us there.

"She's gone," Reese said as a drop of blood plopped onto his boot from the head of the hammer. "Someone *took* her."

"It looks like Peter died trying to help her." Eli pulled the body he'd been dragging into the clearing, and several members of the Lord's Army gasped. I recognized Peter as one of Brother Isaiah's grandsons, a sweet man in his early twenties who'd obviously died from the gruesome dent in his skull. But . . .

"The Unclean didn't do that," I said, and Eli frowned

down at me. "Degenerates would have torn him apart trying to get to his soul, and even a demon in its prime would probably have ripped his throat out or crushed his skull. Most of them enjoy the visceral *experience* of the kill." They'd invaded our world—and our bodies—because their own lacked most physical sensation. They wanted to feel, taste, and hear things. Including death. "Demons only use weapons when they need to avoid exposing themselves to an audience."

The Lord's Army had clearly spent more time killing human hosts than observing the demons hidden within them.

Eli glanced from face to face in confusion, then down at Peter's corpse. "Then who . . . ?"

"Grayson." Devi took the bloody hammer from Reese and held it up to the light from the nearest campfire. "Her weapon, her kill. But she wouldn't have done it unless her life were in danger."

Brother Isaiah made a stern noise in the back of his throat, at the front of the crowd already starting to gather. "That's unthinkable. Peter would never have—"

"He was possessed." Finn turned to Maddock, and his hand tightened around the rifle strap. "Kastor got to her through the Army. Nothing else makes sense." He lowered his voice and whispered the rest, his gaze practically begging Maddock for . . . something. "You *know* I'm right."

Maddock gave him the smallest of grim nods, and when

Devi's gaze met mine from across the dead body, I realized she had heard Finn too.

"You cannot know for sure that Peter was possessed," Brother Isaiah insisted. "Maybe *Grayson* was Unclean."

Eli shook his head, but Devi's explanation came faster. "If Grayson had been possessed, she wouldn't have needed a hammer to kill someone."

"And Kastor wouldn't have needed to kidnap her," Finn pointed out, holding Reese's gaze to reassure him. "If she'd been possessed, she would have just driven off in one of our vehicles, daring us to come get her. But that's not what happened. They had to *abduct* her because they're not *inside* her."

"She's bait," Maddock clarified, his voice so soft that several of us actually leaned in to hear him better. "They want the rest of Anathema to follow her to Pandemonia. They left both of our cars so we can do just that."

Devi shrugged. "If they're on foot, they can't have gotten very far."

"They're on horseback." Eli looked up from where he knelt next to Peter's body. "I saw at least two sets of hoofprints. Are any of our mounts missing?"

A murmur rolled through the crowd as half a dozen members of the Lord's Army went to check on their horses. A couple of minutes later little Joanna pushed her way to the front of the crowd, her pink cowboy hat hanging at her back from its braided cord. She was breathing hard, her dark eyes wide with fear. "Naomi and Serah are gone! So are their horses."

Naomi, I remembered, was Joanna's older sister. She and her friend Serah were among the young women who'd been teaching Grayson and Melanie to bake.

"Did they get kidnapped too?" Joanna fiddled nervously with the knot on her hat cord while she stared up at Brother Isaiah, clearly terrified.

"No, my dear." The elder's joints popped and creaked as he knelt next to her. "It looks like Finn is right. The Unclean likely got to Naomi, Serah, and Peter in their sleep, then took Grayson as bait to draw her friends to Pandemonia."

"I'm *so* sorry," I said, watching helplessly as the news spread in a ripple of somber whispers. By traveling with Eli and the Lord's Army, we'd made them all targets.

It was my idea to help Melanie. *I'd* done this to them.

Before I could figure out how to better express my devastated mea culpa to a girl who'd now lost both her little brother and her older sister, Damaris stepped forward and put one arm around her young granddaughter.

Brother Isaiah stood to address the crowd. "Naomi and Serah are gone, but not forgotten. Our sentinels will free their souls and return them to the well, as is our sacred duty and our honor."

"We'll leave at first light," Eli confirmed.

But all I could think about was that *I'd* brought this loss upon Eli's friends and family when they'd done nothing but help us, and the losses might not be over. How long had Naomi, Serah, and Peter been possessed? How many more of Brother Isaiah's people had already fallen to the invisible predators we'd led straight to them?

Were more Unclean hidden in the crowd, watching the chaos play out in silent glee?

"I'm not waiting until morning." Reese's declaration drew me out of my terrifying thoughts. "Grayson can't afford the delay." Rage exploded across his face, reddening his pale features as fear and grief for his girlfriend crested. "This is *your* fault!" He grabbed Eli by the throat and lifted him from the ground one-handed.

"Reese!" Maddock pulled on one of Reese's massive arms. Finn took the other one, but Reese was too big. Too strong. Too terrified and angry.

"You let her go off by herself before her transformation was triggered. Before she was even trained to fight. *You* did this!"

"Reese, let him go!" I shouted as Eli kicked frantically and the crowd began to close in, many bearing blunt weapons.

Devi's beautiful features sharpened into a scowl. She grabbed a handful of Reese's light brown hair and pulled as hard as she could. Reese shouted as his head was jerked back. His hand opened, and Eli fell to the ground, gasping and rubbing his throat. Devi dragged Reese back several steps, then stood on her toes to speak as close to his ear as she could get.

"Reese. Eli didn't take Grayson. In fact, *we're* the reason three of his friends and relatives are dead. Five, if you count Tobias and Micah. Kastor's after *us*."

When he nodded awkwardly, jaw clenched, Devi finally let him go.

Reese immediately turned to Maddock. "Give me the keys."

"Wait," Eli croaked from the ground, rubbing his throat. "Even if you could track them in the dark with nothing but headlights, they'll go off-road. Somewhere hooves can go but tires can't. Why else would they leave on horseback?"

Reese's cheeks were scarlet with fury. His eyes were narrowed, his jaw clenched. He was still close to losing it.

"We don't have to follow them," I pointed out. "We know where they're taking her, and our cars will go faster than their horses. We'll cut them off before they get to Pandemonia, and we'll get her back, Reese. We'll go as soon as Mellie's had her baby."

The last word was still hanging in the air when the problem hit me. *I* wouldn't be going *anywhere* after my sister had her baby. Not ever again.

But even if Reese and the others waited for her, Mellie couldn't go with them—I didn't want her and the baby anywhere near Pandemonia. Yet Eli and his people were much less capable of protecting my last family members than Anathema was.

There were no good options. My death would give the baby life yet leave no one capable of defending that life.

Oblivious to the choice I was wrestling with, Reese glanced over my shoulder to where my sister was laboring next to our campfire with only Anabelle in attendance. "No. Nina, we have to go *now*," he whispered. "She could be in labor all night. Grayson can't wait that long."

"Son, they've probably already claimed her as a host," Brother Isaiah said, and I turned to find him watching our exchange with many of his followers fanned out behind him. "If that's the case, the most you can offer her is the release of her immortal soul."

"He's an atheist." Eli pushed himself to his feet, still rubbing his throat. "He doesn't believe her soul can find peace."

"It doesn't matter. She's not possessed," Finn said, and we all turned to him in surprise. "Not yet."

Reese swiped one thick arm across his face, wiping away tears that seemed to be part grief, part rage. "How do you know?"

"I know because Peter has a dent in his head rather than a smoking hole in his chest. She didn't exorcise him, so she hasn't triggered her transition yet, and she's safe until she does. Exorcist hosts are a *very* rare luxury, even in Pandemonia, and they all know that if she's possessed before she enters transition, she never *will* enter transition."

"How much time do we have?" Reese asked, and I noticed that his gaze had lost focus. He was concentrating on the plan to get Grayson back.

"As much time as she gives us," Finn said softly. "As long as she refuses to exorcise her first demon, they can't possess her." He cleared his throat and glanced at the ground. "But there's nothing they won't do to try to *make* her trigger her transition. They have no compassion and no boundaries. They have no souls."

His last statement echoed into stunned silence as the rest of us considered what that might mean.

"I almost helped trigger her . . . ," Reese whispered, and I'm not sure anyone beyond our immediate circle heard him. "I could have gotten her killed." He looked up suddenly, and his gaze found mine. "Stay with your sister, if you need to. I understand. But I'm going after Grayson now, and I'm taking the SUV. Any of you who want to come are welcome." His gaze skipped over Finn— probably assuming we wouldn't be split up—and found Maddock and Devi. Before they could answer, I laid one hand on Reese's arm, panic swelling deep inside me.

"Let me check on Mellie. It could be false labor." That was the only hope I had left to cling to. "And even if it's not, maybe it won't take as long as we expect."

Reese nodded. "Check on her. But I'm going in fifteen minutes, with or without you."

I jogged back to our campfire, Finn's footsteps echoing at my back. Damaris was right behind him.

"What happened to Grayson?" Mellie asked when I knelt next to her. She had both hands on her belly, but she wasn't sweaty or pale. She looked pretty good, considering.

"Some of Kastor's demons possessed a few of the Lord's Army's members and took her."

Melanie's eyes widened. "Here? Kastor's people are *here*? *Now*?"

"They were, but they're gone, and I don't want you to worry about that right now." Nor did I want her to know that Reese would be leaving in minutes, with or without us. "How do you feel?" I glanced at Anabelle, who had stopped consulting her watch; then I turned to Damaris, who frowned as she felt my sister's bulging stomach.

"I can't feel any contractions," the midwife said.

"Maybe she's not having another one yet."

"The first two were eight minutes apart," Anabelle said. "But now she's gone ten minutes without one."

I studied my sister's face, brushing her hair back from her forehead. She looked confused and scared but physically comfortable, and it was hard not to get my hopes up. "Is that unusual?"

"Not particularly. I'd like to check her cervix, to rule out false labor." Damaris turned back to the patient. "Honey, we need to get your pants off."

"No, I think I'm fine now." Mellie's arms tightened protectively around her stomach. "The contractions have stopped. It was probably false labor, just like you said. We have to go get Grayson."

"Okay, but we need to be sure," I insisted, while Damaris and Anabelle turned one of our mats to face the fire because no one had returned with a flashlight. "I mean, is there any chance of that? I don't want to move her if she's going to have a baby in the next day or so."

"Nina, I'm fine," Melanie insisted. "It was false labor—the books even have a fancy name for that—but it's over now." She sat up and reached around her belly for her shoes. "Let's go."

"How long would it take to check her cervix?" If I knew for *sure* that we had more time . . .

Please let us have more time. . . .

Damaris glanced at one of the neighboring campfires. "We're still trying to get water to boil so I can sterilize my equipment. That'll take another ten or fifteen minutes."

"I . . ." I frowned, glancing back at Reese, who was carrying a bag of supplies from the cargo truck to the SUV. "If it happens again while we're on the road . . ."

"I'll be there to help." Eli stepped into the circle of light from our campfire with a backpack over one shoulder and a full duffel over the other. His voice was still hoarse and his neck was red. "I'm going with you."

"The hell you are!" Reese stomped toward us from the direction of the truck, his thick arms swinging at his sides, his eyes narrowed in fury. "It's *your* fault Grayson's missing."

"That's part of the reason I'm going," Eli insisted. "I owe Grayson a debt, and I'm going to help you get her back. And it's my sacred duty to release Naomi's and Serah's souls. Also, if Melanie goes into labor, you'll need me," he added, tossing a reassuring glance at both me and my sister.

"Reese," Finn said, "he's a good fighter, and we can't afford to turn down help."

"Fine." Reese stomped backward toward the cargo truck. "But he's riding with *you*."

"Agreed. But we're taking the SUV." I turned back to Finn. "Could you move some of our stuff to the back of the cargo truck to make room for Eli in the SUV?"

"Of course." Finn headed toward the edge of the campsite while Melanie and I said our goodbyes to the Lord's Army, thanking Eli's friends and family for everything they'd shown and taught us, as well as their company. With any luck, we'd be back with Grayson and my sister would still be pregnant. But we'd learned never to rely on luck in the badlands. . . .

By the time we got to the SUV, Finn was on his way to the truck with our extra supplies and Eli was wedging his belongings into the SUV's cargo hold.

"Here, some of that can come up front with me." Melanie handed me her bag, then headed toward the rear of the vehicle, where Eli had dropped his crowbar on the ground to free up both hands for wedging luggage into the tight space.

"Thanks," he said as I leaned into the third row to set my sister's bag on the floorboard.

156

A thud echoed from the back of the car, and I froze, startled. "Mellie?" Goose bumps rose on my arms as I stood. The back hatch closed with a heavy clunk, and the light from the cargo area went out, which left me staring into the darkness behind the SUV. "Eli?"

"He was in the way." My sister stepped into the light pouring from the backseat of the car, and the first thing I noticed was that she held herself strangely. Instead of caressing or rubbing her stomach, which she'd been doing nonstop for months, Mellie stood with both arms hanging at her sides. Her right hand held Eli's crowbar. "I might have swung a little too hard. Let's hope I get it right this time."

She raised the crowbar, and fear leapt into the back of my throat, bitter and acidic. "Mellie?" I tried to back away but bumped into the open rear door of the SUV. Melanie raised the crowbar with a grunt, and in the instant before it hit the side of my head and darkness slammed into me, I realized Mellie wasn't the one swinging a metal club at my head.

My baby sister was already dead.

TEN

I woke up to a crick in my neck and the familiar rhythmic bumps of tires on cracked pavement. *The SUV.* We were on the road again, and I must have fallen asleep after . . .

What happened?

My eyes flew open, and when I lifted my head, pain shot through the left side of my skull. The entire world . . . wobbled.

I moaned, but that only made the pain worse. The daylight shining through the windshield was so bright that we might as well have been driving on the surface of the sun.

"Mellie?" I said, and the syllables came out all mushy, yet they slammed into my head with the force of a sledge-hammer.

"You've got a hell of a concussion," she said, and when I turned to face her—why was she driving?—the world spun around me again. "So you should probably sit still."

"Why are you . . . ?" I tried to touch my throbbing head, but my arm was stuck behind my back. When I wiggled my fingers, pins and needles shot through my hand, as if I'd been sitting on it for too long. "How did I . . ."

I closed my eyes and images flashed across the backs of my eyelids.

Mellie stepping into the light, holding Eli's crowbar.

Light glinting on the metal as it swung.

I moaned again as the pieces fell into place in my head. Shock tightened around me, threatening to squeeze all the air from my lungs, when I realized my hands weren't just stuck behind me, they were *tied* behind me. When I tried to move my feet, I discovered my ankles were bound as well.

I'd been abducted by the demon possessing my sister.

"Noooo . . ." I hardly recognized my own voice. "No, give my sister back. *Please.*"

"You know it doesn't work that way." The monster wearing Melanie's face faked a sympathetic frown as she steered around the stripped-clean corpse of a Jeep blocking the center of the neglected highway. "She's not in here anymore. If I vacated this body, all the organs would shut down and within minutes her physical form would be as dead as the rest of her. Your sister's gone for good, Nina."

Tears blurred the world in front of me, smearing wheat

fields and the occasional rusted hulk of abandoned irrigation equipment. I sucked in breath after breath, trying to control the hitching sobs that shook my entire body and speared my head with fresh, sharp pain.

She *couldn't* be right. If the world we lived in could support demonic possession and flames spouting from the palms of mortal beings and a rift between the fabrics of *two entirely different realities,* surely there was some way to reverse what this monster had done and bring my sister back.

If Eli's God truly existed, how could he deny me one tiny little miracle?

"Eli . . ." The name snuck out on a sob before I even realized what I was thinking about.

Melanie's corpse gave a careless shrug. "He was still breathing when we left. He might make it."

And if he did, he'd tell the others what had happened. That Mellie and I hadn't just run off and left them. He'd tell them, and they'd come after me.

Except that they couldn't, because they had to find . . .

I blinked to clear tears from my eyes, and then I twisted in my seat, trying to see into the back of the SUV. "Where's Grayson? You're working with whoever took her, aren't you?"

"Smart girl. Grayson is on an alternate route—part of a two-pronged attack to divide and conquer Anathema. Either your group will split up, weakening itself to go after both of its members separately, or they will all head to where they know they can find you both in the same place."

"Pandemonia," I said, and she nodded. "Who are you?" I squirmed, trying to take pressure off my numb hands. "How long ago did you kill my sister?"

How long had I been sleeping next to a monster?

"Give it some thought." She steered around a century-old wreck on the right side of the crumbling road. "You'll figure it out eventually."

My mouth was dry and my head throbbed fiercely, but I made myself think through the pain. We hadn't come into direct contact with any of the Unclean since . . .

Tobias. Maddock had called the demon Aldric.

Except Aldric couldn't be possessing Mellie, because I'd fried him right out of our world. But the demon Eli had bashed with his crowbar . . .

"You're Meshara," I said, and the demon laughed with Melanie's throat. With Melanie's voice. But not with her eyes. "You've been with us since that day in the court-house. Almost a week ago." Pain gripped my chest like a giant fist, and suddenly I couldn't breathe.

I squeezed my eyes shut and tears rolled down my face, but I couldn't use my hands to wipe them. My fingers dug into the seat behind me as I silently pleaded with reality to banish the cruel lie sitting next to me and return my sister. But when I opened my eyes, the demon was still there. Still wearing Melanie's body, as surely as it wore her sneakers.

My baby sister—the only true family I had left—had died alone in her sleep almost a week before, and *I hadn't noticed*. Her soul was being slowly devoured by an evil parasite, and *I couldn't tell*.

My mom had been possessed since before I was conceived, so there was never any change in her for me to notice, but I was closer to Melanie than I'd ever been to anyone in my life. Including Finn. I knew her better than I knew *anyone*, but she'd died, and I'd had no clue.

I had *utterly* failed her.

Grief was a weight tied to my feet, dragging me beneath the current of denial. I was drowning, and I had no will to fight the tide.

"I *am* Meshara, but now I'm also Melanie, who came with this convenient little built-in insurance policy." The demon laid one hand on my sister's bulging belly. "We both know you're not going to try anything that might hurt your sister's squirming progeny. Nor would you let someone else put the little monster in danger. Which means that even though I took you prisoner, you're my guardian angel, in case any of your friends catch up with us before we get to Pandemonia. Don't tell me you don't appreciate the irony."

In fact, the irony made me want to vomit up my own lungs. But Meshara was right. Mellie's baby was the only piece of her I had left.

"There was no early labor?" My thoughts felt sluggish, but my concussion was the least of my worries.

"Nope. This little parasite seems quite content where he is for now," the demon wearing Mellie's face confirmed as we bumped over a crack in the highway. "Thank goodness. Playing sweet, knocked-up baby sister was hard enough, but faking uterine contractions is a bit beyond my ken. And there was nothing I could do about the whole cervical issue."

"But you're sure the baby's okay?" The question was ultimately pointless because there was nothing to keep her from lying, but I had to ask.

"As sure as I can be without an ultrasound machine or a prenatal psychic connection. I can't read the little bastard's mind. Hell, I can hardly feel him kicking anymore. Your sister's stomach's gone kind of numb."

"Numb? Is that normal?"

Meshara closed her eyes for a second, evidently searching through my sister's memories, then looked at the road again. "According to one of those stupid pregnancy books, it's from the stretching of the skin. Came on kind of sudden, though. And the book didn't mention the loss of sensation spreading into my limbs." She took one hand off the steering wheel and pressed her thumbnail into the pad of her index finger, then shrugged as if she couldn't feel the touch. "Or that food would lose its flavor. Being pregnant sucks. That's why we usually let humanity bear the next generation for us. Except for a few sickos I know who get off on the whole 'human experience' thing."

Could pregnancy really dull a woman's taste buds and

numb her fingers? Suddenly I wished I'd read more of Melanie's books.

"Then maybe you shouldn't have possessed a pregnant woman."

Meshara rolled her eyes. "We both know Melanie's the only host you wouldn't have tried to burn me out of at the earliest opportunity."

Which meant she clearly didn't expect me to remain tied up for long. Smart demon.

"So why did you fake . . . ?" Suddenly I understood. "You were the distraction." We were all supposed to be caught up with Mellie's early labor so Kastor's spies could get away with Grayson. Meshara had sent Grayson to the truck for her bag. She'd set the whole thing up, and we'd fallen for it.

"*Now* you're getting it. Good to know there's no permanent damage from the crowbar."

"Does it even matter, if I'm just going to wind up as somebody's host?"

"Physical damage matters. A possessed body heals slower than normal, and brain damage is nearly impossible to recover from. That's why we don't possess the mentally impaired. Now, psychological damage—*that* just gives the new occupant an interesting backstory to work with."

"Melanie isn't your backstory," I snapped. "She's my sister."

"She *was* your sister. Now she's a collection of unique memories and experiences, distinct from those of anyone else in the world. She's qualia for me to play with. And I have to say, pedestrian pregnancy aside, hers may be the most interesting life I've ever assumed. An aptitude for study, yet no fondness for it. Sex at the *scandalous* age of fifteen. And love!" Meshara twisted to look at me through my sister's eyes, and the car swerved to the right so hard that I smacked my shoulder on the window. "It wasn't just physical with the doomed Adam Yung. Mellie really loved him. And she loved their baby."

"Stop." Unshed tears stabbed at my eyes like needles, but Meshara obviously enjoyed my pain.

"Then the way he died! They made her watch, and it was too much for her, even just seeing it on the screen. He screamed her name at the end as the flames crisped his skin. She passed out cold. Hit her head on the floor. Did she tell you that? Her anguish must have been *delicious*."

I clenched my teeth and tried to ignore her as I watched fields and small, burnt-out towns pass by my window.

"Melanie thought you'd left her. They told her you'd escaped the city, and that hurt her worse than anything. Worse than being tied to an exam table, prodded with equipment and poked with needles. The worst part of all was that she thought you let it happen."

"I have to go to the bathroom," I said, turning to stare straight out the windshield at the miles of splintered concrete stretching out before us.

"What? Stop mumbling."

"I'm not mumbling. I have to pee."

Meshara rolled Mellie's eyes again, and I realized she'd mastered the human gesture. "No, you don't."

"Yes, I do," I insisted, squirming in my seat to emphasize my discomfort, which allowed me to twist so that my wrist bindings touched the passenger's-side door.

"Cross your legs and hold it." Meshara glanced at my bound ankles and laughed. "Okay, then just hold it."

For the next few hours I tried to tune out the demon's torturous nostalgia-by-proxy while I watched the few remaining highway signs to estimate our distance from Pandemonia. To judge the dwindling window of opportunity I had to free myself and disable the demon without hurting Mellie's baby. I took advantage of every swerve and bump in the road to scrape the thin cord binding my wrists against a jagged edge of plastic in the broken passenger's-side armrest, but I couldn't tell whether or not the rope was fraying. I couldn't even be sure that I was hitting it in the same place with every bump, though I *was* sure I'd gouged my own skin several times.

According to Finn and Maddock, Pandemonia had grown out of a prewar city called Colorado Springs, which was about sixty miles south of the former Colorado state capital of Denver. Denver had burned to the ground during the war—I knew that much from history class. But what the sisters hadn't told us was that Colorado Springs had escaped major damage only to be taken over not by demons disguised as Church officials, as in the other surviving cities, but by demons in no disguise at all.

No wonder the Church didn't want people to travel very far beyond its walled cities. They couldn't afford for us to know about Pandemonia, nor could they afford to lose any of their human cattle to Kastor.

When I gasped at the latest cut in my arm, Meshara glanced at me with a frown.

"I still have to pee," I said, and before she could question my bladder as the source of my pain, I changed the subject. "So, what's the plan when we get to Pandemonia? I'm assuming if you were going to possess me, you would have already tried."

"I would have already succeeded." She reached back between the front seats, and the car swerved while she felt around for something I couldn't see. "I could have taken you while you slept, just like I took your sister."

"Watch out!" I shouted, and she looked up just in time to swerve around a long-stalled minivan on the side of the road. Meshara held a snack-sized bag of cayenne-flavored peanuts, the last from a box no one but Reese could stand to eat because they were so hot. She ripped the bag open with her teeth and dumped an eighth of the contents into her mouth.

Mellie would have been crying from the heat, but Meshara looked disgusted as she chewed. "Cayenne, my ass. False advertising is what that is. These have *no* flavor." She dropped the bag into the center console, and red-powdered nuts spilled into the empty drink holder. "I can't *wait* to get out of this body. Nothing feels right. Nothing tastes right. Nothing even looks right." She leaned forward to peer over the steering wheel at the sky. "Is it getting cloudy? Why does everything look so . . . dull?"

I glanced out the window and found only a few wispy white clouds. "The windshield's tinted at the top. So, why *didn't* you possess me?" I asked. "Why go for a pregnant human who may or may not survive childbirth when you could have had a healthy exorcist body, which will last much longer?" When her jaw clenched and she stopped talking for the first time in *hours,* I understood what she wasn't saying. "You don't have enough rank to claim an exorcist host, do you? Why would you go to this much trouble for Kastor if he won't let you profit?"

"If this errand is successful and I survive, I will have my choice from a selection of beautiful young bodies that have *not* been stretched and weakened and *dulled* by pregnancy." Meshara laid one hand on Melanie's belly, and I wanted to rip her entire arm off. "Anything I want from the stables. Kastor gave his word," she said as we passed another highway mileage sign.

Neither Finn nor Maddock had been willing to talk about geography in any way associated with Pandemonia, so in the interest of avoiding the demon city in future travels, I'd borrowed a very old, very well-worn map from Brother Isaiah. It had taken me two hours to memorize all the highways leading to Colorado Springs, as well as the names of several of the nearby towns.

"And something about the fact that he's a soulless

monster makes you think he can be trusted?" I eyed a faded sign lying in the middle of the exit lane, its pole bent almost in half.

Oakley, Kansas. Prewar geography had never been my best subject, but that was enough to tell me we hadn't hit Colorado yet.

"The fact that he wants to maintain his control of the city means I can believe him. Unfulfilled promises lead to revolt, which is how he came into power in the first place," Meshara said. "If Kastor says I get a new body, I get a new body. And that day can't come fast enough." She squinted at the road. "Is your sister nearsighted?"

"No." But *I* had a mild case of myopia. "So what kind of hoops does a demon have to jump through to earn an exorcist as a host? I mean, who'll be wearing Nina Kane next season?"

"What?" She squinted at the road as if I were nothing more than a fly buzzing near her ear. "Mumbling is a sign of low self-confidence. Speak up."

"What's going to happen to me when we get to Pandemonia?" I repeated, each syllable exaggerated and loud. Pregnancy shouldn't have affected her hearing. Surely she was just trying to scare me.

"Oh. He'll either auction you off or give you away as a political favor," she said as if the details didn't truly matter, and my stomach began to churn. "But—" Meshara frowned and glanced down at her stomach, where her left hand still rested. "This thing's kicking hard enough

169

to bump my fingers, but I can't feel the movements from inside. Is that normal?"

"I don't think so." I frowned and sat straighter, anxiously trying to assess the problem without access to my hands or any medical knowledge whatsoever. "Melanie could definitely feel the baby kicking."

Meshara shrugged and returned both hands to the wheel, her pale brows drawn low.

"If I actually gave a damn, I might postulate that your sister felt what she wanted to feel—you know, because she *cared*—and I don't feel what I don't want to feel. Because I don't really give a shit about your little niece or nephew, beyond its value to me as a human shield."

The truth of that statement made me shake with fear and burn with rage. I could *not* let her get back to Pandemonia, because when she abandoned Mellie for a new form, my sister's body would die and the baby would die along with it.

As best I could tell, Meshara was driving west on what was once Interstate 70, and if her speedometer and my estimates were anywhere near accurate, she'd covered more distance in a single day of driving than we'd managed in the past five days of traveling with the Lord's Army, mostly because—as Reese had pointed out—cars could go faster than horses and they didn't have to stop to eat or rest.

We were already too close to Pandemonia for comfort.

"But I thought the whole reason you guys possess

human bodies is to experience things a demon can't in its natural form."

The demon tilted her head—a decidedly human gesture—and seemed to be giving the question serious thought. "Well, yes, in the sense that we can't experience *anything* in our natural form. We have no sight and very little sound, and absolutely no taste whatsoever. Our sense of touch is limited to pressure, which means we can tell when we bump into something or someone, but that's it. There's no pleasure. No pain. We literally spend eternity crawling around, experiencing nothing."

Which was why our world drew demons like bugs to a porch light. The human form was like a sensory buffet laid out before a child who'd never eaten.

An evil child with no self-control.

Meshara squinted as she guided the SUV off the road to avoid a fallen tree, rotting across all four lanes of cracked pavement. "But we have individual tastes, just like your people," she continued. "Some like to eat—you should *see* some of the gluttons waddling around Pandemonia—and some like music. Some live to dance, some stare at bright colors all day long, and we have an entire faction dedicated to wearing interesting and stimulating fabrics."

She glanced at me as she pulled the car back onto the road, bumping over an unseen chunk of concrete in the process. "And, of course, we have several distinct groups of masochists, who like pain because it's the strongest sensation they can elicit. And then there are those sick bastards who actually like being pregnant." She shuddered at the thought. "The aching joints, indigestion, and feet kicking my ribs from the inside were bad enough, but numbness and dead taste buds are worse than pain. I thought women liked pregnancy for the excuse to eat whatever they want. What's the point if you can't taste anything?" She glanced at me with a wry shrug. "You may think possession is distasteful, but I swear there's *nothing* stranger than growing a human being inside one's stomach."

"The baby's not in your stomach, it's in your uterus." Which she should know, considering that she had access to everything Melanie had ever seen, read, or felt. "But it's not even *your* uterus . . ." My anatomy lesson faded away when what she'd actually been saying finally sank in. Worry tightened my chest. "Wait, you could feel the baby moving before, but now you can't?"

Meshara shrugged. "That part's a relief, really." She squinted and bumped over another rift in the road. "I can still see the little parasité moving. I just can't feel it."

"That's not normal."

"All I care about is that it's *preferable*." The demon suddenly sat up straight and slammed her foot down on the brake. I flew forward, and my seat belt bruised me from hip to shoulder, driving all the air from my lungs. If not for the belt, I might have gone through the windshield.

Before I could suck in enough air to shout, Meshara had released her own seat belt and shoved open the driver's-side door. "What's not normal is how badly I have to pee!"

"Just now?" I'd had to go for *hours,* even with nothing to drink, and she'd had two bottles of water during the drive without so much as a complaint from her bladder, as far as I could tell.

"Yes. Sit tight!" she shouted as she lunged from the car and fast-waddled toward the grass. I lost sight of her when she ducked behind an abandoned car with a sapling growing through the engine compartment, but after a couple of minutes, which I spent sawing the nylon cord against the broken armrest at my back, she returned, still pulling the stretchy fabric of Melanie's maternity pants over her bulging belly. Only, something about her baby bulge looked . . . strange.

"Meshara!" I twisted for a better look, tugging as hard as I could against the frayed cord around my wrists. Being near a demon made me stronger than I'd have been on my own, but not as strong as I'd have been in the presence of several other exorcists. And nylon was very strong, for its weight. "Something's wrong."

"What?" she snapped as she dropped into the driver's seat. "You're mumbling again."

"Your belly. I'm telling you something's *wrong.*"

Frowning, she pulled up the hem of her shirt, and her eyes widened even before she could push down the top of her pants. The fabric seemed to be . . . bunching. As if the flesh beneath were contorting. She pulled the elastic material down to the base of her bulge and we both gasped. "What the hell is *that*?" she demanded, while we watched

173

her stomach roil as if her guts were waging war beneath her flesh.

"I think that's a contraction." My heart pounded and my thoughts raced. It was too early. And how had she not *noticed*? "The baby's coming. For real this time."

ELEVEN

"The baby can't be coming," Meshara insisted calmly, staring at her contorting stomach. "It's too early."

"That's not up to you." Fear plucked at my nerve endings like the strings of a guitar. What was I supposed to do with a demon in labor? Even if she safely delivered her "human shield," enabling me to exorcise her from my sister's body, what could possibly come next? My soul would do the poor child no good if there was no one there to take care of it once I was gone.

Minutes after the birth, I would be sitting alone in the middle of the badlands with the bodies of my sister and her baby.

Of all the ways I'd pictured the birth going horribly wrong, this wasn't one of them.

Panic sharpened my thoughts like the lens of a camera, blurring everything on the periphery so I could focus on the most important part. *One thing at a time, Nina. The baby comes first*. Even if it would only live for a few minutes.

I twisted in my seat, angling my bound wrists toward the demon. "Cut me loose so I can help you."

Meshara ignored my order, still ogling her belly in detached fascination. "Is he trying to rip his way out the hard way?" She reached for the lever on the side of the driver's seat, then pushed the whole chair back to put more space between herself and the steering wheel.

"It's not like there's an easy way." I tore my gaze away from her belly to study her face. "Can't you feel that?"

She shook her head, and Melanie's pale hair fell over her right shoulder. "It's like I'm watching the whole thing from the outside. How long has this been going on?"

"How am *I* supposed to know?" I sank back into the passenger's seat, trapping my hands against the upholstery as anger swelled to rival the fear already storming inside me. I wanted Meshara to deliver my niece or nephew screaming in agony the whole time. Then I wanted to fry her from my sister's body with my left hand while I cradled the baby in my right.

Was that too much to ask?

"You're supposed to be in a lot of pain right now!"

"No, I'm supposed to be in a brand-new body with no appreciable stomach, perfect vision, and *me* as the only parasite!" Her eyes were wide and she kept blinking, as if to clear her sight, but I still saw no sign of pain. "With any luck, we'll be in Pandemonia long before the damn thing pops out." She slid the seat forward again and slammed her stomach into the wheel to punctuate her dissatisfaction.

Anger bubbled up from deep inside me. "Be careful!"

"Let's be clear!" Meshara grabbed my chin and squeezed it mercilessly, glaring at me with eyes that held all of the color and expression of Melanie's yet none of the warmth. "I don't give a shit about this little uterine leech." To demonstrate, she punched her stomach with her free hand. I flinched, tears welling in my eyes, but she didn't even seem to feel the blow. "We're going to Pandemonia, come hell, high water, or motherfucking childbirth, and when we get there, *I'll* get a pretty new body and you'll get . . . whatever Kastor decides to do to you before he gives that tight little flesh-and-blood fortress away." She looked me up and down appreciatively, and my skin crawled even as I noticed her stomach contorting again. "That man does like his toys. And *this* thing . . ." She punched her belly again, and hot tears spilled down my cheeks toward the ironclad grip she had on my chin. "With any luck, they'll cut it out of your sister's corpse and show it to you before they throw it out with the rest of the garbage."

"I'm going to kill you," I said through clenched teeth, glaring into eyes that had seen my most intimate moments of triumph and despair. Eyes that had laughed with me and cried with me and fallen closed in the bed next to me every night for fifteen years.

Eyes that now held nothing of my sister's light or love or beauty.

Meshara laughed and let go of my chin. "No, you won't, because even though *I'm* willing to kill this kid just to watch you scream, you're not. You're going to let me drive you straight into hell on just the *chance* that you might find an opportunity to save this baby, because hope is a disease festering inside you, compromising your aim and crippling your logic."

"You're right about all of that." I twisted in my seat until I felt the jagged bit of plastic against my wrists again. "But you're wrong about the timing. You've had *two* contractions in the five or six minutes since you got back into the car." She might not be able to feel them, but I could *see* them. "You've probably been having them for hours. You're not going to make it to Pandemonia before the baby comes."

"The hell I'm not!" The first thread of anxiety laced her voice. Meshara shifted into gear and slammed her foot down on the gas.

I sawed at the nylon cord as fast as I could while we barreled down the road, terrified all over again every time she rubbed her eyes. Something was wrong, beyond the surprise contractions. The numbness, blurry vision, and hearing loss were *not* part of a normal birth.

"You can't drive while you're in labor, whether you can

feel it or not." I tried to remember everything Melanie had ever told me about the process. "You could vomit. At some point your water is going to break. And you might lose control of your bladder and bowels."

Meshara swerved around an ancient three-car pileup, and my shoulder slammed into the window again. "Okay. That's disgusting. But at least I won't be able to feel or smell it." She stomped on the gas again, and the SUV bumped over a huge crack in the pavement. "That's the only good thing about this stupid, failing body."

"*Why* can't you feel it?" Blood trickled down my wrist, but I kept sawing at the cord.

"Something's wrong with your sister." She squinted at the road. "Nothing feels right. Nothing tastes right. I can hardly hear you." She turned to look at me, and it took a second for her eyes to focus. "If I'd known Melanie was sick, I'd have picked Anabelle, human shield or not."

Fear crawling up my spine, I sawed harder at my bindings. Something was *seriously* wrong. "Melanie was *fine* until you pushed her out of her own body. Something's wrong with *you*."

Meshara shook her head, leaning as close to the windshield as she could get, obstructed by both the baby and the steering wheel. "Demons have no bodies of our own in your world, which means we're at the mercy of human physiology." She finally eased up on the gas pedal. "Looks like you were right about my not making it to Pandemonia, but labor isn't the problem. This body is failing. Fast."

My mind raced as the car began to swerve slowly, erratically, while she blinked furiously. "Are you still going numb?"

"Can't feel the wheel at all now," Meshara confirmed. Then she stomped experimentally on the gas, and the car shot forward again. "Can't feel the pedals either. And my tongue is tingling." She turned to look at me, and the car slowed again. "What the *hell* is wrong with your sister?"

"I don't know. Maybe this is what happens when a demon goes into labor." Had this happened to my mother? To Grayson's? How could it—they'd both survived to have a second in the same body.

Meshara shook her head, and the car swerved again. "It's not. I've hardly tasted anything in days."

I gave up sawing at the nylon cord and pulled my arms apart with as much force as I could summon. The cord creaked and several individual strands popped, but the binding didn't give. "Days?" Details spun through my head, and one of them triggered a vague memory. Someone *else* had complained about taste. . . . "How long, exactly?"

"Since a couple of days after I took Melanie's body."

And suddenly I remembered. Tobias/Aldric had started complaining about the way his food tasted a couple of days after we'd found him. Could he have been sick too? If I hadn't exorcised him, would he have lost his sight and hearing?

Two demons getting sick didn't bother me in the

least—surely sick was one step closer to dead—but could Meshara's illness affect the baby?

And why hadn't any of the rest of us caught it?

"What the hell is happening to me?" Meshara demanded, panic trailing from her words as she squinted at the windshield. "It started out as dull taste buds and some tingling, and suddenly everything I like about being human is just"—she threw her hands into the air, and the car swerved again—"draining away."

I gave my arms another pull, and more strands of nylon popped. "Stop the car!"

"What?" She squinted even harder as the SUV barreled between an off-kilter concrete barricade and the rusted hulk of an abandoned bus.

"Stop the car before you get us both killed!"

Instead, Meshara stomped on the gas, and the SUV lurched forward again while she alternately squinted and blinked furiously at the road, mumbling about making it to Pandemonia before my sister's rotting hull of a body gave out.

"Look out!" I shouted as she swerved around the burned-out frame of what might once have been a police car, and we careened toward a three-foot-high buckle in the concrete. Meshara screamed and took her foot off the gas, but she couldn't hit the brake before the SUV slammed into the jagged fold of pavement.

I flew forward, and my seat belt felt like an iron bar

swung straight at my chest. For several seconds I couldn't breathe. I blinked, but all I could see was the crumpled hood of the SUV, which had popped open to block the whole windshield.

I twisted in my seat to find my sister slumped over, the steering wheel pressing a dent into the rounded top of her belly. "Melanie!" I cried, in the instant before I remembered that Mellie was dead and her body was possessed. And that her baby's odds weren't much better.

"Meshara!" Her eyes fluttered open. She moaned, and her eyes closed again without ever focusing. "Hey!" Terrified and furious, I jerked my arms apart as hard as I could, and finally the cord popped, releasing my hands. "Meshara." I flexed my fingers until the feeling came back, ignoring the blood caked on my wrists, and then I gently pushed my sister's shoulders back until she sat upright in her seat. The demon opened her eyes again. She squinted, trying to focus. "Are you okay? Can you feel the baby?"

"Can't feel anything." Her speech was thick and labored, as if she'd finally lost all feeling in her tongue. "Whass happening to me? I can hardly see you."

Fighting pins and needles of my own from the bindings, I lifted her shirt to expose the baby bump and found the top of her belly already beginning to bruise from the collision with the wheel. And as I watched, her stomach began to contract again, her muscles defining a tighter shape beneath her flesh.

"You're having another contraction." How long had it been since the previous one? "Don't move!" I shouted, to be sure she could hear me.

I pulled my feet up onto my seat so I could free them, but the nylon knots were too tight and my fingers were still tingling.

"I gotta get outta this body." Her words were still labored, as if she were speaking around a mouthful of marbles.

"You'd just get sucked back into hell."

"Thass where you'll send me anyway." She stared slightly to the left of my head, and I realized she couldn't see the difference between my face and the headrest. "At leass I won't see the fire coming."

Nor could she feel the baby kicking or her own bladder filling. She couldn't taste cayenne and hadn't been able to smell Grayson's bread either.

As the pieces began to come together in my head, I twisted onto my knees and leaned between the front seats to pull Eli's backpack closer. "Meshara," I said, rummaging in the zipper compartment. Surely he had some kind of small blade.

But if he had a pocketknife, he obviously kept it in his actual pocket. There was nothing sharp in his backpack at all.

I dropped back into the passenger's seat, scanning the car for anything sharp enough to cut through nylon, and had almost decided to contort my body in order to use the broken armrest on my ankles too, when my gaze fell on the keys in the ignition.

I snatched the ring and identified the key with the sharpest-looking teeth, then began sawing on the bindings around my ankles. "Okay, so you were fine for the first couple of days in Mellie's body, and Tobias was fine for the first couple of days we had him . . ."

"Tobias?"

"Aldric," I reminded her. "But after that, you both started to lose your sense of taste and the sensation in your skin." I stopped sawing long enough to inspect the damaged nylon and was pleased with my progress.

"This is all your fault!" Meshara's words were slushy, but her tone was sharp. "I caught this plague from you and your friends!"

I worked the key back and forth as fast as I could, trying to ignore the friction burning into the pad of my right thumb. "The only people who've caught . . . whatever this thing is, are you and Aldric. Just the demons, Meshara."

"No." She shook her head. "Aldric and I were in Tobias and Micah for two days before we infiltrated your group, and we were *fine*." Her words slid one into the next, and I had to listen closely to understand. "We got this from *your* people, and I wish I'd never laid eyes on any of you. I'd rather be crawling around in hell than trapped in a human body that doesn't work."

"In that case, I hope your little plague spreads! Humanity

couldn't ask for much more than demons voluntarily withdrawing from our world." My hand froze as the last words fell from my lips, and I realized what I'd just said.

Humanity *couldn't* ask for much more than that. A disease that affects only demons, depriving them of the very senses they'd invaded our world in order to experience? That was too specific—too targeted—a plague to have natural origins.

Meshara's illness wasn't merely a miracle, it was a miracle of *science*.

We were looking at the kind of manufactured illness that would have taken researchers years—maybe *decades*—to engineer back before the war. The kind of illness that was completely beyond the abilities of what few scientists and facilities had survived the restructuring of the United States from a democratic republic to a demonic theocracy.

Which led me back to "miracle."

I only knew of one organization in the business of making miracles happen, scientific or otherwise.

The Unified Church.

TWELVE

My hands fell away from my ankles. The keys thumped to the floorboard. "It *is* a plague. . . ."

"What?" Meshara demanded, furiously blinking her unfocused eyes, while I reached down for the keys.

"You've been poisoned by the Unified Church!" I resumed sawing, reinvigorated not just by the stunning—if puzzling—realization, but by the fact that Meshara's stomach was clenching and twisting again in its primitive prenatal dance. The baby was running out of time, and I had no idea what to do.

"Never been to church," she mumbled, and I could hardly hear her over the racing of my own pulse. "Never even been in one of their cities."

I gave the cord around my ankles one last, vigorous

attack, and the nylon finally gave, freeing my ankles. I was out of the vehicle in an instant, but I had to brace myself against the roof of the SUV while I regained my balance after having been tied up for at least twelve hours. From outside the car, I could see the damage from the wreck in its mangled, smoking glory.

The SUV was totaled.

My heart hammered so hard I could feel each individual beat. We were stuck in the middle of an unmaintained prewar highway, with no gun, very little food, and no shelter to speak of, other than the smoking ruin of our wrecked vehicle.

"Okay. We need to get you into the backseat," I said as I rounded the car, with no idea whether or not she could still hear me. Her speech was getting harder to understand, and as far as I could tell, she was almost completely blind. Seeing my sister's body fail was a special kind of torture, even though she was no longer in it. She wasn't even sixteen years old. She did *not* deserve what I'd let happen to her, and the worst was yet to come.

If the loss of sensation limited Meshara's control over her uterine muscles, Mellie's baby was in big trouble.

On the driver's side, I climbed onto the middle bench and began throwing things over the headrests into the backseat, keeping my eyes out for my sister's labor and delivery bag.

"Meshara, can you hear me?" I spread the only blanket I'd found across the bench seat.

"Unfortunately," she called, slurring the syllables.

"Come on." I backed out of the vehicle and took her by the arm, overwhelmed by my mental list of things we needed but didn't have. Not the least of which was a midwife. And a soul. "I need you to stand up. Can you walk?"

"What's the point?" she demanded, staring over my shoulder, and with a fresh bolt of terror I realized she'd gone completely blind. This plague, whatever it was, was progressing even faster than the birth.

"The point is that if you don't get your ass up and deliver my sister's baby, I won't have any choice but to roast you alive, then cut the baby out of you!" But I really, *really* didn't want to do that.

I'd held it together so far because I had no other choice. Because Mellie's baby was still depending on me. But if I had to perform an amateur caesarean only to watch the child die without a soul, I would *lose* it.

How much more could the world expect me to survive?

Meshara didn't resist when I turned her legs toward the road, but she didn't help either.

"You're going to cut the baby out?" Her laughter sounded forced, but skeptical. "With what? A car key?"

"Listen to me." I pulled her out of the driver's seat, and she wobbled for a moment on legs she obviously couldn't feel. "If you don't bring that baby into this world safely, I *will* dig through the car for a glass bottle or a hunk of metal or a tool from the tire changing kit until I find *something* that will cut through human flesh."

Meshara tried to shrug, but her shoulders hardly moved. "I can't feel anything anyway."

I had to clench my teeth to keep from screaming in frustration, afraid to attract degenerates while I was still trying to bring Mellie's baby into the world.

"Okay. Let's make a deal." I half tugged, half carried her three steps to the middle row, where I helped her sit on the edge of the bench seat, facing me. I looked straight into eyes that couldn't see me, hoping she could still hear me well enough to understand what I was about to offer. "You help me deliver the baby, and I'll take you to Pandemonia so Kastor can give you a new body."

She rolled her unfocused eyes. "You're an exorcist. You would *never* let a human die so a demon could have a new body."

I took her by the shoulders and leaned in close, even though she couldn't see me. "There is *nothing* I wouldn't do for a chance to hold Melanie's baby." To make sure that the *only* thing the poor kid would feel in its horrifyingly short life was love.

And heaven help anyone who got in my way.

"If you don't believe me, look back through her memories," I demanded. "I risked prison to steal food for her. I risked my life to rescue her from the Church. Mellie's baby is all I have left of her, and the child won't live long. Maybe an hour. Give me that hour, and I'll give you another human *lifetime*."

"Swear."

"I already—"

"Swear on your sister's name," she whispered, and her tongue seemed to be in its own way. "Swear on her baby's life."

"I swear on the name of my only sister, Melanie Kane. I swear on the soul of her dead lover, Adam Yung. And I swear on the life of their unborn child. Please, Meshara. Help me deliver this baby."

"Fine," she relented. "But I can hardly move my own tongue."

That would have to be enough.

"So, what do we do?"

"Um . . ." I propped both hands on my hips, wishing for the millionth time in the past half hour that I'd paid more attention to the endless series of childbirth discussions. But I'd thought that even if I was present when the baby came, my role would be that of cheerleader.

In truth, I'd always assumed the aunt's chief duty in the whole affair would be cuddling the newborn. I was highly prepared for that.

"Okay, scoot all the way in and lean back against the door. Make sure it's locked. Then I need you to pull up your shirt and put your hand on your stomach, and concentrate, to see if you can feel the contractions. Can you do that?"

She couldn't, and the fact that I had to help her scoot across the bench seat didn't bode well for her ability to push a baby out through girl parts she couldn't feel.

While Meshara scowled at a stomach she couldn't see, I threw open the back hatch and started going through everything Eli had packed before the demon had felled him with his own crowbar.

Melanie's delivery bag wasn't there; it must have stayed in the truck. But I found a clean maternity T-shirt in her personal bag and set that aside, mentally earmarking it for the baby's first—and likely last—swaddle.

Eli's duffel held not one, but two sharp knives, each stored in its own handmade leather sheath, and I wanted to kick myself for not hopping around the car to search the luggage when I'd needed to cut through my ankle bindings. I slid the cleaner of the two knives into the largest of my cargo pockets, intending to use it to cut the umbilical cord.

Cutting the baby out was a last resort. But now it was actually possible, should it prove necessary.

I was rummaging through Reese's bag full of spare parts for a flashlight and some batteries when Meshara called out from the middle row, and her words were now nearly atonal, as well as mushy. "I think it's happening again."

Nearly panicked, I pulled every sleep roll and blanket I could find from the cargo area and set them on the third-row seat, to keep them out of the dusty badlands air. "I need you to start counting the passing seconds as soon as the contraction ends. I don't have a watch, so we'll have to use the revered one-Mississippi method, which I learned in kindergarten." Sister Margaret had been teaching us to estimate the drying time for white school glue, but I was sure she'd be pleased by my unconventional application of the knowledge.

While the demon counted silently, laboriously moving her numb lips with each unspoken number, I spread another blanket beneath her and across the rest of the middle bench seat. Then I dove into the cargo area again in search of the last packet of wet wipes, which Melanie had been saving for the baby's first badlands bath, in case we weren't within reach of a freshwater source when her labor began.

As near as I could tell, we weren't within reach of anything.

When I'd laid out everything we could possibly need—at least, everything we had on hand—I sat on the end of the bench seat and spent the next hour alternately watching for hostile company from the badlands and reading from the pregnancy book I'd found wedged between the passenger's seat and the center console, with one hand on my sister's belly so I could feel the onset of the next contraction. Meshara couldn't feel them anymore, either from the inside or the outside, but she was still able to count out the seconds between spasms.

The contractions started out at six-minute intervals, and I got good at mentally dividing seconds into minutes. But by the time the sun began to sink toward the western horizon, Meshara's water had broken, her stolen uterus was contracting every three minutes, and she was almost sure she felt a little pressure in her pelvic floor.

Even after reading the emergency delivery section of the book four times, I wasn't sure exactly what the "pelvic floor" was, but if she was feeling anything at all, the sensation must have been quite strong.

I told myself that when the contractions were two minutes apart, I'd make myself "check" her cervix. Or at least make sure the baby wasn't about to fall out.

I was trying to wrestle Meshara out of Mellie's maternity pants, with little help from the increasingly useless demon, when the soft growl of an engine startled me upright so fast I actually hit my head on the roof of the SUV.

"Hang tight!" I shouted, to be sure she'd hear me, as I scrambled out of the vehicle and stared down the unmaintained highway at the miles we'd already driven.

"Wha . . . ?" Meshara called, and I wasn't sure whether she was asking a question or starting the contraction count all over again.

Within seconds the approaching vehicle came into sight, a small, dark blur in the distance, speeding around obstacles and spitting up clouds of dust beneath its tires every time it veered off the road to avoid a collision.

My heart thumping painfully, I squinted, trying to decide what kind of car it was, or at least what color. It was coming from the general direction of the Lord's Army, if my understanding of the map was accurate, but that didn't mean that whoever was in it was friendly. Meshara had left Anathema with only one vehicle, and two missing members to chase. Considering that hoofprints would be easier to track through the dirt than tires on pavement, I held out no hope that they'd come after me instead of Grayson.

Not that I would have wanted them to. Grayson was much less able to defend herself.

As the car sped closer I decided it was a dark-colored sedan. Black, gray, or blue. I couldn't swear it wasn't one of the Lord's Army's cars, but I couldn't imagine them coming after me. They'd be busy enough trying to make sure that no more of their own were possessed, then trying to bring peace to the souls of Naomi and Serah.

A minute later I was able to make out two shapes through the windshield. Seconds after that I realized the car wasn't slowing. It hadn't seen me.

Or maybe it had and the plan was to run me down.

"Meshara!" I shouted, backing toward the wrecked SUV, afraid to look away from the car speeding toward us. "Brace for impact!"

The dark car was less than one hundred feet from us when the driver suddenly slammed on the brakes. The vehicle began to skid, and the driver overcorrected. The car spun off the road into the grass and did a complete revolution before sliding to a stop at the edge of the road, its nose ten feet from the bumper of our SUV.

Eight feet from my kneecaps.

I didn't realize I was screaming until the car's engine died, leaving only the soft ticking from beneath its hood and the near-paralyzing sound pouring from my throat.

"Nina!" Someone was getting out of the driver's side of the car. He wore a dark cowboy hat and jeans. "Nina!" he shouted, and I stopped screaming just as the passenger's-side door opened. Anabelle climbed out and slammed her door, and by the time she had folded me into a hug tight enough to squeeze all the air from my body, I understood that the car's driver was Eli.

A thick white bandage peeked beneath the brim of his hat on the left side of his head.

For a moment I could only stand in shock, and after a second Anabelle stepped back to hold me at arm's length. "Nina, are you still . . . you?"

I cleared my throat. "Still me. Are you . . . you?" I asked, and Anabelle nodded.

"Where's . . . Melanie?"

"Meshara," I corrected. "The same demon that killed Micah. She's in the SUV."

Anabelle's eyes watered and she covered her mouth in horror. "Nina, I'm *so* sorry." She'd known Mellie since the day my sister had started kindergarten.

I nodded, numb in the face of her grief. "All that matters now is the baby."

Eli's eyes narrowed as he studied our wreck. "What happened? Is she . . . incapacitated?"

"Kind of. She crashed the car, and . . . ," I started to

explain, but then my gaze flew back to Anabelle. "What about him? Is he still himself?" I was pretty sure I knew what she'd say, considering they'd been driving alone together for hours, but I had to ask.

"Yeah. He has a concussion, and he was unconscious for several minutes, but Finn confirmed that it's still him."

"Finn." I blinked. "Where is he? Where's everybody else? Are they okay?"

"They're fine. They went after Grayson last night," Eli said, and an unexpected wave of disappointment washed over me. I wanted them to save Grayson. It made sense that they'd go after her first.

Yet the truth was that I also *really* wanted Finn to come for me. I wanted him to be so worried about me and so enraged to have lost me that he couldn't *not* come after me, even if he lost the vote.

But I understood why he hadn't.

Eli took off his hat and wiped sweat from his brow, his fingers brushing the edge of the bandage. His gaze kept straying back to the wrecked SUV. To whatever he could see of the monster who'd killed his brother and my sister. "Finn wanted to come after you," he said, and I realized he'd read the disappointment on my face. "But Maddock said that Kastor wouldn't allow either of you to be possessed before they got you to Pandemonia, because that would render you useless as bait. Then Reese said *you* are better able to protect yourself than Grayson is. And that

196

even as a demon, Melanie's speed would be hampered by the pregnancy."

I tried to swallow my dismay and deny how badly my arms wanted to wrap around Finn. How badly the rest of me wanted to be held by him. How badly I wanted to hear him tell me everything would be okay, even though Mellie was dead and the baby had no soul and . . .

Wait. Meshara and I weren't alone anymore. Ana and Eli could take care of the baby once I was gone.

Tears filled my eyes again, and I swiped at them before they could spill over. Mellie's child would live. But I would never see Finn again.

"They were right," I said before Anabelle could try to comfort me. "About all of it." Yet Meshara's hampered speed had nothing to do with the pregnancy. "Are you two alone?" I looked past them to the car, which appeared to be empty.

"Yeah. We left first thing this morning," Anabelle said. "As soon as Damaris was sure Eli was well enough to travel. She wouldn't let him sleep more than an hour at a time because of the concussion."

Meshara had taken no such precaution for me.

"I'm glad you're okay," I said, glancing at each of them, but my gaze returned to Eli. "And I'm even more glad that you found us when you did. I need some help." I headed back toward the SUV, and they followed. "How did you find us?"

"You and Grayson were carried off in different directions, but we knew the destination was the same for you both." Eli jogged to catch up with me. "We took the most direct route and figured—worst-case scenario—we'd beat the others to Pandemonia and wait for them a couple of miles from the gate." He shrugged. "Then we found you in the middle of the road."

"Sorry for almost running you over," Anabelle added. "We didn't recognize you at first. We thought you would have made it to Pandemonia by now."

"We probably would have, if not for that." I waved one hand at the totaled vehicle. "And that." I opened the door wider and motioned for them to peer inside just as Melanie's stomach began visibly contracting again. "The baby's coming. And that's not even our biggest problem."

Eli took one look at Meshara, then removed his hat and dropped it onto the driver's seat. "How long has it been?"

"We're not sure, but the contractions are three minutes apart. I think she's getting close."

"Anabelle, go get my backpack and as many bottles of water as you can carry." Eli turned back to me. "That's the quietest contraction I've ever seen."

"Yeah. She's a real champ." Sarcasm dripped from every word, and he gave me a sympathetic smile.

"I'm so sorry about your sister."

"I'm sorry about your brother. And your cousins. And your stolen horses. And the blunt force trauma." I glanced at his bandaged wound. "*So* sorry."

"Who's there?" Meshara slurred, and Eli glanced at me in surprise as Anabelle jogged back toward their car. "Nina? Who's talking?" The demon was looking in our direction, but her eyes remained unfocused.

"It's Eli. He and Anabelle found us just in time." Although, truthfully, I would have considered them equally on time if they'd arrived at any point during the previous day.

Eli frowned as the trunk of the car behind us squealed open. "What's wrong with her?"

"She's blind. And nearly deaf. She can't taste anything. And she can't feel anything. Which is why we're witnessing the quietest labor in history."

"Wait." He ducked to peer into the vehicle again. "I don't understand. She can't feel *anything*?"

"Only some pressure in her pelvic floor, but that's just in the past few minutes. And she's *totally* blind," I repeated for emphasis.

"Uh-oh." Eli turned back to Anabelle and waved to hurry her. She jogged back and set the bag at his feet, then handed me a bottle of water while she opened another for herself. When she'd drained half the contents, Eli held his hands away from his body, and she poured the rest of the water over them slowly while he rubbed his hands together, rinsing off all of the surface dirt.

When the water was gone, she dug a clean rag from the bag, then patted his hands dry. "Do you have any sanitizer?" he asked as I dug through the supplies I'd laid out on the backseat. I squirted a generous amount onto his left palm from an aloe-scented bottle, and Eli rubbed his hands together again while Anabelle and I helped Meshara out of her pants.

"What's happening?" the demon demanded, shouting as if we were the ones going deaf.

"Eli's going to examine you!" I shouted back.

"What's with all the yelling?" Ana asked as she helped Meshara lie on her back, then positioned her bare feet up on the headrests.

"She's losing her senses," I explained. "All of them. As near as I can tell, it's some kind of disease that only affects demons."

Eli placed one hand carefully on Meshara's stomach, then began the rest of his exam, and I turned away, content to once again be relegated to the role of aunt—for however long it would last.

"I've never heard of a demon disease," Anabelle said. "How do you know it only affects the Unclean?"

"Because no one else has any symptoms. Melanie was fine before she was possessed, and then a couple of days after Meshara took over her body, food started losing its taste and smell. After that, her skin began to go numb. Today she lost her sight and most of her hearing, and that part happened *really* fast."

"Okay." Eli turned toward us, wiping his hands on the clean cloth. "She's nearly ready to push," he said, and warring threads of fear and joy tangled inside me.

It's normal, Nina, I told myself. *Someone* always *has to die for a baby to live. Donating your soul is an honor.*

The Church had been right about *that* much. Right?

At least you'll get to see the baby first. . . .

But suddenly I was scared.

No, I was *terrified.*

"Let's hope it goes quickly." Eli repositioned Meshara's foot on the headrest. "We're losing daylight."

"*Can* she push?" Anabelle asked. "I mean, if she can't feel the contractions . . . ?"

Eli shrugged. "I'm hoping she's only lost the *feeling* in her muscles, not the use of them."

"So . . . now what?" I glanced from Meshara to Eli to the sun as it slipped deeper toward the western horizon.

Eli gave me the first smile I'd seen since "Mellie's" fake labor had foreshadowed the real thing more than twelve hours earlier. "Now we wait for the next contraction. And get ready to meet your sister's baby."

I had a clean towel wrapped over my arm and a knife in my pocket. I was ready to say hello *and* goodbye.

THIRTEEN

"Push!" Eli shouted, and I echoed the command inches from Meshara's largely useless right ear. Having decided that I didn't need to actually *see* the miracle of birth, I'd taken up a position of support at her back, against the passenger's-side door. I sat sideways on the bench with one leg folded on the seat, and between contractions Meshara leaned back against me.

Her hair still smelled like Mellie. She looked like Mellie. And she was about to deliver Mellie's baby. Those subversive facts worked against me emotionally, even though I knew I was holding a demon. Cheering on a monster.

"Okay, stop!" Eli yelled, and I repeated the command into her ear. She still felt no pain, but she'd started to sweat, a clear indication of the effort her body was expending.

"When he was in Tobias's body, Aldric said the same kinds of things," Anabelle said, continuing our discussion of Meshara's mysterious illness between contractions. A discussion that kept me from dwelling on the purpose of the knife in my pocket. "He only took one bite of the chocolate Reese gave him the day you exorcised him. He said it didn't taste right."

"I remember. He couldn't feel his bumps and bruises either. Or that burn from the campfire. It's safe to assume he was infected with whatever Meshara has."

Eli's gaze was still trained on Melanie's stomach. He'd been amazing through the whole thing, though surely nothing in his life with the Lord's Army had prepared him to deliver a demon's baby, from a body that couldn't actually feel the birthing process. "But he never went deaf or blind, did he?"

"I'm guessing he would have if he'd spent much more time in Tobias's body," I said. "The incubation period seems to be about two days. Meshara's been in Melanie's body for six or seven days now—"

Eli looked up sharply. "That long?"

"Yes, and she appears to be near the end phase—total loss of all sensory input."

"You think this is actually fatal?" Anabelle asked. "I mean, she seems fine, other than the obvious." Being completely cut off from the world through the loss of every sense she should have had.

"At the very least, it will lead to demons starving

themselves, either because food is no longer appetizing or because they can't feed themselves when they can't see, smell, or feel their food."

Eli glanced at Meshara again as if to confirm that she couldn't hear us. "This disease, or virus, or whatever it is . . . it seems to be taking away everything demons want from the human experience. I'm guessing that's more than coincidence."

"I think it was engineered. By the Church." I looked up at Anabelle. "Is that possible? Do you know if the Church has the kinds of facilities that would require? The kinds of doctors? Or scientists?" We'd all been led to believe that kind of technology—anything not required for a general medical practice—had been either abandoned or destroyed after the war.

Ana nodded slowly. "They've been actively—if quietly—recruiting science graduates from the universities since long before I was ordained. Rumor has it they kept parts of the Centers for Disease Control up and running after the war, to be sure they could protect what's left of humanity from illness, which is honestly the last thing we need, after everyone we've lost to the demon horde."

Though the truth was that we'd been losing humans and their souls to demons for centuries before the war began. We just hadn't known it.

"It's down south in Miseracordia," she added. "Which used to be called Atlanta."

"So it's possible, then?" Eli said. "They could have

made a disease that would . . . what? Take all the fun out of possession?"

"I think we're well beyond just 'not fun.'" I gestured to Meshara for emphasis. Her head was propped on my shoulder, her eyes closed. Her breathing was normal and unlabored. She was literally experiencing nothing between contractions during the most intense moments of childbirth. "The Church figured out how to isolate demons in our world just like they're naturally isolated in their own world. Total sensory deprivation." Thinking about that, I suddenly understood why some demons and presumably some humans—might rather feel pain than feel nothing at all.

Anabelle frowned. "But the Church is *run* by demons. Why would they develop an illness that would target their own population?"

"Here we go again." Eli glanced at Meshara's stomach, and I looked down to see it convulsing. I leaned toward her ear—the right was still functioning a little better than the left—and shouted for her to push.

"I think *Kastor's* population was their target," I told Anabelle as the demon bore down against a pressure she could no longer feel. I couldn't believe the change in Meshara. In the span of a few hours she'd gone from fiercely fast and deadly to disconnected and virtually helpless. "I've never heard of anyone—Church members or civilians—suffering from anything like this, in New Temperance or anywhere else. Not that they would have reported that on the news." That would have made the Church look powerless in the face of a scary new illness.

"But surely those of us *in* the Church would have heard about it," Anabelle said. "And I don't understand how they could be sure Kastor's people would be infected but the Church's wouldn't."

"They *couldn't* be sure," Eli said. "Unless their members were never exposed but Kastor's people were. Targeted exposure. Like biological warfare in wars of the past." He looked up and nodded at me.

"Okay, you can stop for now!" I shouted into Meshara's ear.

"How much longer?" she said, each word soft and slushy.

"Getting close!" I shouted, without bothering to verify that with Eli.

"How would they target a specific population?" Anabelle asked.

"They'd need a delivery system." Eli leaned against the back of his seat so he could see all three of us. "Someone to carry a vial of the virus—or something exposed to it—into Pandemonia."

I glanced at him in surprise, and Eli shrugged. "It's been done like that in the past. Our textbooks are more than a century old and unedited by the Church." Which meant he'd had history lessons my teachers would never have let me hear.

Anabelle frowned. "If that's their plan, how did Meshara get it? How did Aldric?"

"Double agents?" Eli shrugged. "Maybe one of them was supposed to carry the vial but it broke and they got infected?"

I shook my head. "Meshara said she's never even been in a Church city." Which could have been a lie, but I was unconscious for hours, and . . . "If she's loyal enough to Kastor to resist possessing me on his order, why would she bring a vial of some deadly poison right into the heart of his community?"

"It's not actually deadly, though, right?" Eli said. "Wouldn't anyone infected in Pandemonia just ditch the diseased host for a fresh one?"

"Yes, as long as there were fresh ones available." The fact that we were all conscious was the only thing keeping Meshara in Melanie's compromised body. I closed my eyes, trying to follow Eli's thread of logic back to the Church's intentions. "But then those fresh bodies would just get infected. Eventually there wouldn't be any healthy hosts left in Pandemonia. And based on how fast this thing has reduced Meshara to a senseless bag of bones, 'eventually' is starting to sound more like a week or two, tops. After that, where would they go?" I opened my eyes to frown at Eli. "Is Verity the only city near Pandemonia? How close is it?"

"It's about a day's drive. So they could theoretically get

there in time to find fresh hosts." He sat up on his knees again when he noticed Meshara having another contraction. "Tell her to push. We're almost there now."

I coaxed my sister's killer through another round of pushing, and Eli announced that he could see the baby's head. Goose bumps popped up all over my arms, and my heart got stuck in my throat.

Melanie's baby is almost here.

My eyes filled with tears, and suddenly her death seemed terribly, unbearably real, because she would never get to hold her child. She would never even get to *see* the baby she'd carried for all those months. Her last connection to Adam, who'd died just because he'd loved a girl whose last name was Kane.

The baby would have to make do with an aunt who was too much of a wimp to watch the business end of its birth. An aunt who would have less than an hour to spend with the precious new miracle . . .

I wiped tears from my eyes before Eli could see them, and I refocused my attention.

"Even if Kastor's people could get to Verity before they went blind, there's no guarantee they could get inside the city," I said. "If the Church is really behind this, officials in Verity would see that coming. They'd be fortified, and willing to do anything to keep the virus from spreading." My eyes widened as the potential fallout sank in. "When they're out of fresh bodies to hop into, demons would have to leave our world on their own, or live in useless bodies until they starve and then get sucked out of our world en masse." Which was surely exactly what the Church had intended. "They've come up with a plague that will cause a *voluntary* evacuation of demons from our world, and they *cannot* afford for it to backfire on them."

"Okay, I understand that," Anabelle said, when that round of pushing had ended. "But I'm still not sure how Meshara got the disease if the rest of Kastor's people haven't. She'd know if they were sick in Pandemonia, right?"

Meshara's shock and terror over her own predicament felt real, and I couldn't help but believe she'd never seen anything like what was happening to her. "Meshara thinks she got it from us," I said. "Both she and Aldric were fine until they came into contact with Anathema."

"You escaped from New Temperance, right?" Eli said, and I nodded. "So maybe the Church sent something contagious into the badlands with you, hoping you'd infect the degenerate population."

"I think Kastor was their goal," I said, thinking back to the report I'd read and the hatred in Deacon Bennett's voice when she'd mentioned him. Suddenly that memory triggered a chilling realization. "Holy shit. Kastor *was* their goal. Deacon Bennett actually said she *hoped* Kastor got his hands on us!"

"Yeah, but she didn't mean it like that," Anabelle said.

"She was just kind of . . . cursing us. Like when I used to tell my little brother that I hoped the monsters under his bed got him in his sleep."

"Except that Kastor is real, and the Church really hates him. They're scared of him. What if she *wasn't* just cursing us?" I blinked, and for a moment I saw not the interior of our wrecked SUV in the rapidly darkening badlands, but the inside of the New Temperance courthouse, from which Mellie, Finn, Anabelle, and I had made a miraculous escape.

"What if we didn't truly escape? What if they had *let* us go? What if they had pretended to play into our hands so we could 'escape,' knowing Kastor would come after us? *Relying* on that very thing? Think about it." I counted off the points on my fingers. "They knew Kastor had been raiding their caravans, specifically looking for exorcists to be used as hosts. They knew he had taken Carey James—Grayson's brother—for that very reason. And they *have* to know that the citizens of Pandemonia have been watching their television broadcasts since . . . forever. Which means that announcing on the news that Anathema had escaped into the badlands was like ringing the dinner bell for Kastor. The Church didn't have to send its virus to Pandemonia. They just had to plant it on us somewhere, then let us go. They *knew* Kastor would do the rest of the work for them. And they were right."

"Nina, it's time," Eli said, but I hardly heard him. "This is it."

I propped Meshara up out of habit, still mentally mired in the Church's deception. "Time to push!" I shouted into her ear. I couldn't tell whether she had any awareness of her own position—if she couldn't feel her limbs, could she tell how they were situated?—and I only knew for sure that she'd heard me when she gave a great grunt of effort and curled around her own bulging stomach.

"Good!" Eli called. "Here comes the head!"

Anabelle peeked over his shoulder and her eyes widened. Then her gaze snapped up to my face, and I practically saw her mental gears shift as she tried to distract herself from what she'd seen. "Wait, Nina, you think we're actually carrying the disease?" She frowned. "But we've been through all our stuff over and over, consolidating. Repairing. Replacing. Restocking. Even if they were smart enough to send it in one of the supply trucks, knowing we'd raid it, surely we would have found . . . Wait, how does one store a virus?"

"It could have been in anything," I said. "Probably in something they knew we'd keep. Like painkillers. Or Mellie's prenatal vitamins. They probably didn't stash it in something obvious, like vials or syringes."

"But if it was in something we'd use, wouldn't we just be infecting ourselves?"

"Not if humans can't get the virus." Which seemed to be the case, since only the possessed among us had gotten sick.

"Okay." Anabelle nodded slowly. "But then wouldn't

they just be wasting their virus on us, instead of using it on Pandemonia? And even if they weren't, how did they expect Kastor's people to actually get infected? Accidentally prick themselves on a suspicious syringe in our luggage after we were captured?"

Good question. And there were no syringes. Anabelle was right. We would have noticed. . . .

Syringes. *Needles.*

My hand fell from Meshara's shoulder as something she'd said earlier finally sank in. She'd said the Church had tied Melanie to the prenatal exam table and poked her with needles.

What if they hadn't been just running tests? What if they hadn't been just taking blood out of her, but putting something *into* her bloodstream?

"We *are* carrying the virus," I said, my voice hollow with shock. "But you're right—it's not in a vial or a syringe. It's in *Melanie*. They injected her with it, then *let* us escape, knowing Kastor would come after us.

"My sister is the Church's Trojan horse, and Kastor is still trying like hell to bring her into his city."

FOURTEEN

"Are you serious?" The beam from Anabelle's flashlight wavered as she gaped at me over Eli's shoulder. "You think they infected your sister?"

"Nothing else makes sense. They had unlimited access to Melanie for several days, and they had two reasonable excuses to 'examine' her—pregnancy and suspicion of possession. We assumed they were threatening Melanie to get me to turn myself in." Which I'd done. "But what if they were really trying to get me to break her out?" Which I'd also done. "When we rescued her, there were almost no consecrated Church members in the courthouse. We assumed we'd successfully lured them out, but what if they were running on a skeleton crew already because any of the possessed were at risk of contracting and spreading the virus once Melanie had been infected?"

"Nina, you're about to become an aunt!" Eli called. "The rest can wait."

He had no idea how wrong he was about that, and I couldn't tell him.

"Here comes the head! Push!"

Astonished, I repeated his order into Meshara's ear. Then I watched, shielded from the most graphic moments by my sister's stomach, while her baby came into the world as helpless and precious as I'd expected.

Though quite a bit messier.

"It's a boy!" Eli held the tiny infant up, one hand beneath the baby's head and back, the other holding his rump and feet, and my heart nearly exploded with . . . joy.

There was nothing else in that moment. No worry over what lay in wait in the badlands, or—worse—in the cities. No fury at Meshara for killing my sister and using her child as a human shield. No fear for myself. Not even grief for Melanie. In the moment her son was born, there was room inside me for nothing but celebration of the life she and Adam had created. The life she'd carried and protected. The very last member of the Kane family had arrived, in spite of countless odds stacked against him.

And he was *beautiful*. He was so amazingly, breathtakingly beautiful that it almost hurt to look at him. But it hurt even more not to be holding him.

When the baby didn't immediately begin to cry, Eli laid

him on the clean cloth draping his lap, then folded it over the child and began to massage his limbs. The baby made a mewling sound so soft and weak that fear speared my chest like a bolt of lightning straight to my heart.

"Is something wrong?"

"Nothing that I can see." Eli continued to rub him gently with the cloth, and the baby let out a loud, warbling cry. A strong, *healthy* cry. "He's small, but those lungs sound great. Ten fingers, ten toes. Nothing missing, nothing extra. No club foot. No cleft in his lip or palate. Come meet your nephew!" I helped Meshara sit up long enough for me to slide off the bench seat, then close the door for her to lean against. Anabelle carried the baby to the back of the SUV, where I met her in front of the open cargo area, which we'd already emptied and staged as a receiving area for the baby.

I had to bite my tongue to keep from yelling at her to hurry. I was desperate to hold him, but if I waited too long to free my own soul, my sacrifice would be for nothing.

"What do you think she'd want to call him?" Anabelle laid my nephew on another clean cloth—this one a towel folded in half—while Eli tended to Meshara in the middle row.

I didn't have to think about that for long. Melanie had volleyed names for a girl back and forth, but she'd had a boy name picked out almost from the beginning.

"Adam," I said, and when I looked up, I saw tears standing in Anabelle's eyes.

"After his father," she whispered, and I nodded.

"He's a Kane, and he'll always be a Kane, but he's also part Yung."

Anabelle warmed a wet wipe between her hands, then gave me the package to warm with my own body heat while she carefully and systematically cleaned the baby. If I hadn't known better, I might have thought she'd done it a thousand times, but the truth was that she and Melanie had done all the reading they could, and Anabelle had obviously learned even more from our time with the Lord's Army.

Adam cried until his bath was over and she swaddled him in the clean, soft T-shirt I'd laid out. In all the raids we'd carried out since escaping—being driven?—from New Temperance, we hadn't come across a single article of infant clothing, and the half-dozen baby blankets Melanie had collected were still somewhere in the back of the cargo truck. That old, soft shirt was the best I had to offer Adam.

That and a few minutes spent in the care of the aunt he would never know.

Anabelle put him in my arms, and the sound that bubbled up from my throat was half sob, half laugh. Adam was *so* beautiful. He had his father's straight, dark hair and almond-shaped eyes, but his irises were all Mellie. Light brown, almost golden, those eyes blinked up at me, and for a second I felt as if I had my sister back. As if I'd never failed her and her baby.

"Oh, your mother would have given anything to be here with you now," I whispered as tears rolled down my cheeks. "She loved you so much. She would have done anything to keep you."

"Nina." Anabelle laid one hand on my arm, staring at the baby as he stared up at me. "We need to do something about Meshara."

"She can wait." I couldn't look away from Adam's precious face. "She's not a threat anymore." And I wasn't looking forward to burning a hole through my sister's chest.

"We really shouldn't put it off," Ana insisted. "When the sun goes down, light could draw degenerates, and we don't exactly have shelter out here."

I made myself meet her gaze. "I don't have much time with Adam, and I want him to spend all of it staring at my face. Listening to my voice. That's as close as he's ever going to get to meeting his mother."

"But . . ."

I shook my head, then sat in the cargo area and tucked my feet up onto the upholstery. "Just close the hatch so nothing can sneak up on us."

Anabelle carefully closed the back of the SUV, leaving me wedged into the narrow rear of the vehicle with just enough space to cradle Adam comfortably. He seemed content for the moment, even with nothing to suck on, so I decided not to worry about the fact that we hadn't found either of the pacifiers Melanie had collected from the same shipment that had given us several canisters of powdered baby formula. Which were also in the delivery bag, unless I'd missed something in our luggage.

Having done what he could for Meshara, Eli was outside, going through our things for any baby supplies we might have missed—not that that he thought we'd actually need them—and packing what we couldn't do without into the car he and Anabelle had driven.

The SUV's rear passenger's-side door opened, and Anabelle climbed over the middle bench seat to settle sideways in the third row, from which she could peek into the cargo area for glimpses of Adam.

"He's so sweet," she whispered, and I nodded as the baby's eyes fell closed.

I tensed for a moment, afraid that he'd already slipped from the world after less than fifteen minutes spent in it. But then his tiny chest rose and fell, and I realized he was just napping. I resisted the urge to wake him up so I could stare at his eyes, because I was afraid that would make him cry, and we had nothing with which to console him.

We didn't even have any of the cloth diapers Melanie had made. Not that I would have known how to put them on, anyway. Hopefully, Eli would know what to do about that.

"I wish Mellie could have seen him. I wish he could have seen her." *I wish he wasn't about to lose his last living relative.*

Tears filled my eyes, and every time I blinked them away, they came back. I had to clench my jaw to hold back the sob fighting to be heard. The knife sheath poking me through my pocket was a constant reminder of what little time we had together and exactly how it would have to end.

Then, suddenly, Adam's whole body tensed.

"Ana!" I whispered, terrified, and when her eyes flew open, I realized she'd dozed off, sitting straight up.

"What?"

"He just went really stiff. I need you to take him." Adam's tiny face blurred beneath the tears filling my eyes. "I think this is the end."

Ana pulled herself up onto her knees and peered over the bench seat. "He's still breathing," she whispered, and when I blinked to clear my vision, I realized she was right. "He probably just messed in his blanket. Here." She handed me the package of wet wipes. "Why don't you clean him up while I see if Eli found anything else for him to wear."

She got out of the car before I could object, and in my head the seconds ticked away. Seconds Adam couldn't afford.

If I didn't act soon, my sacrifice would be for nothing.

I pressed the lever to fold the right side of the bench seat in half, then laid the baby on the nearly flat back of the chair.

Adam woke up and started to fuss when I unswaddled him, and sure enough, the bottom of the makeshift blanket was full of a tarry black stool, which might have disgusted me if it had come out of any other creature in the world. I pulled a wet wipe from the package and folded the blanket up to enclose as much of the mess as I could, then began cleaning the baby up.

I rolled him carefully onto his left side, supporting his stomach with my free hand, then realized that the spot I'd been trying to wipe off wasn't residual baby poo. It was a pale brown birthmark.

The patch stretched the length of Adam's small spine and neck and faded into his hairline.

Goose bumps popped up all over my arms. Melanie had the same mark, in that same pale shade of brown. But she'd developed hers over our past few months in the badlands and had attributed it to a hormone-induced change in pigmentation.

How could her baby have been born with exactly the same mark?

Ana opened the door and climbed into the third row, where she sat on the unfolded half of the bench. "He didn't find any diapers, but there's this." She handed me another T-shirt.

"Ana, look." I lifted the baby and held him against my chest, so she could see his back. "Mellie had the same mark along her spine."

Ana squinted to see in the dimly lit cargo area. Her eyes widened. "How weird that you all three have the same birthmark! It must be genetic." She rolled up Adam's soiled shirt and laid out the clean one for me.

"What? I don't have that. And it can't be a birthmark. Mellie didn't have hers until a few months ago."

"Well, whatever it is, you have it too," Anabelle insisted as I laid the baby on his back on the clean shirt. "I saw it when we bathed in the river, back in Ashland." She frowned. "That seems like a lifetime ago. So much has gone wrong since then."

I couldn't argue with that, but . . . "You're sure? Here." I swaddled the baby as best I could and handed him carefully to Ana, then turned my back to her. I lifted my shirt and angled my back toward the dim interior light. "Is there really something there?"

"Yes. A stripe straight up your spine. Light brown. Just a shade darker than your skin. It seems even weirder, knowing all three of you have it."

I frowned, staring out the rear windshield into the darkened badlands. "And you're sure it's the same as Adam's and Mellie's?"

"Yes." The SUV shifted, and her reflection in the glass leaned in for a closer look at my back. "It *must* be something you inherited, if all three of you have it."

"Not unless you're secretly related to Grayson," Eli said. "Because she has the same mark."

Startled, I let my shirt fall into place, then turned to find the sentinel standing in the open passenger's doorway.

"What?"

Eli flushed. "I wasn't . . . I didn't . . ." He cleared his throat and started over. "She turned around to put on a fresh shirt after a sparring session a couple of days ago, and I saw it. A pale brown stripe up her spine. Lighter than my skin, but darker than the rest of hers. I wanted to ask, but . . ."

"But you didn't want her to know you'd seen," I guessed, and he nodded.

"What *is* it?"

"I don't know." I took the baby back from Anabelle and noticed that Eli held a canister in one hand. "Is that what I think it is?"

He glanced down, as if he'd forgotten what had brought him back to the SUV. "Oh. Yes. I didn't find any diapers, but this was in the bottom of a box with some protein bars and a jug of water. There's a baby bottle too."

When he held up the canister of powdered baby formula, I remembered that Reese had packed it in the box of emergency provisions and put it in the back of the SUV when we'd left Ashland, "just in case" our two vehicles got separated.

"Thanks," I said when he set the canister on the folded bench seat. "Could you mix one up for me?"

"I'll do my best." Eli took the formula and headed back to the other vehicle for water and the bottle.

"I guess I'll try to find a bag for this." Ana held up the soiled shirt, wadded into a tight ball. "Until we can wash it." When she followed Eli toward the other car, I cradled little Adam in my arms and paced a few steps between the vehicles.

"Okay, little man, this is it," I whispered as I walked, and he closed his tiny eyes against the glare from the setting sun. "I love you. I know you can't understand what I'm saying, but I hope you'll always know that. And your mother—she would have moved heaven and earth with her own two hands to be here with you if she could have."

I lifted the little bundle, and his eyes fluttered, then fell shut again. I laid a kiss on his impossibly soft cheek, and my tears left dark spots on the makeshift blanket.

"Nina, he might be okay," Anabelle said, and I jumped, startled by her quiet approach. "You never know."

"I do know." I wiped my cheeks with my spare hand and tried to smile at her. "He *will* be okay. I need you to take him now." I held the baby out to her, and she smiled and started to take him—then looked closer at my face.

"Nina . . . *Noooo* . . ." Her eyes widened and she crossed her arms over her chest, refusing to take the baby. "Don't you even *think* about it."

"There's no other way. I failed Mellie—I can't let her son down too. Take him, Anabelle."

"No." She shook her head and took another step back. "Just wait. He might make it on his own."

But if that wasn't the case, we wouldn't know until he'd already died, and by then I couldn't help him.

"Take him. Please don't make me put him on the ground, Ana."

"Nina, please . . ." But she held out her arms, tears standing in her eyes. "Don't do this to me. Don't do this to *him*. He's already lost his mother."

"I need you to take care of him. Anathema will help you, and if they can't, Eli's people will. Tell Adam about Melanie for me. Tell him about his dad. Tell him how much he meant to all of us."

"Nina, wait . . . ," she begged as I placed the baby in her arms.

"And tell Finn . . ." I sniffled and wiped tears from my face. "Tell him I love him." I pulled the knife from my pocket and dropped the sheath onto the ground as I backed away from the edge of the road, toward the overgrown field beyond. "Tell him I love him *so* much. But this is how it has to—"

Gravel crunched at my back, but before I could turn to look, something whistled through the air behind me.

The world went dark again.

* * *

I woke up on the third-row bench seat, my knees tucked up to my chest. After a disorienting moment spent blinking into the dark, everything came back to me and I sat up straight, terror clawing at my insides like a cat in a cloth bag.

"Adam!"

But there was no one else in the car.

Eli had hit me. There was no other explanation for the crunch of gravel behind me before I'd lost consciousness.

I climbed over the seat and opened the back door, then stepped out into the night. Metal squealed behind me, and I turned to see the interior of Eli's car light up as he opened the door and got out. Another silhouette sat in his passenger's seat, and I recognized the outline of Anabelle's hair.

"How *could* you?" I marched toward him, fire raging in my gut even as agony squeezed blood from my heart one miserable beat at a time. "I wanted him to *live*! That was *my* choice!" Two feet from him I pulled back my fist, but Eli made no move to defend himself.

"Nina." Anabelle pushed open the passenger's-side door and stood. "Adam's alive. He's been waiting for you to wake up."

"Wha . . . *What?*" Shock drained the blood from my face, but I didn't believe her until I saw the squirming bundle cradled in the crook of her arm.

"He got lucky," Eli said. "Sometimes there's a soul or two in the well, Nina. The Lord *knows* we work hard to put them there."

"But you didn't know he'd live when you hit me." Anger roiled within my voice. "You were willing to let him die."

"I was willing to keep you alive," he insisted. "The Lord isn't done with you, Nina. He wouldn't have given you the gift of exorcism if he wanted you to throw it away, and I trusted that if the Lord has a purpose for Adam as well, he'd find a soul for the child." Eli shrugged and glanced over his shoulder at Anabelle and the baby. "I guess I was right."

I didn't even realize I still wanted to punch him until my fist crashed into his jaw. Eli's head rocked to the side and he stumbled back a step, but he took the blow without complaint. "I guess I deserve that."

One punch was the very *least* of what he deserved, but . . .

Adam's cry pierced the night and I turned to him, startled. And that's when it hit me. He was *alive*.

I was going to see Mellie's baby grow up.

Anabelle smiled. "Get in the car. We can't let him cry out here."

I sat in the backseat, startled to see Meshara buckled in next to me, and Anabelle put Adam in the crook of my arm, then handed me a bottle. While he drank, she and Eli climbed back into the front.

"How long was I out?" I couldn't tear my gaze from the baby's face, and the soft little sounds of contentment he made while he ate touched some fragile part of me I hadn't even known existed. I'd never seen anything so tiny and helpless. So utterly dependent upon the world to keep him alive.

But Adam was not born into a kind world.

Anabelle angled her watch into the moonlight. "Just less than an hour. He's about eighty-five minutes old."

Still so new. So fragile. So . . . precious. "And we're sure . . . ?"

"I've never seen one die after a full hour," Eli assured me, rubbing the red mark across his jaw. "Hell of a punch," he added as an afterthought.

"Exorcist, remember?" I decided not to tell him how badly my hand hurt. "How long has she been like that?" I nodded at Meshara, whose labored breathing had gotten loud.

"Since not long after you went down. We wanted to put her out of her misery—for Mellie's sake—but couldn't until you woke up." Because if they'd released the demon while I was unconscious, Meshara would have gone right into my undefended body. She would have done that on her own, if she'd had any idea my body was undefended.

"She looks so miserable." Her eyes were unfocused and she didn't react to our voices or Adam's cries. She wasn't blinking anymore because she couldn't feel how dry her eyes had become. When I put my hand on her shoulder, she didn't jerk in surprise, or even look up. I gently pressed my thumbnail into her skin, leaving an indentation but not breaking the surface, and got no reaction at all.

My sister's body had become a prison for the monster inside it, cut off from all sensory input, and though her breathing sounded horrible, it showed no sign of stopping. Meshara would live until her stolen form literally starved to death. Or choked on its own spittle. Or was torn apart by degenerates.

She was a startling, horrifying vision of what the Church had in mind for Kastor's people, and it was no less than they deserved. But it was too hard to watch while it wore my sister's face.

"I'm ready to let her go," I said finally, and Ana took the baby without being asked. Eli carried Mellie's body to the wrecked SUV, and her still form blurred beneath my tears as he laid her across the middle bench seat. He left me alone with her, and for several minutes I could only crouch on the floor, resting my head on her stomach. Listening to each labored inhalation.

"I'm so sorry, Mellie," I said as tears rolled down my face to soak into her shirt. "I'm so sorry I let this happen to you. I hope there wasn't any pain. I hope you didn't even know. . . ." I sat up and wiped snot from my face before it could fall on her. "I wish I could undo it all. . . ."

But the only thing I could still do for her was set her free.

My entire body hitched with sobs as I placed my left hand over her chest. Twice I tried to call forth the flame that would fry the parasite from her ruined body, and twice I failed, because when I looked at her, I saw not the demon, but my sister.

Finally, I took a deep breath and spoke to Meshara. "From whence you came, bitch." Fire burst from my palm and shot through her chest. Meshara's eyes opened wide.

She jerked once, twice, then a third time, but never made a sound.

"For Melanie," I whispered as I removed my hand from the smoking hole in her chest. Then I pulled a blanket from the backseat and draped it over her.

I cried all the way back to the car.

FIFTEEN

While Anabelle and Eli cut an extra shirt into strips of cloth with which to pad the baby's diaper area, I changed Adam's soiled wrapping by moonlight on the backseat, suddenly wishing I'd paid more attention to what would happen *after* the baby came. At the current rate of consumption, we would run out of wipes in a few days, and I had no idea what to do with the messy clothes until we had a chance to clean them.

Adam sucked on his palm while I rolled him onto his side to make sure his back was clean, and the mark on his spine caught my eye again. "Hey Eli, have you ever seen anything like this, other than on Grayson's back?" *And on mine . . . ?*

He turned to look at Adam from between the front seats. "I've seen some interesting birthmarks, but—"

"It's not a birthmark. Mellie, Grayson, and I didn't have it until . . ." I frowned. "Actually, I don't know when Grayson and I developed the discoloration, but Melanie's showed up a couple of weeks after we escaped from New Temperance. It was just a small spot at first. Like a bruise." But Adam had been born with the full version.

Eli folded his stack of cotton strips laid across one knee. "Maybe it's an allergic reaction to something you came across in the badlands."

"But Grayson lived out here with the rest of Anathema for months before they found me and Mellie." My thoughts flew so fast my head spun. "We all three got the mark after we left New Temperance, but none of the guys did." Reese, Finn, and Maddock regularly sparred with their shirts off, and while the scandalous display of flesh had shocked me at first, after a month or so it had seemed routine. And . . . nice.

"But it can't be gender specific, because Adam has the mark but Devi and I don't." Anabelle added her strips of cotton to Eli's pile. "And it can't be something that affects just exorcists, because Melanie wasn't an exorcist but Devi is."

"We had an outbreak once, when I was a kid," Eli said while I carefully reswaddled the baby the way he had shown me. "Two of our members died, but *everyone* who got sick developed a rash."

Anabelle stuffed the soiled blanket into the bag of clothes Adam had already gone through. "What kind of sickness?"

"Sore throat. Fever. Brother Isaiah said it was some kind of virus—lots of them cause rashes."

My goose bumps doubled in size. "You think the demon virus could have caused the stripe on Mellie's back?"

Eli shrugged. "It's all conjecture, but for Melanie to transmit the virus, she'd have to be infected with it, even if she's just a carrier. Or *was* just a carrier, until Meshara possessed her. If that's true, then humans actually *can* get the virus—they just don't exhibit the full range of symptoms until and unless they're possessed."

"Then how come the rest of Anathema isn't infected?" If that *was* what the mark indicated.

Eli shrugged. "We won't know that until we know how it's transmitted."

"Well, obviously Mellie transmitted the virus to the baby in utero. So we know it's blood-borne." Anabelle tied the stack of cotton strips into a bundle with a piece of twine from Eli's backpack. "If the virus were airborne, the Church wouldn't need a carrier, and using one would be too dangerous—any demon she breathed on would be infected. But she passed it to you, Nina, which suggests that it *can* be transmitted through direct contact." Anabelle shrugged. "You're the one she had the most direct contact with."

"She spent a lot of time with you too," I pointed out as I

stroked Adam's soft cheek with my thumb. "And Grayson spent most of her time with Reese, yet she's evidently infected and he's not." The baby stared up at me, and when I slid my pinkie finger against the tiny palm that had escaped the T-shirt blanket, his fingers curled around mine.

"So, what's the connection between you three Kanes and Grayson?" Anabelle asked, kneeling on the front bucket seat so she could see the baby over the headrest. "Grayson's the outlier. You three are all genetically related, and she's not. You're from New Temperance—even Adam was conceived there—and she's not."

"Grayson is from Constance, right?" Eli asked with a glance at the baby.

"Yeah. She and her brother, Carey, were bred as hosts there, just like . . ." *Just like Melanie and I were.* "That's it!" I sat up straight with the revelation, startling Adam, who began to fuss. "Grayson, Melanie, and I were all born to demons." I stared through the window at the darkened SUV, where my sister's body still lay. "And so was Adam."

Melanie hadn't passed the virus on to her son. *Meshara* had done that. "Growing inside a possessed body must do something to us genetically. Or at least physically. Something that enables us to carry the virus. And the Church would have known that about Melanie. The second our mother was exposed, they'd have known Mellie was an ideal carrier for their plague. But my guess is that they didn't expect Kastor to take so long to get his hands on us. And they probably didn't expect Melanie to get possessed."

"Their Trojan horse isn't going to make it to the gates." Anabelle sank back into her chair with a defeated sigh and stared at the SUV. "It's not that I'm rooting for the Church to win, and I *hate* that they used Melanie as their weapon. But Kastor is our enemy too, and since Mellie's not going to make it to Pandemonia, it kind of feels like she died for nothing."

I closed my eyes, stunned. Meshara had stolen *everything* from my sister—even the chance for her death to have meaning.

I *couldn't* let her death mean nothing.

"Melanie wasn't their only Trojan horse." I'd caught the virus from my sister, which meant that whether they'd meant to or not, the Church had turned me into a walking contagion, capable of spreading their virus to any demon I came into contact with without ever even having to expose myself as a threat. "Kastor wants me?" I glanced from Anabelle to Eli as they twisted to look at me from the front seat. "He can have me. But he's going to get a *hell* of a lot more than he bargained for."

It only took them a second to catch on. "Wait, Nina, let's think about this," Anabelle insisted, and Adam began to fuss in my arms as if he knew exactly what was going on. "If they've got Grayson, the city's already infected. You don't need to go."

"With any luck, Reese and the others caught up with

234

Grayson before Kastor's people could get her to the city. If that's the case, the demons who took her are dead, which means neither they nor Grayson will be infecting Pandemonia. And if Grayson *is* in the city, the others will need help getting her out. Either way, I have to go."

"But what about Adam?" Ana looked horrified. "You can't just abandon Melanie's baby to . . . what? Go spread disease in the most dangerous city on earth?"

"I'm not abandoning him. You two are going to watch him for me." I tried to hand the baby to Anabelle, but she frowned and crossed her arms over her chest.

"You're all the family he has left, Nina!"

"And the most important thing I can do for my nephew"—now that he didn't need my soul—"is make sure Kastor will never, ever get his hands on this little guy. I *have* to go to Pandemonia, Anabelle."

Ana turned to Eli, desperation shining in her wide eyes. "Say something! Talk some sense into her."

Eli opened his mouth, his forehead furrowed, and I held up one finger to stop him. "Don't even start. *You* said the Lord gave me an exorcist's gifts for a reason." I was far from sure I believed in Eli's warrior religion, but I *did* believe in purpose, and the Unified Church had unwittingly given me a hell of a one. They'd given me a way to avenge Melanie and protect Adam.

They'd given me the ability to bring all of demonkind to its knees.

Eli nodded, then turned to Anabelle. "She's right. Nina's been given two gifts—exorcism and contagion. And they both seem destined for Pandemonia."

"But . . . what about the baby?"

I looked down to find him sleeping in my arms, and suddenly I wanted nothing more than to stay there, holding him, looking for signs of Mellie in his tiny features. "With any luck, I'll make it out and come back for Adam, but the odds aren't in my favor. Anabelle, I need to know that if I die, you'll do everything you can to protect him and give him a good life."

"Nina . . ."

"Please, Ana. For Mellie."

"Yes. Of course." She exhaled heavily and stared at the baby with tears in her eyes. "You know I will. I just don't want to lose you too."

"And will you help her?" I turned to Eli. "Can Ana and Adam stay with you and your people?"

"Of course they can. But we get raided too, Nina. Ours isn't an easy life, or a secure one."

"I know." But those both applied to my life too, ever since the moment I'd discovered that I was an exorcist. "Just do your best for Adam, and I'll do my best to come back for him. That's all any of us can ever promise."

* * *

We buried Melanie on the side of old Interstate 70 as the sun rose over the badlands. Eli and I took turns digging with our only shovel while Adam napped and Anabelle wrapped my sister's body in the nicest blanket we had, to cover up the smoking hole in her chest. Though I could hardly see it anyway through the tears steadily blurring my vision.

Eli closed the grave with shovelful after shovelful of dirt while I clutched the baby to my chest. In the hundreds of times I'd pictured Melanie's labor and delivery, I'd never once pictured my sister lying in the hole I'd known would have to be dug afterward.

We marked Melanie's grave with a cross Eli made from scraps of wood and the nylon cord from my bindings. He'd carved her name on the short length of the cross with surprising aptitude. But as the crimson morning sun shone down on my grief, I realized I would probably never again see either the cross or my sister's grave.

I had little confidence that I would leave Pandemonia alive.

I held Adam snugly, feeding him his third bottle, while Eli and Anabelle loaded up everything they could fit in the car except what they'd insisted I carry in the bag Ana had packed for me.

"Okay." Eli set the full backpack at my feet. "Remember, we'll be traveling down old Interstate 70, toward what used to be Salina, Kansas. If you make it out of Pandemonia anytime in the next week, you should be able to catch us in a car. Adam will be waiting for you."

"Thank you," I said. Anabelle held her arms out for the

baby, but I clutched him tighter until he began to squirm. "If you run into the rest of Anathema, tell them what we've figured out and how. Tell them where I am and why. But stay with the Lord's Army, Ana. Promise me you'll keep Adam with Eli and his people."

She frowned. "But Maddock and Devi and Reese . . . They're stronger and faster, and they'd do anything to protect us—"

I laid one hand on her arm to be sure I had her full attention. "The Lord's Army fights demons when they have to. When evil brings the fight to them. Anathema will always be *looking* for that fight. That's what exorcists were born to do. But even if any of them knew how to take care of a baby, that kind of life isn't safe for Adam."

"But you're an exorcist," she pointed out. "All that goes for you too."

"I'll worry about that if I survive Pandemonia." But the chances of that were slimmer than either of us wanted to admit.

"But . . ."

Eli stepped between Anabelle and me and pulled me into a hug, careful not to squish the baby. "Meeting you and your friends has been among the greatest honors of my life."

Ana pulled him away from me by one arm, scowling. "She's not going to die!"

Eli frowned down at her. "Life holds no such guarantee, and the odds don't improve when you march into a city full of demons." He turned back to me while Anabelle watched us through wide, worried eyes. "You're going to need this." He removed his cowboy hat, turned it around, then set it on my head, over my objections. "Sunscreen only goes so far. This will shade your face and protect your eyes from the glare."

"Thank you," I said when I realized he wasn't going to change his mind.

"In about thirty miles, you might run into another division of the Lord's Army. In the spring they like to harvest patches of spinach, radishes, and asparagus that grow wild a few miles north of I-70. Their elder, Brother Malachi, is my maternal grandfather, and our divisions share many relatives. If you see them, show them the hat and tell them I sent you. They will give you shelter and watch over you while you rest."

"Thanks again, Eli."

He smiled and began walking backward around the front of the car. "Go with the Lord, Nina Kane." His words had the ring of a final goodbye, and my throat tightened at the thought.

I placed the baby in Anabelle's arms as Eli slid into the driver's seat, and when she got into the car and closed the door, I leaned in through the open window to kiss my nephew on the forehead. He smelled like wet wipes and formula, and I was sure that for the rest of my life, even if I lived to be a hundred years old, I would forever associate that combination of scents with grief, hope, determination, and the cruel suspicion that I would never again see any of the people I loved the most.

As Eli and Anabelle drove east on old Interstate 70, carrying with them my last living relative, I picked up the bag they'd packed for me and tossed it over my shoulder. I watched the car until it disappeared into the horizon, and then I turned and headed west, with nothing but the bag on my back, determination in my step, and my eyes on the goal.

Pandemonia.

Ready or not, here I come.

* * *

By my estimate, I'd been walking for eight or nine hours, not counting several stops to relieve myself, when I saw smoke rising into the sky to the north. I felt like I'd maintained a good pace, but since I had no watch and lacked Eli's ability to accurately tell time by looking at the sky, I could only guess that I'd gone about thirty miles. Which meant I might be seeing smoke from a campfire built by the Lord's Army's sister division Eli had mentioned.

I left Interstate 70 to veer north, and after walking for another quarter of an hour, I realized that the smoke plume didn't look right. It was too thick—more like a bonfire than a small hearth for each family unit. And the smoke was too dark, as if they were burning gas or oil rather than wood.

Something was wrong.

My pulse swishing in my ears, I pushed myself faster in spite of my aching feet and legs, and half a mile later the source of the smoke came into sight. It wasn't a bonfire. It was the charred remains of a camper similar to the one Damaris drove while two of the Army's young women held school for the children in the back.

On the ground next to the camper lay two dead horses. Scattered in all directions from the fire were other signs of violent chaos. Clothing stomped into the dirt. Dented pots and pans. Scattered piles of freshly picked radishes and unwashed spinach. Hand-carved wooden toys and home-made leather pouches. Cowboy hats, most stomped into the ground and stained with blood.

Eli's sister division had been attacked, and other than half a dozen horses now grazing several hundred feet across a field full of knee-high wild grass, I couldn't find any signs of life. But the closer I looked at the carnage, the more death I found.

Two bodies lay on the ground near the dead horses, one a young man about my age whose leg had been crushed by the fallen animal, probably only moments before his head was crushed by . . . something else. Something blunt and deadly.

Two older women lay near an unlit campfire, both twisted into unnatural positions. Their arms were covered with defensive wounds—one was obviously broken—and both had succumbed to gaping wounds in their chests. When my horrified gaze snagged on a gore-covered ax on the other side of the camp, I recognized the instrument of their deaths.

There were several more corpses scattered around the campsite, and as I inspected the damage I realized three things about the slaughter I'd missed by no more than a few hours. One: not one of the bodies was ripped open, which told me they hadn't been attacked by degenerates. Two: most of the bodies wore soft leather sleep clothes, which told me they'd been attacked late at night or early in the morning. And three: assuming this division was at least the size of Eli's, there were far too few corpses.

Most of the victims had been taken.

Or so I thought, until metal squealed behind me.

I spun, my pulse pounding in my throat, to find a girl around Melanie's age standing in front of the open door of an old, rusty sedan. She held a tire iron in both hands like a bat, clearly ready to swing. "Who are you?" she demanded in a shaky voice, and behind her, movement from the sedan drew my attention to several small heads peeking over the backseat.

"My name is Nina Kane."

Her eyes widened, and she took an unsteady step backward into the embrace of the open car door.

"What happened here?" I asked when she seemed frozen with indecision. "Demons? Was it Kastor's people?"

"It was *our* people. Only they weren't really. They woke us up before dawn. Four of them, wearing the skins of our friends and parents. One of them was my mother. Only she wasn't. Not anymore." The girl sniffled and wiped her eyes with the back of one hand. "They killed the ones who fought, and burned Brother Malachi in the camper." Her eyes filled with tears again when she glanced at the burned-out vehicle over my shoulder. "They took everyone else and only left me to care for the little ones."

Because they found child-rearing tedious but didn't want to waste the potential future hosts.

"But this is *your* fault," the girl continued, and I frowned, confused. "They were looking for *you*!"

"Me?" I stepped forward, hoping to hear her better, but she raised the tire iron and made a threatening noise deep in her throat. The children ducked out of sight in the sedan. They were all terrified, and I didn't know how to convince them I was no threat.

"They wanted to know if any of us knew Nina. Or Maddock. Or Finn," she said, and horror tightened my chest. This *was* my fault, at least in part. Anathema had been the target. "There were other names, but those were the ones they said the most. Were they talking about you? Are those your brothers?"

"Yes, that's me." I exhaled slowly, my mind racing. "The boys are my friends." They were more than that, of course, but the fact that Kastor was out looking for us, leaving carnage in his path, underlined the urgency of my mission. "Eli Woods is my friend too. Do you know him? He's a sentinel in another division of the Lord's Army."

"Eli is my cousin," the girl said.

"Good." I glanced past her into the car, where the children were peeking again, scared, their dark-eyed gazes trained on me. "Does that car run? Do you have gasoline?"

She nodded.

"Can you drive?" Church cities wouldn't issue a driver's license to a girl so young, but nomadic children seemed to learn everything early.

Her second nod confirmed my guess.

"Good. Pack up everything you can still use, then drive those children east on old Interstate 70 until you catch up with Eli's division. Don't stop for anything or anyone. They're planning to spend a few days in what was once Salina, Kansas, before they move on. They'll take you in. And with any luck, I'll see you there on my way back through."

When I backed away from the car full of children, headed for one of the other vehicles, near the perimeter of the ruined campsite, the girl finally lowered her weapon. "Where are you going?"

"Into the Lion's Den."

"That's where they took our people," she called as I turned toward the nearest intact car, crossing my fingers that it had gasoline and that someone had left the keys behind. "Why would you go there?"

"To kill the lions and set the lambs free." I pulled open the driver's-side door of a rusted, formerly slate-gray vehicle with large wheels, a high center of gravity, and a solid-looking roll cage. It was the kind of car Reese would have chosen. It would go fast if I had to run, and it wouldn't get crushed if I flipped it over.

Not that I was planning to flip it over.

"They'll kill you," the girl warned, and I glanced back to see her holding a handmade leather back pouch, half-full of whatever supplies she'd been able to salvage.

"Probably. But hopefully, by then the damage will already have been done."

The girl gave me a strange look while I searched the gray vehicle for the ignition key. "They're usually over the visor," she called. Then she straightened her shoulders, got into her sedan, and drove the car full of orphaned children east on I-70. I spared a moment to send up a prayer to Eli's Lord that she and the children would make it unscathed.

Then I slid into the driver's seat of the gray car and pulled down the sun visor. Shade fell over my face and a set of keys dropped into my lap. I started the engine, and the arrow in the gas gauge swung up to just beneath the three-quarters-of-a-tank line.

I took off toward the west as fast as I could drive.

* * *

The sun had just slipped beneath the horizon when Pandemonia came into sight, its buildings blazing in the distance like torches in the dark. Other than two periods of unconsciousness, I hadn't slept in two days, and I had no expectation that that would change anytime soon.

I hadn't come to Pandemonia to rest.

The glow from the demon city was an extravagant waste of energy and resources that Deacon Bennett would have condemned on sight. Where the Church subsisted on careful rationing of everything from city utilities to human hosts, I could see at a glance that Pandemonia was a bastion of excess.

And if that wasn't enough to set the two demonic civilizations apart, once I passed the abandoned suburbs and industrial districts and could see downtown, I realized that Pandemonia's walls were as representative of the anomalous population they contained as were any of the Church's city enclosures.

Rather than a tall, smooth steel wall, welded and virtually seamless, Pandemonia's defenses were a patchwork of metal—chair legs, chain-link fences, traffic barricades, car frames, shopping carts, garden gates, street grates, ladders, scaffolding, steel pipes—all apparently fused together by welders high on some sort of psychotropic drug. The effect was that of a metal briar patch surrounding the entire former downtown area, as far as I could tell, easily penetrable by light and sound but not by any creature larger than a cat.

The only gap in the bizarre fusion of steel was the city gate, facing almost due east.

I parked my borrowed car in the middle of the road a hundred feet from the gate, and for a moment I could only stare up at Pandemonia while I took deep breaths, trying to avert sheer panic. This was it. My chance to succeed where the Church had failed. To drive the worst of the demonic presence from earth and reclaim the badlands in the name of humanity.

If I survived, I swore to myself, I'd go after the Church. Starting in New Temperance.

First things first, Nina.

Metal squealed when I opened my car door. I turned off the engine—and with it, the headlights—then got out of the car, leaving my stuff in the front passenger's seat because they'd only confiscate it if I tried to bring it with me. I'd taken seven steps toward the gate when light flared with a fizzy-sounding pop, trained right at me.

I was literally in the spotlight.

"Who the hell are you?" a voice demanded, followed by a high-pitched squeal I associated with every PE teacher I'd ever had—someone was using an electric megaphone. "Identify yourself or you will be shot."

"That'd be an awful waste," I shouted, shielding my eyes from the light with one hand at my forehead. "My name is Nina Kane, and I'm an exorcist. Tell Kastor I've come to talk."

SIXTEEN

"Where'd this one come from?" A pink-bra-clad woman in her late thirties reached for me as Felix pulled me down the dark, narrow hallway by my left arm, and the steady flow of adrenaline that had been keeping me both awake and alert spiked like electricity run straight through my chest. "She's pretty. Tired, and kind of smelly, but very, very pretty." Her fingers brushed my shoulder, and I shuddered in revulsion.

I'd been in Pandemonia no more than an hour and had yet to leave the building built into the city gate, yet I'd already seen at least twenty people. All of them had wanted to touch me. Few of them had any impulse control whatsoever. And if I were to add up the clothing worn by all of them combined, I wouldn't have had enough material to cover two high school students attending any Church school in the world.

Pandemonia's dress code appeared to be "clothing optional."

I hadn't lived a covered-up, buttoned-down, bottled-up Church-run existence in months, but even close-quarter cohabiting with boys in the badlands hadn't prepared me for the flagrant immodesty inside Pandemonia. The display of flesh was disorienting. Unnerving.

No matter where I looked, I wanted to avert my gaze. And sanitize my hands. And scrub my eyeballs with a scouring agent.

"Don't touch." Felix slapped the woman's hand away from me, and when she lunged at him, hissing, her brightly painted nails flashing in the overhead light, I realized her bra wasn't a bra at all. It had the structural integrity of armor—something like a corset from the pages of my history texts—intended to both to support and display the flesh it hardly covered. Based on the lacy straps and ribbon trim, I could only conclude that the garment was actually meant to be seen rather than covered up.

That bra was her actual *shirt*.

Felix pinned the woman in pink against the concrete wall by her neck, without letting go of my arm. I could easily have pulled free, but if free was what I wanted, I wouldn't have surrendered in the first place.

"That's *Nina Kane*," Felix growled, his nose inches from the choking woman's forehead. "No one touches her, Dione. Kastor's orders."

"Nina Kane the exorcist?" Her eyes brightened with interest.

"Thus the order not to touch." Felix let her go, and Dione circled us like a cat on the prowl, waiting for the chance to pounce again, heedless of the red mark around her throat from his fist.

"She's even prettier than the other one. . . ."

"The other . . . ?" Horror washed over me like the first wave of heat from a bonfire. "Grayson? Is she here?" If so, where was the rest of Anathema?

"The one with all the curls?" Dione said, and I nodded. "I heard her screaming. Would you like to know what Kastor has done with her?"

"Yes," I said, though I wasn't sure that was the truth—knowing what had happened to Grayson yet lacking the ability to stop it was like torture.

But when Dione only laughed instead of answering, I realized she knew that. And she—like the rest of demonkind—wanted to see me suffer.

When I wiped all emotion from my face, determined to deny her any further pleasure at my expense, she pouted and turned back to Felix. "Who caught this Nina Kane?" Her movements were fluid and eerily graceful, and if she ever decided to attack me for real, I'd probably never see her coming. "My money's on Aldric."

"Aldric's gone." I shrugged, my hands zip-tied at my back, and gave her my best taunting smile, hoping she couldn't smell the fear behind it. "So's Meshara. I burned them both out."

Dione laughed, and light from the dusty fixture at the end of the hall shone dully on her spiky hair, the tips of which were dyed a contrasting shade of pink. "That's what you think you're going to do to me? Burn me out?"

I shrugged, careful to exhale in her direction in case the demon virus *was* somehow airborne. "I don't think I'll have to," I said, and her smile faltered but the hunger in her eyes swelled. "And no one caught me. I came to see Kastor."

"Wait." Dione stepped in front of us and held her hand out like a stop sign. "You came here on purpose?" She turned to Felix without waiting for my reply. "What *is* it with Kastor? I swear, back in the Stone Age, fish used to jump out of the water and impale themselves on his spear."

"Kastor was here during the Stone Age? Or was that hyperbole?"

Dione laughed. "Yes to both," she said, and for the first time it occurred to me that some members of his species had actually lived in our world hundreds of times longer than any human ever could. They'd seen the rise and fall of governments and technologies I'd only read about.

How much of our world had they shaped, unbeknownst to us?

Felix pulled me around Dione, but she only growled and

followed us. Even before he opened the door at the end of the hall, I could hear raucous yelling, as if the members of an angry mob were trying to out-shout one another.

We entered a large courtyard, bordered on three sides by two-story prewar buildings. A crowd was gathered at the center of the open space, around a raised stone square much like the one in the center of New Temperance. But my hometown had never seen a gathering like this. The audience—it really was a mob—was half-dressed and roisterous. The din was deafening, and I couldn't see whoever stood on the stone platform for the thick press of the crowd.

"You got here just in time," Dione taunted from my right, while Felix tugged me by my left arm. "They brought in a fresh haul of hosts this morning. Biggest lot we've seen in years. Half were from a raid on some nomads, half from a captured Church caravan."

Dismay sank through my chest as Felix led me past the back of the raised square—the only side not surrounded by men and women shouting out numbers. On the platform, facing away from me and toward the crowd, stood a line of people wearing more steel than actual clothing. Their hands were zip-tied at their backs, like mine, but they were all connected by a chain threaded through steel shackles around their ankles. Their heads were bowed, as if refusing to see the spectacle playing out in front of them might somehow save them from it, and I understood the psychological need for denial.

In retrospect, I could see that I'd lived it for the first seventeen years of my life.

"Up next, we have a human female, approximately nineteen years of age, in perfect physical condition." Onstage, a man wearing only a ridiculously tall black hat and matching black satin boxer shorts pulled a girl about my height forward two steps. The young men chained on either side of her were jerked forward with her, and though I couldn't see any of their faces, I could tell from her trembling arms and from the violent hitch each time she sucked in a breath that she was crying. "She has no noticeable scars or deformities, and as you can see, her face boasts an aesthetic symmetry certain to make her occupant the envy of his or her peers."

I realized with a jolt of horror that the people onstage were being auctioned off as hosts to a crowd of demons gathered to bid.

As Dione had said, about half of the hosts up for sale wore the remnants of unembroidered Church cassocks of various colors, cut away in strategic places to show off lean torsos and strong limbs. They, I realized, were human Church members who'd been kidnapped from a caravan taking them to their consecration ceremony.

What they didn't realize was that if Kastor's people hadn't stolen them, the Church would have put them through a similar ordeal. The private "consecration" ceremony was really a mass possession, where Church elders deemed worthy were given fresh bodies, as well as the new identities that came with them.

The other half of the hosts up for sale wore handmade leather accessories, similar in style to what Eli's division of the Lord's Army had been teaching us to make. My chest ached even more fiercely when I realized these were the people who'd been taken away from their children that morning at the burned-out campsite.

"Let's start the bidding at three hundred," the man in the tall hat said, and bidders began shouting numbers again. I stared at them as Felix pulled me past, and I was surprised and horrified to realize that none of the bidders looked old or in any way used up, as my mother had begun to look during her last few months in the human world, when the demon inside her had used up the soul it had stolen. Her arms and legs had grown long and bony, and her joints had begun to crack with every movement. Though I hadn't realized it at the time, those were the first physical signs of demonic degeneration—the result of a demon remaining in its human host for too long.

But the oldest of the Pandemonia bidders appeared to be in their midthirties, and none of their faces looked hollow or jaundiced. Their limbs didn't look disproportionately long, nor had their hair started to thin.

No one in that crowd actually *needed* a new body.

The demons in Pandemonia weren't merely evil, they were *wasteful*. They were throwing away human hosts that still held half-consumed—yet irrecoverable—souls, like the more affluent girls at my school who'd bought new uniforms before their old ones were truly worn out, simply because they could afford to.

But at least those girls had donated their used clothing to the less fortunate—like Mellie and me. Demons had no equivalent charity.

"When does *she* go up on the block?" Dione asked as Felix dragged me around the corner of a building into a dark, narrow alley.

"Don't know that she will," he said. "That's up to Kastor."

"She'd bring a fortune."

Felix huffed. "You don't have a fortune to spend on her, so why do you care?"

"Where are we going, anyway?" I asked when Dione didn't answer. "I'm here to see Kastor."

Felix's reply was swallowed by a new clamor when we emerged from the alley into a marketplace teeming with customers, even well after sundown.

The auction square was lit by torches mounted on the walls of the surrounding buildings, which painted the grim proceedings with an eerie flicker of shadows. The marketplace, however, was lit with electric streetlamps, which cast cold, clear pools of light at regular intervals in the ambient darkness. The rooflines and balconies of buildings on either side of the wide lane were lit with a thousand tiny lightbulbs strung together on plastic-coated wires, which I recognized from pictures I'd once seen of prewar winter holiday decorations.

The extravagant, celebratory display of light gave the entire shopping district the look of a nocturnal wonderland, like something out of one of Melanie's storybooks. I was fascinated by the spectacle, even knowing I was being led toward some fate no doubt much less . . . entertaining.

As we passed through the middle of the market I stared at the stalls and carts on either side of the center aisle, alternately amused, horrified, and baffled by the wares for sale: Garments made of too little material to rightly be called clothing. A menagerie of animals on jeweled leashes—tiny pigs, strangely clothed monkeys, bright birds, exotically patterned lizards, and even several long, thick breeds of python. One booth sold a wide array of food on thin wooden sticks dripping with melted chocolate, caramel, or cheese. Another sold meats I couldn't identify and bright, fragrant fruits I'd never even seen pictures of.

Booths peddled jewelry, cosmetics, and prosthetics of a disturbing and personal nature. Carts sold hats, feathered or sequined sashes, and shoes with dangerously high platforms and spindly heels. Liquor and beer flowed from taps in refrigerated carts. Colorful, icy concoctions were served in clear glasses, garnished with olives, edible flowers, or berries speared on brightly dyed toothpicks.

People danced and sang their way from one stall to the next, and more poured into the marketplace from stores and restaurants lining the wide lane, their doors open, spilling exotic aromas into the air.

Pandemonia seemed devoted to stimulating the senses

in every way imaginable. My eyes were so wide they actually ached, but I couldn't seem to close them for more than an instant at a time. The whole thing made me dizzy. I'd never seen so strange or lavish a display of wealth and plenty, and the people who consumed it all were just as colorful and bizarre as the market itself.

They came in every size, shape, and skin tone. Some were dimpled and plump, others bizarrely muscled. Some had more hair than they could contain on their heads, chests, and beneath their arms, and others were as hairless as a newborn, and everyone seemed proud of every bald patch of skin, be it pale, tanned, toned, soft, or painted to match their pets, their clothes, or their jewelry.

Several, in fact, wore nothing *but* paint, and I felt myself flush each time my gaze landed on what I at first mistook for a snug top or lumpy pair of pants.

They wore silk and satin and leather and sequins and feathers and ribbons. Their hair was dyed every color of the rainbow, and their shoes seemed designed to make walking impossible, which might explain why they stumbled from place to place instead.

If the Church's unspoken credo was "Cover yourself and behave," Pandemonia's seemed to be "Show yourself and have fun." No one stood still. No one spoke quietly. No one seemed out of place, uncomfortable, or self-conscious. And if there were any rules, laws, or policies, I couldn't tell.

As Felix marched me through the madness, people turned to stare as if *I* were the oddity.

Nina Kane, someone said, and soon the rumor had caught on like fire burning through the crowd around and ahead of us.

"Who caught her?"

"Is Maddock with her?"

"Will they sell her?"

"She looks pale. Is she sick?"

". . . smaller than she looked on television . . ."

". . . so young . . ."

People reached for me, and I let them touch me, hoping that each invasive touch would spread the demon virus far and wide. Someone pulled a hair from my head, and when I flinched, they all laughed. Hands ran over my arms and up my legs. Noses dove into my hair and inhaled. Fingers explored my ears and the hollows above my collarbones.

"Hands off!" Felix shouted, but he might as well have been whispering.

"Back away!" Dione yelled, but they only pulled her aside, and after that they were pulling me.

Hands crept beneath my shirt and over my stomach, and I clenched my teeth to keep from screaming. A tongue slid into my ear, hot and wet, and I shuddered all over.

". . . skin tastes amazing . . ."

". . . so young and healthy . . ."

"She'd last for decades . . ."

". . . so tight and firm!"

Another hand grabbed my right arm and tugged me so fast and hard that Felix lost his grip. The world spun around me, and then a strange mouth closed over mine and I nearly choked on the metal-pierced tongue shoved into my mouth.

I tried to scream, but my attacker swallowed the sound. I tried to pull away but found resistance from at least a dozen hands wandering all over me while the whispers about my various gifts and advantages as a potential host continued.

A familiar warmth burst from my bound left hand, and flames blazed to life at my back, nearly scorching my thigh. Screams ripped through the night behind me. The demon stuck to my face continued to abuse his position, but all the other hands were abruptly gone. The crowd shuffled backward, and suddenly I stood in a circle all my own, except for the kissing demon.

A hand grabbed my left arm again, and Felix ripped me away from the man still trying to strangle me with his tongue. I gasped for breath, blinking up at the monster who'd assaulted my mouth, and found a man in his midthirties, his hair just beginning to gray, his eyes a deep, piercing greenish-hazel, practically glowing against smooth, light brown skin.

"Fire!"

"Do you see?"

"Think of the power. . . ."

The whispers continued all around me. My heart pounded, and I couldn't suck air into my lungs fast enough. Everyone was staring at me. Hands reached for me again, adorned with glittering rings and shimmering bracelets, some with artwork drawn straight onto their skin, and they were held back from contact only because my left palm still blazed behind me.

"Don't get too close."

"Stunning!"

"I bet it's a blissful pain."

"I warned you!" a single, youthful voice boomed over the crowd. I gasped and looked up to find a man not much older than I standing on the balcony above one of the restaurants, staring down at the chaotic marketplace. "Nina Kane is off-limits for your own safety!" The young man's gaze met mine and his smile bloomed, slow and full of some secret promise.

I wanted to look away, but not watching this man seemed as dangerous a prospect as letting him watch me.

Kastor. His identity was obvious from the authority he clearly wielded and the confidence in every single aspect of his bearing.

"Welcome to Pandemonia, Nina Kane," he said, and though he'd lowered his voice from public-address to just-for-you, I still heard him with perfect, eerie clarity. In fact, I seemed to be hearing intent he hadn't actually vocalized.

Then, finally, he blinked and readdressed the crowd, dismissing me. "Someone take Nedes to the kennels."

"No!" someone shouted, and when I turned, I found the kissing demon backing away from me as several of his fellow citizens closed in on him, vicious satisfaction shining in their eyes, the potential for violence resonating in every tensed muscle as they reached for him. "I only wanted a taste!" Nedes insisted, his hands held palms out as if to show that he was unarmed. "I wasn't going to possess her, I swear!"

At his protest, the memory surfaced of my mother trying to possess my body through a frigid, soul-sucking kiss, and I suddenly understood Nedes's crime.

"Kastor!" he shouted as hands grabbed for him. They tore his clothes and ripped hair from his head, each fighting for the privilege of hauling one of their own to the kennels, where—I assumed, based on what Finn had told me—Nedes would be locked up until his human host began to degenerate and he devolved into one of Kastor's hounds.

"Take Nina Kane to the stables," Kastor ordered without even looking at me. "Lock her up alone." With that, he turned his back on the crowd and returned to the loud, lavish party I could hear raging inside, without bothering to make sure his orders were carried out.

While the crowd hauled a screaming, bleeding Nedes toward the kennels, Felix and Dione tugged me in the opposite direction, toward a stately three-story building crowned with a bell tower, which had probably been the city's prewar courthouse. The building's brick exterior might once have been white, but only the hardest-to-reach corners and crevices remained untouched after a century of unchecked graffiti and no structural maintenance at all, that I could see.

"That was Kastor?" I twisted to glance at the now-empty balcony behind us as the market settled back into its ambient chaos. In spite of the apparent youth of most of his citizens and my understanding that a demon's appearance said nothing about his strength or his true age, I was surprised by the face Kastor wore. "I expected him to look older." More like a leader.

"If he looked old, no one would listen to him," Dione said. "No one respects the elderly."

I frowned as we approached the courthouse. "Human authority figures are always older because they have the most experience."

Dione laughed. "That doesn't make any sense!"

Felix gave her an exasperated look. "Throughout human history, age has been an indicator of good health and wisdom. Only the strongest and healthiest lived long enough to learn much."

"Well, here the younger a demon looks, the more power he has. Only the wealthy and influential can afford to trade in slightly used hosts for brand-new ones," Dione said. "It's an expensive lifestyle."

And incredibly wasteful.

"Youth is a status symbol," I said, and she nodded enthusiastically, as if she'd just taught a dog to speak.

"Exactly."

"But it's only the *appearance* of youth. You guys are all ancient, right?"

"By human understanding, yes. We don't really have that concept. We have no beginning and no end, so none among us is really old, just like none is truly young."

I knew that, but I didn't truly *understand* it. I couldn't imagine something that had always been and would always be, even if the earth were swallowed by a star or frozen into a ball of ice hurtling through the universe.

But the reverse was not true. Demons seemed to have no problem grasping the concept of impermanence.

Felix hauled me up the front stairs of the courthouse, and I stared in awe at the designs crawling over the steps, the stone railings, the bricks, and even the windows. Words in ancient languages. Pictures of forgotten lands. In places, just bright blobs of color in seemingly random arrangements. Some of them meant nothing, that I could understand, and others were familiar—if psychologically uncomfortable—renderings of the human condition. I recognized an arm here and an eye there, as if people were buried beneath the stones and the colors and only certain parts of them had managed to fight their way through.

I'd seen something similar once, in a prewar art book Melanie had borrowed from Adam Yung's father. The paintings inside were classified as "abstract," and while some looked like very deliberate swirls of color, others looked like people made of odd shapes and angles.

Pandemonia's courthouse seemed to have popped up

from the pages of that book, and the longer I looked, the more uncomfortable I became with the images. Strong strokes of red and yellow looked like flames. Crimson blotches looked like blood. Blues and greens and grays became trees, flowers, and storms, yet they were also eyes, bruises, and dead flesh.

There was too much of . . . everything. Yet little logic to be found.

"I don't think she likes the decor." Dione pulled open a door painted to look like a window opening into a world made up of fields of fire and skies full of ocean currents that never quite met the flames.

"Don't take it personally," I said. "I haven't liked anything I've seen so far."

Felix pulled me through an empty, echoing lobby toward a staircase that spiraled down into an ominous darkness. "So then why did you come?" he asked, pushing me ahead of him onto the first slick-looking marble step.

"You haven't figured that out yet?" I glanced at Dione, who'd waited at the top of the stairs. "I'm only here to kill Kastor."

SEVENTEEN

The "stables" turned out to be the courthouse basement, which had clearly been retrofitted as a prison after the war. Felix put me in a cell of my own, empty except for a filthy bucket against the back wall. The bars were roughly welded steel, and my cell shared one wall with the pen on my left and one with the pen on my right.

The only source of light in the long, narrow basement was a series of wall sconces—torches, burning with actual fire—mounted well out of reach on the brick walls. The light wasn't bright enough to reach the farthest corners, but the flames made the entire huge room seem to flicker. The effect was like being in the castle dungeon from one of the scary stories Melanie had loved as a child.

Had Maddock been locked up here, waiting for Kastor

to take him as a host? Had Finn sat here with him, unseen, his only friend throughout an ordeal that might otherwise have psychologically obliterated a boy taken from everything and everyone he'd ever known?

How long had they been captives? Maddy had said Finn got him out. But how? Could I possibly effect my own escape without Finn's body-hopping ability? Had it even helped him, if everyone with a key to the cell was already possessed, thus off-limits to him?

Grayson wasn't among the prisoners, and I couldn't decide whether or not to be happy about that. I couldn't imagine Kastor selling an exorcist on the auction block, so I was pretty sure that wherever she was, her conditions were better than mine.

Unless he'd already given her to someone.

For several minutes after Felix left the stables, I sat at the back of my cell and concentrated on bringing heat into my left hand. That was difficult, with no demons present to trigger the flames, but I finally managed by mentally reliving the moment I'd discovered Meshara in my sister's body.

Slowly, carefully, I angled the flames toward my right hand, blistering my palm in the process, and managed to soften the plastic zip tie holding my hands together, so that I could pull it apart.

The blisters were worth it.

A quick head count of my fellow prisoners told me there were at least forty of us, and based on the grime that had accumulated on about half of the population, I was guessing prisoner hygiene wasn't a big priority for our captors. Normally, that would have disgusted and outraged me, but considering that I'd come to spread germs, I considered it a good sign.

For *hours* I sat in my cell, ignored by my captors and prevented from distributing the contagion I carried. Kastor was obviously in no hurry to meet with me, and making me wait felt like an obvious display of power.

I tried to introduce myself to the people in the adjoining cells, but they were too traumatized to tell me more than their names, and after several attempts at further communication, I understood why.

The human hosts I'd seen up on the auction block had all been young and healthy. Most had been attractive, and they were all relatively clean. They'd obviously recently arrived in Pandemonia, but the prisoners all around me had clearly been in their cells for quite a while. They were grimy and thin. Many were pale and pasty from lack of sunlight. And they were all at least thirty years old.

These were the hosts who hadn't sold during previous auctions. They were leftovers—the bodies that the poorest and least powerful demons in Pandemonia would have to choose from when their current hosts started to degencrate.

My suspicion was confirmed when Felix finally came down the stairs again, this time with a customer—a pale, thin woman in a short skirt and what appeared to be an athletic bra. Her knees and elbows had started to stand out from her flesh, and her hair had begun to thin—both signs of early degeneration I recognized in retrospect from seeing the process in my own mother before I'd known she was possessed.

"The ones on the left are fifty." Felix gestured to the row of cells across from mine with one outstretched arm. "The ones on the right are between seventy and eighty." His next gesture encompassed my half of the basement.

"Not one is worth half that," the woman spat, as her gaze traveled over the men and women caged across from me. Most of them were in their forties, and they were all filthy and half-starved. "Does fifty cover a shower?"

Felix shrugged. "You pick one out, and we'll hose him down for you. Five more will get him deloused."

"Outrageous . . . ," the woman mumbled as she turned to my side of the basement. Her eyes widened when her gaze fell on me.

I stood and wrapped my hands around the bars at the front of my cage. The woman limped closer and stopped just feet away. Her greedy gaze roamed my body, and I had to stifle a shiver of disgust when she seemed to see right through my clothes to assess what lay beneath. "Can I get this one for eighty?"

"Hell, no, Tullia. She's not for—"

"She's skinny," the woman insisted, but I could see the bluff in her face. "I don't think she's worth more than seventy-five."

"That's Nina Kane," Felix snapped, and Tullia's eyes

widened. Then they narrowed as she stepped closer to study my face.

"Nina Kane the exorcist? From the Church broadcasts?"

"The very one. She's not for sale. Kastor's just keeping her here until he gets around to dealing with her."

"He'll never get around to it," I said, and they both glanced at me in surprise. Evidently the other prisoners didn't talk much. "He knows I've come to kill him, and he's afraid." I stuck my left hand through the bars.

Felix frowned at my unbound hands. "How did you . . . ?" But the woman was bolder. She stared into my cupped palm as if it might hold the secret to eternal youth, and I let loose the flames waiting just beneath my skin.

Tullia shrieked and jumped back, but the thin tuft of hair over her brow was already ablaze.

Felix cursed and smacked at her forehead to smother the flames while Tullia screamed.

People in the other pens began to murmur softly to their cellmates, as if they'd all just woken up.

When Felix finally put the fire out, Tullia's thin bangs were scorched and her forehead was blistered. Fury danced in her dark eyes. Or maybe that was the reflection from the torches.

"You had that coming." Felix pulled her farther from my cage. "I told you she was an exorcist. Now pick out a host or stop wasting my time."

Tullia growled, then turned to the woman caged across the aisle from me. "Fifty?"

"Fifty-five with the lice shampoo."

"I'll take her." The demon woman dug some cash from her sports bra—I didn't recognize the currency—while Felix unlocked the unlucky host's cage. He dragged the poor human woman from her cell while she kicked and screamed.

Tullia followed Felix as he pulled the host down the aisle into a room at one end of the basement. She closed the door behind them, and seconds later I heard running water as pipes groaned and squealed behind the brick wall at the back of my cell.

Several of my fellow prisoners stared at the door with their hands over their ears. Some cried silently, and others made high-pitched whining noises deep in their throats.

After a while the water and the screaming from behind the door stopped. Several minutes later the door opened and the human woman stepped out unrestrained. Her hair hung down her back in wet strands, dripping on the concrete beneath her feet as she marched down the aisle toward the marble steps leading up to the courthouse lobby. She wore Tullia's clothes, and when she passed my cage, she paused and turned to glare at me.

I stuck my hand through the bars again and flames burst from my palm.

Tullia flinched. Then she scuttled across the aisle and jogged up the steps as fast as her new middle-aged legs would carry her.

At the other end of the basement the door still stood

open. Movement in the room beyond caught my gaze, and a chill raced the length of my spine when Felix pulled the body Tullia had just abandoned past the door by one arm.

I didn't want to know what they were going to do with the corpse.

* * *

I had no way to measure the time that passed while I sat in the dark, watching torchlight flicker against cinderblock walls, steel bars, and the grimy flesh and dirty hair of my fellow prisoners. After a while my mouth went dry and my stomach started to rumble. The pressure from my full bladder became urgent, but I refused to use the bucket at the back of my cage on general principle.

My thoughts strayed to Melanie, and I wondered if she'd had it better or worse in her jail cell in New Temperance. I was pretty sure they'd fed her, but they'd also bound her to the floor on her knees—the posture of penitence—for hours on end. Maybe for the entire two days she'd been there.

Thinking about Melanie led to thinking about her death, and about how I'd failed to prevent it. How I'd failed her. How I'd lost her, and how I might not survive in Pandemonia long enough to ever see her son again.

But at least I got to say goodbye to him, and to Anabelle and Eli. But Finn . . .

If I didn't make it back, he might never find out what had actually happened to me.

When I realized I was crying, I forced myself to redirect my thoughts toward the reason I was in the demon city in the first place. To figure out how to effectively spread a virus I knew almost nothing about to the population of an entire city. The most obvious answer seemed to be poisoning the water supply, but I had no idea where that was or how to gain access to it, or how to poison it, other than drowning myself in the reservoir.

None of my other ideas—sneezing, kissing, or licking the face of everyone I came into contact with—seemed as effective on a large scale, and if transmission actually required direct contact with contaminated bodily fluids, the only person I was *sure* I'd infected since I'd walked through the gates was Nedes, who'd effectively committed suicide via sloppy kiss.

My plan needed work. Not that *any* plan would help if I never got out of my cell.

While I waited, thinking over everything I'd ever learned about the prevention and communication of contagions in health class, Felix brought two more down-and-out customers into the basement, and there was nothing I could do to stop them from picking out inexpensive hosts and leaving their dead, used-up former bodies in the room at the end of the aisle.

At some point I fell asleep on the floor, using my arm for a pillow, and I have no idea how long I slept. With no windows or doors open to the outside world and no meals to establish the time of day, I'd lost all track of time.

By the time the four-person contingent marched down the marble stairs and headed for my cell, I thought I was going out of my mind.

"Nina Kane?" the young man in front asked, and it was immediately obvious that these men—these *demons*— were cut from a different cloth than were the anarchy-prone buyers in the market and at the auction. These men all wore long black pants and snug black shirts— easily the most clothing I'd seen on anyone since entering Pandemonia—and they moved with purpose. With an intent that clearly went beyond the hedonistic search for pleasure.

"That's her." Felix stepped out of the room at the end of the aisle, where he'd been hosing down what appeared to be a room-sized shower stall. "You'd better use cuffs. She burned right through the plastic zip tie."

"What kind of idiot would put an exorcist in plastic restraints?" the young man in front demanded, and Felix shrugged, as if he weren't the one who'd done that very thing. "Turn around and put your hands through the bars."

I took me a second to realize he was talking to me now. "Why on earth should I do that?"

"This is your chance to kill Kastor," Felix called. "These meat sacks are his personal guard."

Kastor had a personal guard? Meshara hadn't mentioned that. So he wasn't in power *solely* because he kept his word.

"Kill Kastor?" The man holding the key to my cell laughed with his head thrown back, his tight, dark curls bobbing with the movement. "Child, put your hands through the bars before I break them off."

"I'm an exorcist." I stared boldly up at him. "Do you have any idea how many of you I've fried?"

"Do you have any idea how many exorcists Kastor has kept as pets over the years until he's ready to take them as host?" the man with the cuffs asked. "Or how many he's killed?"

"The question"—I stepped forward until the bars actually brushed my nose—"is how many have *you* killed?" Flames burst from my palm as I shoved my left hand between the bars and pressed it to his chest. He screamed, then thrashed as he hung from the fire blazing between us as if he weighed nothing.

His fellow guards backed away, and one of them pulled a strange-looking rifle. "Shoot her!" one of the others shouted, and soft shuffling noises came from all around the basement as my fellow prisoners turned to watch the commotion.

Felix jogged toward us from the end of the aisle. "Shooting her won't save Atticus," he yelled as Atticus the guard convulsed in front of me, his eyes rolled back into his head, smoke rising from his scorched clothing.

"But it'll make her easier to deal with." The man with the rifle fired, and something slammed into my left side. I stumbled backward, thrown off balance, and the flames coming from my palm died. Atticus crumpled to the concrete floor in the aisle, unmoving, as the smell of scorched cotton rose from his body.

Pain radiated from my side, just above my hip, and as darkness closed in on me from the edges of my vision I looked down to find a dart sticking out of my shirt. If I passed out, any demon who wanted me could jump into my body.

Panic made my heart race, probably pumping the sedative through my body even faster. "Oh shi—"

I didn't even feel it when I hit the floor.

* * *

Light glared red through my closed eyelids, and when I opened them, pain speared my head. I blinked rapidly, trying to adjust to the light, and it took me a couple of minutes to remember what had happened.

I'd lost consciousness for the third time in . . . what? Two days? Three? I had no idea how long I'd sat in that basement cell, and no idea how long I'd been unconscious this time.

I blinked again and took a deep breath, and finally my surroundings came into focus: A sideways chair, with intricately carved legs in the shape of an eagle's claw grasping a ball. A musty-smelling rug with a repeating red-and-gold pattern hanging vertically. Against my face.

After one more blink, I realized the rug and chair weren't sideways. I was lying on the floor.

When I tried to sit up, I discovered that my hands were bound at my back, this time with metal cuffs.

Pandemonia.

I was still in the demon city. Yet somehow, inexplicably, I was also still in my own body despite having lost consciousness *surrounded* by the Unclean.

"You killed the captain of my guard."

I gasped, startled by the sudden voice, then rolled onto my opposite side to face the source. Kastor stood on the other side of a room ornately decorated with antique rugs and furnishings. I saw a velvet loveseat. A mirror with a golden beveled frame. Several small tables and a desk that all matched the chair behind me. The room looked like it had been frozen in time long before the war against the Unclean.

It took me another second to remember Kastor's guard—Atticus—and what had happened to him. The boss looked angry over his loss, in a detached sort of way, yet I saw no grief or distress. He'd lost an asset, not a friend. Which made sense because demons lack human emotions and attachments.

"We're nowhere near even." I looked up at an awkward angle from the floor, watching for his reaction to see how scared I should be. "Your lapdog Meshara killed my sister."

Kastor's brows rose. "The pregnant one?" My furious glare must have been enough of an answer because he chuckled. "Huh. She knew you wouldn't burn her out, because of the baby. Clever. I wouldn't have given her that much credit."

"You still shouldn't. I sent her back to your homeland." I sat up—the motion was awkward with my hands cuffed behind me, but not impossible. "Just like Aldric and the captain of your guard. But from what I understand, they're still alive and well in your native land. You guys can't really die, right?"

"And you 'guys' are notoriously fragile." Kastor crossed his arms over his chest and sank onto the arm of the stiff-looking sofa. "Even exorcists." The implicit threat made my heart pound, but . . .

"Then why am I still alive? And unpossessed?"

Kastor crossed his toned arms across his chest. "Because you're still useful to me. And because I haven't yet de-cided whom to gift you to as a host."

I tucked my knees up to my chest, then rocked forward onto my feet and stood. "Better decide quickly. You don't have much time left."

He laughed out loud, and my skin crawled.

I squatted and stepped through the loop formed by my cuffed wrists with first my right, then my left leg, so that when I stood, my hands were bound in front of me. My captor looked surprised but made no objection. He clearly didn't consider me much of a threat.

"So, how exactly am I useful to you? Is this still about luring Maddock back to Pandemonia?"

"Back?" Kastor's brown eyes widened. He looked almost impressed. "He told you about his time here?"

"He didn't have much choice, with you sending your henchmen all over the badlands to bring him in. Why do you want him, anyway?" I gave Kastor a long, assessing look. His host was young and healthy. And attractive, in a carefree, confident way boys in New Temperance had never been. His thick brown hair was longer than the Church would allow, and his thin T-shirt showed off defined arms and the outline of a toned chest. His eyelashes were thick and dark, and his skin was tanned to a golden brown. "Your host is, what? Eighteen?" Kastor made evil look *good,* in a way I hadn't been prepared for.

But evil was evil, no matter how pretty the package.

"Nineteen," he corrected.

"And he's the very picture of health and power."

He nodded, and the reflection of the overhead lights shone in his eyes. "More so than you even know." He held out his left hand, and flames kindled in his palm.

I jumped back, startled. "You're wearing an exorcist." Of *course* he was wearing an exorcist. Why would the most powerful demon in Pandemonia settle for anything less? "Wow. Okay, then I don't get it." I gestured at his form with my cuffed hands. "You have a body any other demon would kill for." True, most demons would kill for a snow cone, but that was beside the point. "So why do you want Maddock so badly?"

"You think I want to *wear* Maddock?" He shrugged,

still perched on the scrolled sofa arm, and the realization that I had no clue what he was really up to chilled me from the inside out. "That might have been the plan once, but as you've pointed out, I'm no longer in need of a new host, and I won't be for at least two decades, thanks to the longevity of an exorcist body."

I frowned, my brain racing as fast as my pulse. What was I missing? "So why go after Grayson and me as bait for Maddock?"

Kastor laughed, and the sound grated against my spine like metal scraping metal. "Child, you're not bait to draw Maddock into Pandemonia. Maddock isn't even the fish I'm trying to catch. You and Maddock are *both* bait—for Finn."

EIGHTEEN

"Finn?" I frowned, struggling to fit that new piece into the puzzle.

"You don't even know who I'm talking about, do you?" His voice oozed with condescension. "Finn is Maddock's—"

"Of course I know who Finn is," I snapped. "Are you sure *you* do?" What could he possibly want with a human who had no body to be possessed?

He gestured for me to take a seat in the chair with the eagle claw legs. I sat, but only because I hadn't had real food or any true rest in at least two days. "Nina, I've known Finn since the moment he was born. Two minutes after Maddock. His brother."

"What?" If I hadn't already been sitting, I would have fallen into the chair. "You're lying." Finn would have told me if he and Maddy were brothers. If he'd known Pandemonia's demonic overlord all his life. If he'd once had a body, capable of being born in the traditional sense.

Kastor leaned forward on the sofa arm, evidently fascinated by the conclusion I'd drawn. "Finn and Maddock are twins. Why would I lie about that?"

"I don't know. Because you're *evil*?"

He stood, then headed for a tall cabinet against one wall. "Evil is a human concept. Demons aren't evil. We're simply unburdened by the human conscience and moral codes." He opened the top half of the cabinet and took a short glass from a high shelf. "Actually, we're not really demons either. That's a concept your species assigned to us, assuming us to be denizens of some mythological underworld. It's all a bunch of bullshit." Another shrug. "We're simply the dominant species." He opened a small refrigerator hidden behind a door in the lower half of the cabinet and scooped several ice cubes into his glass. "Would you like a drink?"

I considered reminding him that I was underage, but that felt like a ridiculous concept under the circumstances. "I could use a bathroom break, if you're feeling civil."

He tilted his head to the left, as if considering. "I have lived in your world through many iterations of the concept of civility."

"Is that a yes?"

He pointed toward a door at the back of the room. "Through there. Leave the door open."

The bathroom was small, but the toilet wasn't in direct sight of the sitting room, even with the door open, and that was infinitely better than using the bucket from my cell.

In the semi-privacy of the restroom, I considered my options. I could try to get close enough to Kastor to exorcise him, then free Grayson—assuming I could find her—but once his guard discovered their leader dead, there would be a citywide manhunt, which would complicate both our escape and my effort to infect as much of the city as possible.

Also, with Kastor dead there'd be no one to keep the rest of the demons from trying to possess Grayson and me, and we couldn't possibly fight the entire city, even if her transition had already been triggered.

The only other option I could think of involved getting close enough to Kastor to be sure he was infected, then somehow disabling him so Grayson and I could make our break. With Kastor infected but alive, he would transmit the virus for us, as would anyone else we managed to contaminate during our escape.

"Did you fall in?" Kastor called from the sitting room.

I finished up in the bathroom and washed my hands out of habit—awkward, because of the cuffs—then immediately wished I hadn't. I was trying to *spread* germs, not kill them.

"Are you sure you wouldn't like a drink?" Kastor held up a short glass half-full of amber liquid when I came out of the restroom. "Our status as mortal enemies doesn't have to mean we can't share a beverage."

I was pretty sure that was the very *least* of what our status meant. But the more chances I had to physically interact with him—up to a point—the better my chances of infecting him.

"Um . . . sure. Water would be great. Service in your stable was disgraceful."

"Alas, we no longer have bottled water. We can grow our own food and raise our own livestock, but for everything else we have to make do with what we're able to confiscate. I suspect you and your friends have been living much the same way?" I nodded as Kastor took another glass from the cabinet. "You're welcome to fill this from the sink in the bathroom."

In spite of the anxious rush of my pulse in my ears, I let my fingers brush his as I took the glass, desperately wishing I knew whether or not the virus could be spread by such casual contact.

"Are Maddock and Finn really brothers?" I called as I ran water into the glass with my wrists still cuffed together—if he wanted to pretend this was some kind of social visit, I could certainly oblige him with some self-serving gossip. "Were you really there when they were born?" I drained the short glass in three long gulps, then refilled it.

"I was." Kastor watched me through the open doorway. "They were born right here, almost eighteen years ago, to a human woman about your age. She was an exorcist named Abigail. A beautiful woman. The boys both got her eyes."

Finn had eyes? And they were hazel, like Maddock's? Not green?

So presumably he'd had a body too?

"Abigail was human? Not a breeder?" Instead of returning to the chair with the eagle claw legs, I boldly crossed the room to sit on the loveseat, opposite the arm he'd perched on. "Why wasn't she possessed?"

Kastor's brows arched over my decision to move closer, but he made no comment. "I didn't award her to anyone as a host in part because she was completely insane, and we couldn't be sure that the problem was purely psychological."

As Meshara had told me, if any of Abigail's issues stemmed from brain damage, she would not have made a suitable host.

"And in part because she was carrying my child," he continued, as if that first bombshell hadn't already blown me away. "We didn't realize there were two of them in there"—his vague gesture at my stomach gave me the creepy-crawlies—"until they came out."

"Insane . . . ? Two of . . . ?" Phrases swirled through my head like debris caught in a storm, and nothing seemed to settle long enough for me to grab on to. I could no longer feel the glass in my grip. "*Your* child?"

He nodded perfunctorily, and a strand of brown hair fell over his forehead. "We weren't sure it would be a boy, but we were hopeful." His smile took on a boastful cast, and for a second it was hard to keep in mind that he was actually an ancient evil being rather than an arrogant teenage boy. He'd selected his host very well—Kastor's stolen face was coldly handsome, and difficult to look away from. "As it turns out, it was actually *two* boys. I believe your people would call that a miracle."

He was right about that—in fact, the *only* miracles I believed in anymore were babies.

"We?" I took another sip of water, then cleared my throat. "Who's we?" Did an insane pregnant exorcist count as part of a demon's "we"?

"Everybody." Kastor's grand, wide-armed gesture seemed to take in the entire planet. "All of Pandemonia knew about Abigail's pregnancy. It was celebrated. She was revered. It isn't every day that a human woman carries a demon's child."

"It isn't *any* day that I can conceive of." I looked up from my half-full glass to frown at him. "In what sense could Maddock and Finn *possibly* be your children?" Demons didn't have any true physical form in the human world, which meant they had neither the parts nor the . . .

fluids necessary to create a child. "Did you possess their biological father's body?" I couldn't see any other way for the conception to have happened.

"Child, they weren't conceived by a human father, possessed or otherwise." His patronizing tone felt extra insulting coming from a face not much older than my own. "Finn and Maddock are the first—and as far as I know, the *only*—children ever fathered by a demon in his natural state. And they were conceived in *my* native world."

What?

"How is that possible?" I was so stunned I could hardly get the question out. *Surely* he was lying.

Kastor shrugged, but the gesture was too casual to be believable; he was bursting with pride over whatever he was about to say. "Abigail is the first human in history to survive a trip to our world. And she came back pregnant. Insane." Another shrug, from the arm of the velvet loveseat. "But pregnant."

"I don't . . ." I took a deep breath, and my tongue suddenly felt dry in spite of the water. He *couldn't* be serious. "Do you have any proof?"

"*Finn* is the proof." His brown eyes shone with feverish excitement. "Haven't you ever wondered how he's survived without a body of his own? How he can take over anyone else's whenever he wants?"

"No . . ." I wasn't answering his question. I was denying the implication. "He's not a demon. He's *not!*" The only thing Finn had ever been truly sure of in his entire life was that he was human. "He has a conscience. And he never gets sucked into hell. And he can't access his hosts' memories. And he doesn't hurt their souls!"

"I know!" Kastor looked almost insanely giddy. "He's a very nearly perfect hybrid of our two species. The best of both worlds—except that he can't access human memories. But that's an acceptable loss, considering that he doesn't need a physical form to stay in your world, and that the hosts he takes are *reusable,* because he doesn't have to consume their souls!"

Finn was half-demon. So was Maddock. Their insane exorcist mother had been impregnated by the ruler of a secret all-demon city, in the demons' native world. My horror on their behalf was so profound it defied expression.

"How?" I asked at last, and the question sounded hollow with shock. "Why doesn't he need a body?"

"We assume it has something to do with his demon genetics. He has an incorporeal form, like his father. . . ." Kastor laid one hand over his chest. "But he's native to this world, like his mother. However it happened, Finn is the key to unlocking the same abilities in the rest of us."

"You want to study him?" I really should have seen that coming. Why else would he try so hard to orchestrate a reunion with a son he couldn't even see?

But Kastor shook his head on his way across the room toward a large, neat desk. "I don't just want to study him. I want to *replicate* him." He plucked a notebook from the desk and held it up so that I could see a handwritten list of names, most of which had been crossed off. "I've been collecting the Church's scientists as hosts, to give us access to what they know. One day one of them will help us understand Finn's unusual state and figure out how to bestow it upon the rest of us."

He'd kidnapped Church scientists and turned them into demons, and now he was grinning at me from across the room like a child eager for his parents' praise. Could he actually think I would *approve* of what he was doing?

Although I didn't *hate* the idea of the Church having fewer scientists to use against what was left of the human population. . . .

Wait. Church scientists . . .

Did any of them know about the virus? Did Kastor know? Surely if he *did* know about the plan to drive Pandemonia's demons from our world, he couldn't know it had already been implemented. . . .

"But we can't study him until he comes home," Kastor continued, oblivious to the turn my thoughts had taken. "That's why I need Maddock, as well as anyone else Finn has grown to care about during his sojourn."

Which was why he'd abducted Grayson and me. "How do you plan to study Finn if his natural state is incorporeal?"

He shrugged, but the gesture looked stiff and forced. "That is for the scientists to figure out. I won't pretend to understand the specifics, because I've never possessed a scientist. Hell, I didn't know about Finn's incorporeal potential until he died."

"He . . . died?" It took a second for the horror of that thought to truly sink in. I'd never met anyone as *alive* as Finn. Even stuck in a body with only average physical abilities, he conspicuously enjoyed every warm breeze, every cold dip in a river, and every single time we'd ever touched. When others had only complaints about our living conditions, Finn was quick to point out that cold, hard, and dusty just made warm, soft, and clean feel even better by comparison.

Maybe that was because he'd never felt any of those things on a regular basis before. At least, not that he could remember.

"Did you think he'd been *born* without a body?" Kastor picked up his glass and crossed the room toward me again. "How would that even work?"

"I don't . . ." I shook my head, mentally wiping the disturbing question from my mind. "What happened? How did he die?"

"Abigail killed him."

"His own . . . ?" I couldn't finish the thought. My mother'd tried to kill me too.

"Insane." Kastor shook his head and clucked his tongue, like one of the elderly teachers from my elementary school. "It's a shame, really. She was catatonic when I got her back into your world, and I was fine with that. I mean, *you're* a decent conversationalist." He tossed a magnanimous gesture my way. "But all Abigail ever really did was scream, so I much preferred her silence. When the boys were a couple of years old, she woke up." Kastor snapped his fingers. "Just like that. She saw the twins, but she didn't love them." He frowned. "I thought that was a human mother's entire raison d'être? Loving her kids? But Abigail took one look at her boys—a matched pair of them, identical down to the double crowns on the backs of their heads—and started shouting that they were Unclean."

I shuddered at the thought. Poor boys. Even if they didn't remember any of it.

"We didn't know she was half-right at the time. We thought they were human. We were only keeping them around in case they grew up to be exorcists like their mother. But Abigail just yelled that they were demons, and then she lunged for the boys. She got to Finn first. Only we didn't call him Finn yet then."

"You couldn't stop her?" I demanded, tears standing in my eyes while my hand clenched around my glass. "You're a *demon*. You're faster than humans."

"She was an *exorcist*. And I was in the next room." He pointed to a closed door on the other side of the room, seemingly insulted that I would doubt his strength and speed. "I heard the shouting, but when I got to the doorway, she'd already crushed Max's throat. The boy was dead before I could get to him." Kastor shrugged. "I thought it was a shame at the time—the loss of a potential exorcist host. But in retrospect, if he hadn't died, we'd never have known his true potential."

"Max? Finn's name was Max?" That wasn't the most important of the questions flying around in my head, but it was the only one I couldn't seem to set aside. Finn wasn't even really Finn?

"Maxden. Maddock renamed him later, and by then he seemed to have no memory of ever having a brother."

My hands felt cold, and that had nothing to do with the cuffs around my wrists. "What happened to Abigail?"

"I ripped her throat out." He sipped from his glass. "It was a messy solution, but swift and efficient."

"A messy . . . ?" I stared at him with utter incomprehension. "You pulled Maddock's mother's throat out in front of him when he was two years old? After he'd just seen her kill his brother? No wonder he doesn't remember Maxden! He probably blocked the memory to escape psychological trauma! How could you do that to your own *son*?"

Kastor stood, and he seemed to swell with the motion, as if the threat he embodied was suddenly even greater. "My native language does not have words for the concept of parenthood." His voice sounded deeper. Harder. "Just as we cannot die, we were never born. We are *truly* eternal. None of us has ever conceived a child before—much less two—so you see, I am a *pioneer* among my people. I've done something no one else has ever managed to do, and unless it someday becomes clear that someone else *can,* both my existence in this world and my authority in this city are secure. But don't mistake my genetic donation to a set of half-breed human twins as any kind of emotional attachment.

"I tried to stop Abigail from killing Maxden because he was *mine*. But I did not mourn his death. I did not miss his presence. I have been more disappointed over misplacing my favorite shirt than I was by the death of my son." He leaned so close to me that I scooted back until I hit the end of the sofa, and then I had nowhere else to go. "So do not lecture me on how I should have anticipated Maddock's trauma or empathized with it. His screams did not bother me. I simply had him removed from earshot so I would not have to hear them."

Furious on the boys' behalf, I didn't realize that nervous sweat had compromised my grip on my half-full glass until it slipped from my hand. It shattered on the floor, spraying water and sharp shards everywhere. "Damn it. Sorry." I slid from the couch onto the floor to pick up the largest pieces, which was more difficult than I'd expected with my hands still cuffed, and suddenly I realized an opportunity was staring me in the face. I gripped the next piece of glass too hard, and it sliced into the pad of my thumb. "Shit!"

Kastor set his own glass on the coffee table and headed into the bathroom. When I heard him rummaging beneath the counter for a towel, I spit into his glass as quietly as I could, then let a single drop of my blood fall into it, to be sure he got a good dose of whatever virus I was carrying.

The blood hung there for a moment, suspended in amber whiskey, so I stuck my finger in and stirred until the color disappeared.

"Finn doesn't know, does he?" I said when my demonic host returned with a towel and a small trash can, which made him look slightly more service-oriented than evil. "He doesn't remember any of it."

Kastor handed me the towel for my finger, then watched while I picked up the rest of the glass and dropped it into the plastic trash can. "He knows Maddock is my son, but considering how surprised *you* were by the knowledge, it doesn't sound like he's realized that they're brothers. Maddock didn't start talking to him until more than a year after he died, and it was at least a year after that before we discovered that his imaginary 'friend' was real. And that he could possess a human host. Just. Like. Me."

My goose bumps were back, and they were bigger than ever. "So, if Finn can jump from body to body, why can't his brother?"

"Maybe Maddock could, if he were deprived of his own body, as his brother was." Kastor shrugged. "I intend to find out when I'm done with him."

"You're going to *kill* Maddock?" I dropped the last of the glass into the trash can, suddenly wishing I'd put a couple of the smaller slivers into Kastor's drink. They would have looked like ice, and I would have enjoyed watching him choke on blood as they sliced his throat open from the inside.

"Not until we're sure he can't sire a half-breed child of his own." Kastor took a long drink from his glass, and it took effort for me not to sigh in relief. I'd just poisoned the leader of an all-demon city. No matter what else went wrong later, that much couldn't be undone, and Kastor was now a walking contagion. "Who knows what miracles those born of my genetic line have to offer," he continued. "Someday my species will exist as permanent residents of your world. Like Finn. If Maddock can play a part in that process, he is safe. If he cannot, we'll see if freeing him from his human body sets his incorporeal spirit loose, as it did for his brother. If that's the case, don't you think it's cruel to leave him tied to a less evolved physical form?"

No, I did *not* think that.

His eyes narrowed in my direction as he took another drink. "How close are you to my boys, Nina?"

"Why?" An uneasy feeling settled into my stomach—something told me story time was nearly over.

"They were sired by a male demon and carried by a female human exorcist. We've been waiting a long time for a chance to replicate the process."

I felt the blood drain from my face when I realized what he intended. "You can't *breed* me!" I stood so fast my head swam.

"Of course I can. Which of my boys would you prefer? Maddock?"

That time when I refused to answer, his smile spread to take over most of his face. Evidently I was the worst liar in the entire world. "Finn, then. I should have guessed. Either way, you shouldn't find our little experiment *too* terribly unpleasant."

I almost told him that he was out of luck—that the Church had made sure I could never reproduce—but I was afraid if I took that possibility off the table, he'd have no further use for me, thus no reason to keep me alive. "Not even if you possessed me first," I growled instead, and Kastor shook his head.

"That won't work, I'm afraid. Abigail wasn't possessed when she conceived, and we really need to replicate the process as closely as possible."

"But Abigail wasn't impregnated in our world."

"Well, we don't have much choice about the location. I'm not sure whether you've heard, but the door between our worlds only works one way now, so even if we could get you there, we couldn't get you back. We'll just have to make do, under the circumstances. Fortunately . . ."— Kastor crossed the room toward the unopened door on the far side, then threw it open with a dramatic flair—"we're going to get two shots at this."

When he stepped out of the way, my stomach heaved, threatening to send up whatever scraps of food it still held.

Framed in the doorway was a bed draped in satiny green linens and covered by a beautiful, if old, canopy. On that bed lay a girl in blue jeans and a wrinkled tee with some kind of gag tied between her lips. I would have recognized her from her curly brown hair even if I couldn't see her face.

"Grayson!"

NINETEEN

Kastor let me push past him into the bedroom, and Grayson's damp, reddened eyes widened when I sank onto the bed next to her. She tried to say something, probably my name, but couldn't through the gag.

I pulled the material from her mouth, and it sagged against her collarbones like a cloth necklace. "Nina! Help me sit up."

"Are you okay?" I pulled her upright on the bed, and she rolled onto her back, then tucked her bent legs through her arms so that her wrists were cuffed in front, like mine. "Did they hurt you?"

"Not yet, but their plans are *disgusting*. . . ."

"I know, I—"

"Finn's here," she whispered, hardly moving her lips,

and my eyes widened as fresh tears welled in hers. She'd always been able to hear Finn, even when he didn't have any vocal cords with which to speak. And he'd obviously given up Carter's body so he could sneak into the demon city. His hometown.

"Finn," I whispered, blinking away tears of my own before they could fall. I hadn't expected to see him again. Not that I'd actually seen him yet.

How long had he been there? Had he heard what Kastor had just told me? Were Maddock and the others in Pandemonia?

Her tears spilled onto her cheeks, and when I helped Grayson off the bed, she stumbled into me on purpose so she could whisper directly into my ear when I righted her, blocked from Kastor's sight by my head. "He wants us to—"

"My men brought her in yesterday, shortly before you showed up on my doorstep." Kastor leaned against the doorframe. "If good things really come in threes, I'm expecting the rest of your friends to turn themselves in at any moment." He laughed at his own joke, and I realized he had no idea how close his prediction might be to coming true. "Would you two like to decide for yourselves who'll be the first to give our little experiment a go, or should I just flip a coin?"

"Carey . . ." Grayson sobbed as more tears fell from her eyes. "Please don't—"

"Carey's dead," Kastor snapped. "But I have access to all his memories. I know how much he loved his baby sister. You were the last thing on his mind before he died."

"Carey . . ." Shocked, I sank onto the edge of the bed. Kastor had Grayson's brown curls and her chocolate-colored eyes. They had the same skin tone. Hell, he even had her freckles.

How had I not seen it?

"I'm so sorry, Grayson." I took her hands in both of mine and had to close my eyes to keep them from watering again. "They got Mellie too." I wanted to tell her the rest—about Adam—but I didn't want Kastor to know my nephew existed.

He shrugged. "The only surprising part of this is that you two are surprised. The best way to defeat one's enemy is to get to know him, and the best way to know him is by stealing the memories of those closest to him. Or her, in your case. Your sister was the obvious choice."

"Finn wants us to exorcise him," Grayson said softly, and Kastor stood straighter. Stiffer.

"Finn is here? Now?" He glanced around the room as if his incorporeal son might suddenly become visible. "How do you know?"

"Grayson's always been able to hear him." And I'd always been jealous of her gift.

"He wants us to exorcise you. But I can't do it." She turned back to me, frowning. "I mean, I *can*. I exorcised the demon from Serah, so I've been triggered, but I *can't*. It's *Carey*."

Kastor shook his head slowly. "Sentimentality truly was the downfall of your species. I am not Carey James. He's been dead for quite a while now."

"Don't worry," I said to Grayson, mentally fitting together the beginnings of a new plan. "We don't need to exorcise him. How long has she been here, exactly?" I said, standing to meet Kastor's gaze. "How many hours?"

He crossed his arms over his chest, his brows arched, as if my question piqued his curiosity. "Okay, I'll play along. It's been about twenty hours. Since shortly before you arrived. But she's been unconscious most of that time, sleeping off her body's physical transition to exorcist. What does that have to do with Finn?"

"Has she been here the whole time?" I asked, instead of answering. "Have you touched her?"

"I'm not sure what you're implying, Nina, but—"

"Have you had any physical contact with her at all?" I demanded. "Are you the one who tied her up? Did you put the gag on her?"

"Yes," Grayson answered for him. "When I woke up. We had the same discussion you two just had. But that was hours ago."

"Good," I said, my gaze glued to the demon. "Kastor, you're about to be a very sick man."

His laughter was loud and hearty. "I'm all ears," he said, and I realized he still thought *he* was playing with *us*.

"Do any of your possessed Church scientists have memories of working on a virus?"

"I don't know." Kastor looked intrigued, but not truly threatened. "None that have been reported. They haven't all been possessed yet, though. We're saving some for after we have Finn in custody, so we don't wear the host bodies out before they can be of use."

"Then here's what you've been missing." I could hardly resist a smile. "While you were here playing monarch, the Unified Church was developing a virus that only affects possessed human hosts. They injected my sister Melanie with their virus, and then they let us escape with her, knowing that you'd try to capture us if you knew we were in the badlands." I shrugged at Kastor. "Looks like they were right."

Grayson's eyes were huge. I could tell she wanted to ask if I was serious, but she was exercising self-control.

"Very clever, Nina," Kastor said. "But you're lying. There is no such virus."

"There is, and Grayson and I are both contagious. We don't have any symptoms because we're not possessed, but because we were each born to a possessed mother—as was my sister, Melanie—we make ideal carriers. I spit and bled in your drink while you were in the bathroom, so you're definitely infected," I said with a pointed glance at his empty glass on a table in the next room. "But if you had direct physical contact with Grayson when she first arrived, chances are good that you were actually infected

301

then, which means you're farther along the time line than I knew. You should start to exhibit symptoms sometime tomorrow."

"Bullshit!" Kastor roared. He was no longer amused.

"I can prove it." I turned to face the wall. "Grayson, will you lift the back of my shirt?"

"Okay." Grayson hesitated for a moment, then lifted the cotton with her cuffed hands to expose my spine. She gasped. "What is that?"

"The discoloration along my spine? That is the only visible sign we've found so far in the human carriers. Melanie had it too."

When Kastor's footsteps stomped toward me for a closer look, I turned, pulling my shirt from Grayson's grip in the process. I held my hands out and let flames burst from my left palm.

He stopped in midstep, still several feet away.

"Look back through Carey's memories of Grayson," I said, and he scowled, obviously unaccustomed to being given orders. "Look for memories of her as a small child, or wearing a swimsuit." Even modest swimwear would have shown part of her back. "Does Carey have any memories of his sister's back? Does he remember any birthmarks or discolorations?"

Kastor frowned, and when his gaze lost focus, I knew he was sorting through his collection of stolen memories.

"No," he said at last, and I knew from the angry furrow

in his brow that he understood exactly what I was about to show him.

"Turn around, Grayson," I said, and she gave me a single wide-eyed glance, then turned. I lifted her shirt, and we both saw the pale brown stripe stretching up her back. "My guess is that the color develops there because your nerves run through your spine, but that's really just a theory."

"Nerves?" Kastor's voice sounded strained. "What kind of so-called virus is this?"

"It affects your senses. In fact, it kills them. You're about to lose the very things your species loves about being in our bodies."

"I don't believe you," Kastor spit. He glanced at Grayson as she turned back to us. "She clearly has no idea what you're talking about. You're lying."

"Grayson wasn't there when Meshara lost her sight, her hearing, her sense of taste, and, by the end, all physical sensation. But if you don't believe me, go get whoever brought Grayson in. The host would be a woman, around twenty years old. Her prepossession name was Naomi, and she kidnapped Grayson, what? Two days ago?" I glanced at Grayson for confirmation, but she could only shrug. She'd lost all sense of time just like I had. "She should be exhibiting symptoms by now. Tomorrow you and Felix will as well. Oh, and that guy from the market! The one who kissed me. Nedes. He's *definitely* infected."

303

Kastor's scowled deepened, and I saw the first flash of true fear in his eyes. "Don't move." He backed out of the room and closed the door. When something clicked softly, I realized he'd locked us in. Not that that mattered. Two exorcists could easily bust through the door or climb out the window, but escape was no longer my plan.

Finn's arrival had changed everything. I'd never been more grateful to not see someone.

Through the door we heard Kastor shout for someone to go get Naomi, Felix, and Nedes. "And tell the scientists Finn is in Pandemonia but he hasn't taken a body," Kastor said. "I need to know how to deal with him *now*." After that there was more clinking of glass against glass as he poured himself another drink.

I tugged Grayson's arm until she sank onto the bed next to me. "You okay?" I whispered.

"No."

Our cuffs clanked together as I squeezed her hands. "Is Finn still here? Can he hear me?"

Her gaze lost focus for a moment, then found mine again. "Yes, to both."

"Finn, are the others here?" I glanced around the room as if I might actually see him.

"He says no," Grayson whispered. "Not that he knows of, anyway. He broke away from the rest of Anathema when they came after me instead of you."

My heart thumped harder and heat surfaced in my cheeks. He *had* come for me!

304

"He says he's sorry about Mellie. So am I, Nina," Grayson's eyes filled with tears. "Was it really a virus?"

"Yes. But she'd already been gone for days by then, and none of us noticed. We failed her. *I* failed her. But the baby . . ." I couldn't resist a small smile in spite of all the tragedy.

"The baby made it?" Grayson sat up straight, staring at me in disbelief.

"A boy. Adam. He's a carrier too. Eli and Anabelle have him. I'll go back for him if we make it out of here."

"We *have* to!" Grayson practically squealed, bouncing a little on the bed in excitement. "I want to hold him!" She smiled. "Finn's thrilled too."

"Good, because if my plan works, we *will* get out of here. And we're going to take the city down in the process. Here's what I'm thinking—"

A loud knock from the room next door severed my thought. "Where is she?" Kastor barked, and Grayson and I moved closer to the door so we could hear better.

"We couldn't find Naomi, but the others are still looking," a new voice said. "Felix is on his way, but Nedes is . . . Kastor, something's wrong with him. He's gone blind."

Blind? Already? I glanced at Grayson, and her eyes were huge again. She looked terrified.

"Bring him in," Kastor ordered.

We heard more shuffling from the next room, and then the bedroom door flew open so suddenly Grayson and I both jumped back. Kastor lunged forward and grabbed my arm, then hauled me into the sitting room. "You did this?" he demanded, pulling me to a halt in front of Nedes, who stood in the custody of two of Kastor's black-clad guards.

"I assume you're not talking about the bumps and bruises." Nedes was covered in marks presumably inflicted when the angry mob had hauled him off to the kennels. "I had nothing to do with those."

"He's blind," Kastor snapped, then turned back to the prisoner. "Nedes. Tell her."

But Nedes didn't seem to know what to say, so I stepped closer. "Relax," I said, when Kastor's grip on my arm tightened. "I'm not going to exorcise him. A dead demon spreads no germs."

At that, both of the guards frowned, and I realized they had no idea what was going on, other than that whatever their prisoner had contracted was evidently communicable.

"Nedes!" I shouted, and the blind demon jerked upright, startled. "He's not just blind," I told the rest of the room. "He's very nearly deaf."

"You said two days." Panic echoed in Kastor's voice, and I wasn't the only one who heard it.

"Obviously, direct contact with bodily fluids accelerates the process. He's the only one I've swapped spit with. Except for you," I added with a smug smile, and his scowl darkened like storm clouds. "I'd guess you have another day, at best, before you go blind, deaf, and numb."

"Kastor . . . ?" the guard on the left said, his young face lined with fear. "What the hell is she talking about?"

Their leader let loose a fierce roar of fury and lunged past me. I stumbled to the side, then turned to see Kastor holding a dripping, crimson chunk of flesh with what appeared to be a tube dangling from it.

I choked on my next breath, and Grayson squeaked in shock behind me. The guards let go of Nedes, who fell to his knees, then onto his side, the gaping hole in this throat pouring blood onto the floor.

When I'd recovered from my shock enough to look away from the fresh corpse, I saw the guards wiping sprays of blood from their faces with their sleeves. "Way to go." I turned back to Kastor, who still held Nedes's severed trachea in his right hand. "If they weren't infected before, they are now."

Kastor threw the bloody chunk of flesh at Nedes's body. "Go downstairs to the auction room and take two hosts for yourselves. Anyone sleeping, so that you don't have to touch them to possess them. Bring a third one here, but leave him in the hall."

"But those hosts are all sold," the guard on the right said. "There are only a few that haven't been picked up."

"I don't care!" Kastor roared. "Just take clean hosts for yourselves and get one for me. Knock on the door when you get here. Do *not* allow any contact between the bodies you're wearing now and the new, uninfected ones."

"What's wrong with those two?" The guard on the left waved one hand at me and one at Grayson.

"They're carriers," Kastor snapped. "They *brought* this thing here."

I gave the guards a big smile, and they both stepped away from me, more terrified by the contagion I carried than any demon had ever been by the flames I wielded.

"You've already got it, dumbasses," Grayson said, and I was pleased to realize that she'd followed the entire discussion.

"Go!" Kastor shouted. "Hurry. And don't touch or talk to anyone on your way."

"You can't stop it," I called out as the guard closed the door behind them. "Everyone who touched me in the marketplace has already been infected." That was a bluff. I couldn't be sure how easily it spread through casual contact, but Kastor didn't need to know that. "Soon your whole city will have the virus, and there won't be any uninfected hosts left. Your people will flee our world voluntarily rather than live trapped in bodies that can't see, hear, or feel anything."

"I won't be here to see that happen." Kastor advanced on me, and I saw violent intent in his eyes. We were no longer useful for his plan to breed another Finn. "Neither will you."

"Stay back!" I held my cuffed hands out, and flames burst from my left palm. Kastor hesitated, but only for a second. Then he lunged at me so fast I saw little more than a blur. He grabbed my arms and twisted them away from us both. Pain shot through my wrist and elbow, and the flames in my palm died.

I could have revived them. I could have fought to slam my flaming palm into Kastor's chest, but exorcising him wasn't part of the plan. I needed Carey's body alive.

Kastor pinned me to the floor, one hand gripping my left arm. His other hand reached for my throat. I bucked and twisted beneath him but couldn't throw him off.

A sharp, high-pitched sound of fury came from behind me, and Grayson appeared over Kastor's shoulder. She blinked Finn-green eyes at me, then grabbed him by the back of the neck and pulled him off me. Kastor flew across the room. His back slammed into the wall, and he slid to the floor.

Grayson blinked, and her brown eyes were back.

Kastor shook his head sharply once, then twice. He stood unsteadily, but his eyes never lost their furious focus.

I pushed Grayson behind me to protect her, my heart slamming against my chest.

Someone knocked sharply on the door. "Kastor?" an unfamiliar voice called. "We got you a new body. Rufus choked him out. He's all ready for you."

Kastor gave me an evil smile, one hand on the wall to steady himself. "Nice try, Nina," he said. Then he closed his eyes and crumpled to the ground.

Kastor had left the building.

"Finn!" I whispered urgently, racing across the room toward the door. "Take Carey's body!"

"But it's infected," Grayson hissed.

"Yeah, but it shouldn't start showing symptoms for at least a day, and Finn can leave it whenever he wants."

But as long as he wore Kastor's face, we had the keys to the kingdom.

Carey's eyes opened, and they were Finn-green. The strength and beauty that had looked cold and arrogant on Kastor suddenly looked warm and . . . hungry for me.

My heart leapt into my throat, and the thrill of a minor victory mingled seamlessly with my delight and relief at seeing him again. Even in a body that had been trying to kill me seconds earlier.

We adapt quickly or we die. I was more than willing to take the demons' lead on that one.

"Brilliant as usual, Nina." Finn reached for me and I helped him up. Then he pulled me close for a kiss I didn't want to end, even though his beautiful new mouth tasted like whiskey.

"That is *so* strange!" Grayson stepped closer and ran one hand down his cheek, staring up at him. "You look like Carey, and you sound like Carey." Her eyes watered again. "At least, more like Carey than Kastor did. But you're clearly Finn."

"Yes. It's both weird and wonderful. And I'm sorry about your brother." I tugged them both toward the door.

"But we have to get to Kastor and his guards before they can tell anyone what's going on." I let them go and threw open the door just in time to see several men disappear into a stairwell at the other end of the hall.

"Come on!" Finn raced down the hall with Grayson and me on his heels, and his new speed and strength caught me by surprise, even though I'd known what Carey's body was capable of. We gained ground on the stairs, and when Finn got within reach of the closest, he grabbed the man by the back of his neck. "Heads up!" He turned and threw the demon up the stairwell toward me.

The guard landed on his back on the stairs, and I heard the distinct crack of bone. He screamed, and when I knelt to slam my flaming palm down on his chest, his pitch reached an inhuman range. In seconds his newly stolen body was dead and the demon was cast out of our world.

Grayson raced past me, and seconds later Finn shouted "Heads up!" again. A second demon flew toward us, and Grayson pressed her back to the wall of the stairwell just in time to avoid being flattened. I raced down the steps toward them both, my hand already in flames again, but Grayson dropped onto him without a moment's hesitation, her own fire already ready to go.

She was a natural. And it probably didn't hurt that she'd spent the past year watching her friends and surrogate family do that very thing on a daily basis.

We took off after Finn again and found him frying a third demon, as the fourth disappeared through a metal door into another part of the building. I leapt over them both onto the first-floor landing, then threw open the door and stepped into a hallway lined with closed doors.

The hall was empty.

"Damn it!" I stepped back into the stairway. "The last one got away."

"So, was one of these Kastor?" Grayson gestured up the stairwell toward the three burned-out bodies.

Finn shrugged Carey's broad shoulders. "There's a seventy-five percent chance the answer is yes, but we won't know unless we find the one that got away. Maybe not even then." Because even if we caught Kastor, he probably wouldn't admit who he was.

"Doesn't matter whether he got away or not," I said. "What matters is that *we* have Kastor's face. And I know just how to put it to use."

TWENTY

Finn pressed me against the kitchen counter, his hands at my waist. His breath stirred my hair, and I breathed him in, marveling at his new scent. His new build. Yes, his body had once belonged to our greatest enemy, but before that, it had belonged to Carey James, an innocent and, by all accounts, noble fellow exorcist, who'd loved his sister as much as I'd loved mine.

I couldn't imagine a better home for Finn's spirit, even if it was only temporary.

His lips brushed my ear, and warmth trailed down from the point of contact to settle into my stomach. "I was really hoping you had something more personal in mind when you said you knew how to put me to use," he said as

Grayson finished filling the third small spray bottle, then turned off the kitchen sink.

"I would have if I'd said 'you.'" I stood on my toes for a kiss, but it was really his arms around me that I loved most. Melanie's death had been devastating, and there'd been no real time yet to mourn. But going through that without him was even harder. "But I didn't say 'Finn,' I said 'Kastor.'"

I took one of the three cylindrical plastic bottles and handed another to him. "Okay. Cheers." I lifted my bottle, and Grayson and Finn both tapped theirs against mine. Then we each took a big drink, but rather than swallow the water, we swished it in our mouths, then spat it carefully back into the bottle.

"This is *so* gross," Grayson said, holding her bottle up for a repetition of the process.

"This is biological warfare." At my signal, we all three drank, swished, and spat again. Then we screwed the spray nozzle lids on our bottles and shook them up to spread the germs.

"Are you sure this will work?" Finn gave his an experimental spray into an industrial-sized drawer full of silverware.

"No, but I spent hours considering every possible manner of distribution, and what I learned from Nedes is that transmission through shared bodily fluids is the fastest, most effective means of infection." Unfortunately, that

x

314

meant that Finn wouldn't have much time in Carey's infected body. "So other than kissing everyone in Pandemonia, this is the best I could come up with. But if you have a better idea, I'm all ears."

Finn shook his head. "Kissing *anyone* else sounds like a really bad idea."

Grayson peered skeptically through the clear side of her tap water weapon. "Considering that the alternative seems to be urinating in a spray bottle, I fully support the saliva tactic."

"Okay, then. Everyone understand the plan?"

"Finn is Kastor." Grayson opened the massive commercial refrigerator and sprayed her bottle inside. "He should be able to carry that off since he grew up here," she added, and Finn nodded, grimly acknowledging that fact. I still wasn't sure how much he'd heard about his parentage, but if he was traumatized, he was keeping it all inside, at least for the moment.

With any luck, we'd both have time to grieve and vent after we'd dealt with the demon scourge.

Grayson sprayed a metal bin of tomatoes and potatoes, then turned to me. "You and I are his guards. Rufus and Gidri."

Those were the names of two of the guards we'd killed in the stairwell, and Finn recognized them both as having been with Kastor for years.

"They're both assholes," he'd said. "Rufus has a sweet

tooth. Red licorice is his favorite. Maddy and I used it to bribe him to look the other way when we wanted to sneak out of the apartment."

Gidri, he'd told us, loved weird hats—when he was off duty—and snacked on beef jerky.

We hadn't found any jerky on hand, but I'd discovered a bag of cherry-flavored licorice in the kitchen pantry. I slid several ropes of the candy into my pocket so that they hung out into plain sight, and held up my spray bottle. "Ready?"

"As I'm ever gonna be," Grayson said.

"Kastor, lead the way!"

Finn scowled—he didn't like his assigned part—but tucked his small spray bottle into a large cargo pocket over his right leg, then led us out of what turned out to be a prewar hotel, long ago converted into an apartment building for Kastor and those he deemed most worthy to live near him. Maddock—and Finn, unbeknownst to anyone else—had grown up in a suite on the top floor, mostly raised by a series of human nannies.

On the street Finn took the lead, and Grayson and I walked behind and on either side of him, like a proper entourage. I snacked on Rufus's candy, trying to get into character and forget that I hated licorice. There were no cars. Pandemonia—the downtown section, at least—was a walking city, and we'd gone less than a block from the hotel when people began appearing on the street.

Everyone stopped to wave at or yell a greeting to Kastor,

which confirmed my suspicion that we would not be able to go unnoticed. We'd have to hide in plain sight and convince everyone else that we belonged.

"Most of Kastor's guards are gruff and generally unpleasant," Finn whispered, waving at a very large woman in a very small top across the street. "They don't let anyone get too close to him, and they don't say much, other than 'Move along' and 'That's close enough.'" Finn stopped and turned to confer privately with Grayson and me. "He told you that he's Maddy's father?"

"He told us more than that," Grayson said, and the color drained from Finn's face.

"I've heard rumors." He cleared his throat softly and looked right into my eyes. "I've heard a lot more than Maddock has, because I've always been able to go places he couldn't, without being seen." Finn frowned. "Well, I guess that hasn't *always* been the case. But my point is that everyone knows Kastor is Maddy's dad. No one else has ever fathered a child in demon form. Kastor is like a celebrity here. Everyone expects to see him, but no one expects his guards to let them get too close. You can use that."

Grayson and I understood. Finn should be visible, but untouchable.

We'd just begun to hear the racket from the marketplace when the first bystander recognized me, an event I'd been expecting but dreading. "Is that Nina Kane?" The man turned to walk backward in front of Kastor, the bright purple legs of his boxer shorts swishing with every step.

"Not anymore," Finn said, and the man took a closer look at me as I bit off a chunk from a red rope of candy.

"Rufus?" he said, and I nodded. "I thought you didn't like walking around . . . like that." He held both hands in front of his chest in a cartoonish imitation of breasts.

Finn stepped in before I could answer. "My guard needed an upgrade." He twisted to glance at me. "Show him the fire."

I finally caught on when he glanced pointedly at my left hand. The man in purple gasped and stumbled backward when flames burst from my cupped palm.

"Holy shit!" he whispered.

I took another bite of licorice and maintained a gruff silence, trying to hide the fact that my pulse was racing with nerves and I was starting to sweat. Finn nodded and glanced back at Grayson. "A matched set," he said, and she showed off her own handful of flames. "Gender is irrelevant. What matters is power. Make it known."

The man's eyes widened, and then he nodded and spun to run toward the market.

"Nice save," Grayson whispered.

Finn made a satisfied noise deep in his throat. "This just might work."

I wasn't quite ready to agree, but we had no better plan.

Everyone turned to stare when we walked into the

market, and my heart pounded deep in my chest. I saw the problem almost immediately. We wouldn't be able to spread our contagion while everyone was watching us. "Kastor," I said softly, and Finn stiffened. "Perhaps the people would like a demonstration of your power."

Kastor had been in Carey's body for at least a year, but if I was right, he hadn't done much to show it off before, and if there was anything all of demonkind had in common, it was the love of a good spectacle.

"Of course. Gidri, help me give the people a show."

He stepped into the center of the marketplace, and Grayson cleared a circle around him, as any good guard would. Then "Kastor" began to talk, and while he had the crowd's attention, I slowly, quietly backed toward the edge of the gathering until I stood next to a meat vendor's cart. When I was sure the vendor was captivated by the demonstration, I gave his cart several good sprays, concentrating mostly on the unused kabob sticks and paper cups, for fear that the heat cooking the meat itself would kill our virus.

I moved from one cart to the next while Finn and Grayson performed, listening for the oohs and aahs for timing, and contaminated every item of food and clothing I could find with a generous helping of my own germs.

"Show us the true power of fire!" someone from the crowd shouted as I worked my way back to Finn's side, having infected every edible or wearable thing I could get my hands on. "Burn someone!"

Everyone else cheered, and the demand became a jovial but bloodthirsty chant.

I probably shouldn't have been surprised by their willingness to kill one of their own, considering how many humans had cheered when the Church lit poor Adam Yung on fire in New Temperance. But at least most of my fellow citizens had thought they were saving his immortal soul.

The demons just wanted a show.

"Rufus!" Finn shouted as soon as he saw that I was back. "Give the people what they want!" His eyes sparkled with amused irony, and with a secret jolt of excitement, I realized I'd just been given permission to exorcise a demon in the middle of the marketplace in Pandemonia with total impunity. In fact, the crowd was demanding that very thing.

"Do you have someone in mind, sir?" I asked, and "Kastor" shook his head.

"Ladies and gentlemen, I'm sure you all recognize the infamous Nina Kane, scourge to our kind the world over. Now I present her as a host, defeated and worn by my own loyal guard Rufus, who will now wield her appropriated power for your entertainment. Rufus!" He turned back to me and gestured to the crowd. "Choose from among the volunteers."

No one was actually volunteering. In fact, the crowd had gone silent, brimming with an almost tangible mix of fear and excitement.

I looked out over the possibilities and found Dione

among them. I was seconds away from singling her out when I realized that she was blinking a lot. Heavily. Her eyes were struggling to focus, which told me that she'd already been infected through casual contact with me the day before. Until she figured out what was happening to her and abandoned the infected host body, she was a walking contagion. A soldier unknowingly fighting for the good guys.

So I selected a man from the gathering at random. "You." It was the man in glittery purple boxers, who'd first spread the word about "Rufus" and "Gidri," at "Kastor's" request.

The crowd burst into fierce whispers, and several people pushed the man in purple to the front. He didn't try to run, but he looked more terrified than I'd ever seen a demon look. I marched toward him, and the crowd backed away, widening the ring around us.

I held my left hand up in front of him, and flames leapt from my cupped palm.

The man in purple began to visibly sweat. I pulled him toward me by one arm—his shirt didn't contain enough material to grab—and whispered into his ear. "I'm not Rufus. I'm still Nina Kane. Soon all your friends will join you in hell." His eyes widened, and he opened his mouth to scream.

I slammed my hand onto his nearly bare chest.

The roar from the crowd around me almost drowned out the screams of the demon as I burned him from his host's body. They cheered as if I'd won an election or low-ered taxes, but as near as I could tell, they were actually celebrating their fellow citizen's excruciating pain and expulsion from the human world. The same thing could happen to any one of them at "Kastor's" whim, yet they *reveled* in the pain and terror of one of their own.

When the flames in my left hand died, the man in purple collapsed to the ground, smoke curling from the charred hole in his chest. I backed away, and the crowd descended on him, pulling off scraps of his clothing and handfuls of hair from his head. He was a celebrity in death, and every-one wanted a souvenir.

Finn, Grayson, and I slipped out of the crowd and into the nearest restaurant, where they repeated their exorcist exhibition while I went into the kitchen, ostensibly to pre-pare a snack for my revered boss, and took the oppor-tunity to spray down everything edible with a generous helping of my germs.

We spent the next couple of hours touring the down-town district, going from party to party, each weirder than the last. Grayson and I took turns playing first the distraction, then the infector. Finn didn't get to spray from his bottle at all because everywhere we went, everyone watched him.

In spite of his reluctance to let *me* go around kissing demons, he couldn't entirely escape the same fate. Kastor, evidently, was popular with the lady demons, and several wanted to stake their claim on his mouth. Publicly.

I eased my rage at the sight with the knowledge that in less than a day, none of those women would be able to see, hear, taste, or feel a damn thing. Finn's mouth was poison, and they were drinking straight from the bottle.

By midnight we'd hit the kitchen of every open restaurant and made a second trip through the marketplace. People were actively ingesting our germs. Part of me wanted to wait around long enough to see the virus take hold, but the rest of me knew better. Anyone who'd seen me spray from my bottle and dismissed it as an eccentricity of one of Kastor's top men would know better the minute the virus became public knowledge.

We needed to be long gone before that happened.

"So, how do we get out of here?" I whispered to Finn as we headed back toward the converted hotel, ostensibly so that Kastor could take care of city business.

In the lobby he waved to some people eating and blasting music I'd never heard before, and I hoped they'd all gotten their food from the infected hotel kitchen.

"Quietly. Covertly," Finn said once the elevator doors had closed behind us. "Kastor and his guards never leave the city. Not once in the seventeen years Maddy and I lived here."

"We need a distraction," I said. "Something big that will draw everyone's attention while we escape."

"Something that doesn't require Kastor's presence, or that of his two top guards," Grayson added. The elevator bonged as it came to a stop, and then the doors slid open.

Finn led us back down the deserted hallway and into Kastor's suite.

"Finn, do you have any idea where Maddy, Devi, and Reese are?" I asked as he locked the door of the sitting room behind us.

He shook his head. "They were tracking Grayson when I left. I told Maddock to stay away from Pandemonia at all costs. Considering how little he likes being ordered around, that probably means he's right outside the gate." He crossed into the bedroom and began rifling through Kastor's dresser drawers. "But I have to hope he's being smarter than that. We can't count on their help."

"Fire." Grayson sank onto the loveseat, running one hand over the red velvet upholstery, and I glanced at her in question. "For the distraction. I suggest fire. They're fascinated with it here, in case you haven't noticed. They cook meat over open flames. They set alcoholic drinks on fire before they drink them. While you were in the kitchen at that last place, they offered Finn and me some kind of flambéed dessert. It was basically sugared bananas set on fire, then served over ice cream. It was good. But in an evil kind of way." She shrugged, and I couldn't resist a small smile. She was starting to sound more like herself and less like a kidnapping victim who'd just discovered her brother had been killed and possessed by their worst enemy.

Hopefully, seeing the demon run out of her brother's body had helped with that.

"Hang on," Finn called from the bedroom. "I have to

get out of this shirt. It smells like whatever that demon sycophant in the gold bra spilled on me." He shrugged out of Kastor's button-up shirt and was reaching for a tee from the second drawer when the overhead light shone on his back, and I froze.

A jolt of astonishment shot through me, all warm and tingly. "Finn, wait!" I jogged into the bedroom, and Grayson glanced at me in surprise.

"What?" He frowned as I turned him by his shoulders.

"Grayson, look at this." I touched the base of his spine, where a small but distinctive pale brown line had just begun to stretch toward his neck. It was only an inch and a half long, but I would have recognized that mark anywhere.

"But . . ." Grayson knelt for a closer look at her brother's back. "But he's infected. And that wasn't there before. I saw Kastor change shirts earlier. Or yesterday. Or whenever that was."

"There's a mark on my back?" Finn asked. "Like the ones on yours?"

"Yes." Grayson stood. "I thought only human carriers got that mark."

I shrugged, frowning. "That's what I thought too. Unless . . ." My eyes widened as the implication of Finn's carrier mark finally sank in. "Carey's not possessed anymore. Maybe this means the infection has been halted. I think that as long as Finn stays in Carey's body . . . he's just a carrier."

"Wait, are you saying I can keep him?" Grayson's eyes were as wide as I'd ever seen them. "I mean, I know Carey's dead, but he still looks like my brother, and Finn's always been like a brother to me, so . . . this kind of fits."

Finn pulled Kastor's shirt on and smiled. "So you're okay with this?" He spread her brother's arms, and she stepped into the hug. "Because you only get to keep him as long as I get to keep him." If Finn left Carey's body for more than a few minutes, Carey's organs would shut down and he would die.

"Keep him," she sobbed against Finn's shoulder. "This is what Carey would have wanted, considering the circumstances."

When she finally let him go, Finn turned to me. "So, do you approve? Would you be okay with it if I looked like this for the rest of my life?" His green eyes were practically glowing. I could see how badly he wanted a body of his own, and an exorcist's body was more than he'd ever hoped for, because he would never have stolen one from someone else.

I pulled him close, and my eyes closed when his hands slid slowly down my back. "It's like this was meant to be." I glanced at Grayson over his broad, firm shoulder and grinned. "Your brother's not bad-looking. Now let's see if we can get him out of here in one piece."

TWENTY-ONE

"You're sure about this?" I asked as Finn pulled a match from the box. The gasoline fumes were giving me a headache, and honestly, I knew we'd already gone too far to back out. But I had to ask.

"There is no building I'd rather burn." He dropped the match onto the gasoline-soaked loveseat, then stepped back as it burst into flames. "Let's go." Finn ushered Grayson and me out the door and into the hall as flames crackled behind us, already well on their way to devouring Kastor's apartment.

I'd never committed arson before, but evidently it really *was* as simple as "pour accelerant; light match." Especially if leaving evidence wasn't a concern.

We were much more concerned with leaving town.

On the bottom floor we lit secondary blazes in several custodial closets and unused offices, avoiding the kitchen and lobby areas, which were the only parts of the downstairs still regularly used.

Originally, there had probably been a sprinkler system and an alarm built into the hotel, but those had ceased functioning several decades earlier, by Finn's best guess, so when we fled the burning hotel through a little-used side entrance, no one else had yet realized the building was on fire.

No alarm had been raised.

We took several narrow back alleys on our path away from the hotel, avoiding the crowds still gathered at the auction square and the outdoor market, and when we finally turned back to look up at the building in which Finn and Maddock had spent their childhood, the flames were just becoming visible through windows on the top floor.

"They'll see that soon," Grayson whispered, fear and awe echoing in her voice.

"And I'll make sure they know exactly who's to blame."

We spun as one, startled by the voice behind us, to find an unfamiliar group of about a dozen fairly conservatively dressed demons facing us from the other end of the alley.

"Finn?" The one in front stared right into Finn's green eyes. "You always were the troublemaker," he said, and we all came to the same conclusion at once.

"Kastor," Finn said.

The leader of Pandemonia *was* the demon who'd escaped

us in the stairwell, and he'd since convinced a dozen of his citizens that the Kastor they'd all loved in the marketplace that evening was an impostor.

"Assuming you haven't already been infected," I said, stepping up to Finn's right side, flames tingling just beneath the surface of my left palm, "your best bet would be to flee the city. Now. We're all three highly contagious, and by this point, so is most of your city."

"We've been spraying our saliva on your food all night," Grayson added, and I almost laughed at how ridiculous our plan sounded, boiled down to its basics. But it was a good plan, and I had no doubt it would work, assuming no one warned the citizens in time for them to flee the city.

Kastor's brows rose, and I recognized the expression, even on his new face. "So you think we're just going to let you walk out into the badlands and spread your disease worldwide?"

But I could see through his intentions as if they were made of glass. "You know the Church won't let that happen. As soon as they're sure we've taken out Pandemonia, they'll hunt us down like dogs in the street. They wanted a *targeted* exposure." But we were willing to spend the rest of our lives widening that target.

Kastor didn't give a shit whether we spread the demon plague to his enemies or not. The anger raging in his eyes said he was after revenge, pure and simple.

"If you think you can stop us from leaving . . ." Finn spread his arms. "Come—"

Kastor pulled something from the waistband of his jeans.

"No!" I shouted, the instant I realized he held a pistol.

Grayson lunged as Kastor fired at Finn. If she hadn't been triggered, she would have been too slow to get in front of the gun. But exorcist Grayson was just fast enough to catch the bullet high on her right side.

She flew backward from the force and landed on her back on the pavement. "Nina . . . ," Grayson gasped, and I dropped to her side.

A rage-filled sound ripped from Finn's throat. He lunged at Kastor, faster than I'd ever seen him, or anyone, move. He was amazing in Carey's body—but he couldn't fight twelve demons on his own.

I charged down the alley half an instant behind him.

Finn slammed into his father's new, young body, and the gun went off again. One of Kastor's men screamed and stumbled into the wall of the alley, blood blooming high on his chest from the bullet hole. Four others fled, evidently terrified to make contact with us and our contagions.

The other five all pounced at once.

I kicked aside the first demon who came at me. My left hand burst into flames. Finn's was already burning. The alley flickered with shadows of violence, cast by fire.

Finn growled and tossed a demon over his back. He threw a punch, and Kastor's gun slid down the pavement toward Grayson, where none of his men were willing to go while she leaked contaminated blood all over the ground.

I burned through the next demon that lunged at me, then used his flailing body to deflect the next. When the first demon collapsed, I turned my flames toward the next. A third grabbed my neck from behind, and when he hauled me off my feet, the monster hanging from my palm came with me, stuck to the flames like a magnet to metal. Blisteringly hot, flesh-melting metal.

On the edge of my vision, Finn stood and kicked his father's corpse aside. Another demon leapt for him, and Finn shoved his fiery left hand into the air. The demon landed on his hand in midair, speared by the flames and seemingly weightless.

The demon behind me squeezed my neck, and I gasped in pain as cartilage popped. The flames in my hand blinked out, and the monster that hung from them crumpled at my feet. I tried to twist and fry the monster behind me, but he grabbed my left arm and held it away from us both.

Thunder boomed through the alley, and the hand around my neck loosened. Something thudded to the pavement behind me, and I turned to find the demon who'd had me by the neck now lying on the ground with a small hole in his chest.

Shocked, I spun again to find Grayson still aiming the pistol in her right hand, her left pressed against the bullet wound in her side. "Good shot!" I said, but she only shook her head.

"I was aiming for his head." Her voice was weak. Her face was pale, in what little moonlight shone into the alley.

"Finn!" I raced toward her.

He finished frying the last of the demons, then pulled his shirt off on his way down the alley. "Here. Press this against the wound." He laid the wadded-up material over her side, and I held it there with as much pressure as I could apply. "We have to get her out of here."

"Where can we get a car?"

"At the gate. They're mostly used for trips into the badlands." Finn picked up Grayson, then carried her down the alley and across the street. Everyone we passed was headed for the blazing building. None of them even looked closely enough to realize who we were.

Until we got to the gate five endless minutes later.

"What's the plan?" I whispered, eyeing the nearest guard and his gun.

Finn glanced at the vehicles parked near the gate, and I realized that unlike in New Temperance, there was no patrol assigned to walk the perimeter. Evidently no one wanted to break into a city openly full of demons.

The only guards were four armed men standing in front of the gate itself.

"The plan is to put Grayson in a car and drive right through," Finn whispered. "Don't stop for anything."

I searched the three nearest cars for keys as quietly as I could, and on the fourth, I finally found a set hidden in the visor.

Finn laid Grayson across the backseat, and I sat on the floorboard in the back to keep his shirt pressed to her stomach. Finn slid into the driver's seat and started the car. He backed it carefully out of its spot, and the nearest of the guards walked toward us, carrying his gun.

"Kastor? Is that you?" he called.

Instead of answering, Finn stomped on the gas.

The remaining gate guards scrambled out of the way. One of them fired his gun, yelling for us to stop, and a bullet went through both our front and rear windshields.

The grille of the car rammed into the gate itself, which ripped free from its hinges with the spine-scraping squeal of metal and clunked onto the roof of the car hard enough to dent the center. Finn hit the gas again, and we lurched out of Pandemonia and into the badlands. The broken gate flew off our roof and hit two of the guards running after us.

We veered wildly around the gray car I'd abandoned when I'd turned myself in, then shot off into the badlands.

I stared out the rear windshield, watching to see if we'd be pursued, but no one came out of the city after us. A second later I understood why.

If Pandemonia had been extravagantly illuminated upon my arrival, it was lit up like a bonfire in the wake of our departure. Through the holes in the steel patchwork fence, I could see that not one, but at least *three* buildings were now on fire, and the residents—blissfully unaware that their hosts had become ticking time bombs—were no doubt more concerned with saving the city than with pursuing the invaders who'd set it on fire in the first place.

My pulse raced in my ears as I watched the flames blaze smaller and smaller in the rearview mirror, and I laid one hand on Grayson's sternum so I could feel her breathe. I'd already lost one sister, and I had no intention of losing another one.

Half a mile later headlights suddenly lit the interior of our car, and I twisted toward the front to see a vehicle headed straight for us from the depths of the badlands.

"Brace yourself." When Finn lifted a pistol in his right hand, I realized he'd picked up Kastor's gun on the way out of the alley.

"Wait!" I cried when the left headlight of the vehicle in front of us winked out for a split second. "Don't shoot! That's our truck!"

Finn blinked into the headlights and finally slammed on the brakes. Our car swerved on the crumbling road, then skidded to a stop. The cargo truck we'd appropriated from the Church slowed to a much more civilized stop beside us, winking headlight and all. Reese leaned out of the passenger's-side window with Carter's rifle aimed right at us.

"Who the hell are you?" he demanded, and I peeked up from the backseat.

"Reese. It's us. That's Finn's new body. It used to be Carey's."

"Carey James?" He set the gun down on the floorboard and threw his door open. "Where's—"

"Grayson is back here," I called. "She's hurt, beyond what we can fix. We need to get her to the Lord's Army and hope they know how to remove a bullet." That, and because the Lord's Army had baby Adam.

"She got *shot*?" He was out of the truck in an instant.

"We can't stop here," Finn warned as Reese circled the truck toward our car. "We have to get away before the demons get their shit together."

I climbed into the front seat to make room for Reese in the back. "You really think they'll come after us?"

"The ones who don't know about the virus will," Maddock said from the truck's driver's seat, and I realized they'd talked to Eli and Anabelle. "Once they get that fire under control." He nodded toward the demon city, which still blazed in the distance. "I assume that's your work?"

"Damn right," I said as Devi slid into the passenger's seat of the truck. She looked impressed for the first time since I'd met her.

"Kastor's dead, Maddy," Finn said. "And soon all the rest of them will be. Nina figured out how to infect the whole damn city."

Devi pushed her long braid over her shoulder. "You mean we drove like hell and *still* missed the party?"

"You can tell us about it down the road," Maddock said. "Let's get out of here."

Finn revved his engine, and Devi closed the cargo truck door. Then Maddock turned the truck around and we followed him into the badlands, his taillights ahead of us, the blazing hulk of Pandemonia still flickering through the rear windshield.

* * *

"Well?" Finn said, and I looked up from the potato patties grilling over the morning campfire to find Anabelle standing in the entrance to Damaris's tent, wiping her bloody hands on a scrap of cloth. "How's Grayson?"

"Damaris thinks she's going to make it." But the tension in Anabelle's frame told me how close it had been. Grayson had lost a lot of blood, and the Lord's Army had neither a sterile environment nor a trained surgeon.

Fortunately, we'd collected a good supply of antibiotics and painkillers during our cargo raids over the past five months, and even after sharing with our hosts, there would be enough to help Grayson.

Reese hadn't left her side for a single second of the twelve hours since we'd caught up with the Lord's Army on the outskirts of Salina. Neither had Damaris or Eli. But Eli, I'd noticed, kept stealing starry-eyed glances at Ana as she assisted his mother. Evidently they'd bonded during and after their road trip in the badlands, and in retrospect, their mutual attraction wasn't surprising.

Both had dedicated their lives to faith. Both were interested in caregiving in general and childbirth in particular. Both had more courage than any other human I'd ever met. Finn and I were happy for them.

Reese was *thrilled* for them. And for himself.

"Want me to give you a breather so you two can have a few minutes alone?" Anabelle sat on the grass mat next to me and ran the back of one knuckle down Adam's cheek. He stirred in my arms, but his eyes never opened. He'd turned out to be a very content baby, as long as he was well fed. But we'd already used half our store of formula in the few days he'd been alive, and when that ran out . . .

But that was a problem for another day.

"That's okay." Finn rubbed his hand up and down my back. "We like having him, and you must be tired."

"Not gonna lie—I could sleep." Ana pushed her hair back from her forehead, and even in the flickering light of the fire, I could see exhaustion drawn all over her face. "But tomorrow I want to hear about what happened out there. Every bit of it."

"There's a lot to tell." I stared down at Adam's tiny little lips, pursed in his sleep as if he were sucking on his bottle. Finn's hand slid into my grip on the mat between us, and his thumb brushed my knuckles. The only thing missing from that near-perfect moment was Melanie, but it was her sacrifice that had made the whole thing possible. I smiled at Anabelle and squeezed Finn's hand. "But the short version is that the world has changed for good."

And for the first time in centuries, humanity might come out on top.

EPILOGUE

Crickets chirruped as I ran across the street into the shadows, already regretting my decision. But it was too late to change my mind.

"Are you sure about this?" Finn asked as I slid into the passenger's seat and closed the car door as softly as I could.

"Hell no." I peered out the car window at the featureless brick building, its windows dark except for a few on the top floor and one at the southwest corner. That one was Sister Tabitha's office.

The light over the front porch flickered, and I caught my breath, hoping it wouldn't go out. I stared at the box on the stoop and my stomach began to twist again.

I felt like I might throw up.

But we were doing the right thing. I'd been over and over it and kept coming to the same conclusion.

"The Church is hunting us. They'll be hunting us for the rest of our lives. They know Eli helped us, so the Lord's Army is a target. We have enough of a handicap with Grayson still healing. If Adam got caught in the crossfire, I'd never forgive myself." Neither would any of the others. We'd only had him for a couple of weeks, but no baby in the history of mankind had ever been more loved.

"We can't keep him safe, Finn, even if we had something to feed him." We were nearly out of formula, and there wasn't a wet nurse to be found among Eli's friends and family. "But *they* can." I stared up at the building again. "And they will. They won't let a child die. Souls are too precious."

"Unless they figure out who he is. . . ."

"They won't," I insisted. "They don't even know he exists. If they know Pandemonia fell, they'll assume Melanie fell with it."

This was the best place for Adam, at least for now. We were doing the right thing. Even if the right thing felt like a thousand white-hot swords being run through my body all at once.

I'd just put Adam down, yet my arms already ached to be holding him.

Finally the door opened, and I caught my breath.

I didn't recognize the sister who stepped out onto the porch, and from across the street I couldn't tell whether her robes were embroidered. But for once that didn't matter. Adam would be safe with her for the next few months.

And we would come back for him before things got dangerous. Before they had a chance to put it all together.

"It's kind of fitting," Finn said. "Letting it all end here, where it began."

"Do you think Melanie would hate us for this?"

"I think she'd love you for doing what's best for him even when that's the hardest thing you've ever had to do."

"We'll be back for him," I said for the thousandth time in the past hour. "Soon."

"How long do you think it'll take them to figure it out?" he asked while we watched the sister lift my nephew from the blanket-lined box.

"I don't know. He's a passive carrier, and he'll mostly be in the care of the unconsecrated. But eventually a possessed sister will change his diaper or ease his teething gums with her finger. Someone will be infected, and that someone will infect someone else, and Melanie's little Trojan Pony will bring Troy to its knees. And they'll have no idea how it happened."

"I think she'd like that," Finn said as the sister took my nephew inside and closed the door. "Bringing the virus back home."

My chest ached fiercely. "I think she would too." The light over the porch flickered, and my gaze snagged on the sign next to the door as Finn started the car.

NEW TEMPERANCE CHILDREN'S HOME
ALL INNOCENT SOULS WELCOME

ACKNOWLEDGMENTS

A big thanks to my critique partner, Rinda Elliott, who helped me figure out how to kill a demon and who is the very best sounding board.

Thanks also to Jennifer Lynn Barnes for weekly writing days, opinions, ideas, and good company.

A huge thank-you, as always, to my agent, Merrilee Heifetz, who gets things done. I have many irons in the fire, and you keep me from getting burned.

Thank you to my amazing editor, Wendy Loggia, for all her support and enthusiasm, and for asking the question about this story that most needed to be answered.

Thank you to all the readers who liked Nina and came back for more.

Read Me. Love Me. Share Me.

Did you love this book? Want to read other amazing teen books for free online and have your voice heard as a reviewer, trend-spotter and all-round expert?

Then join us at **facebook.com/MIRAink** and chat with authors, watch trailers, WIN books, share reviews and help us to create the kind of books that you'll want to carry on reading forever!

Romance. Horror. Paranormal. Dystopia. Fantasy.

Whatever you're in the mood for, we've got it covered.

Don't miss a single word

 twitter.com/MIRAink

let's be friends

 facebook.com/MIRAink

Scan me with your smart phone

 to go straight to our facebook page